4/29/23

"Her Unexpected Roommate"

Bulbs, Blossoms and Bouquets #1

By Laura Ann

HER UNEXPECTED ROOMMATE

First edition. February 3, 2021.

Written by Laura Ann.

DEDICATION

Every first book is dedicated to my husband.
Without your support, I would never had put
pen to paper. Here's to eternity.

ACKNOWLEDGEMENTS

No author works alone. Thank you, Brenda.
You make it Christmas every time
I get a new cover. And thank you to my Beta Team.
Truly, your help with my stories is immeasurable.

NEWSLETTER

You can get a FREE book by joining my Reading Family!
Every week we share stories, sales and good old fun.
To get in on the action, visit me at
lauraannbooks.com

CHAPTER 1

"**M**s. Winters?"

Genni forced her eyes away from the spring-filled sight outside. The bright light that radiated in nature was in sharp contrast to the darkness and despair sitting inside her chest at the moment. "Yes?"

"Are you ready to hear the will?" Mr. Filchor asked kindly. His nose twitched, causing his full mustache to shift like a squirming caterpillar.

A small part of Genni wanted to chuckle at the image, but laughter hadn't been a part of her life for a long time, and it held even less of a place now. "Go ahead, but I already know what it says." She clasped her cold hands together.

Mr. Filchor cleared his throat. "I'm sure you do," he agreed with a heavy nod. "Maggie...Mrs. Winters planned for this a long time ago."

Genni nodded and let her mind wander again. Other than the lawyer, she was the sole person in the room. *Because I'm the only one left.* Her mother had died when Genni was a little girl, leaving her in the hands of her widowed grandmother. Her mother had no siblings and no one knew Genni's father to be able to contact any other family. It had always been assumed he was a passing tourist. A simple one-night stand. Genni grimaced and shifted in her seat. Nothing gave a girl confidence like knowing she was an accident.

Most would say Genni's upbringing had been difficult. Grandma Maggie wasn't exactly known for being warm. While not cruel, Margaret Winters was not the cookie-baking, bun-wearing, cheek-squishing grandma in the fairy tales. No...Margaret Winters had

4

known loss. Too much of it, causing her to go through life with a stoic expression and a "get it done" attitude.

With that as her example, it was no wonder that Genni had given up her teenage years and any chance at college in order to care for Margaret as she slowly withered away from lymphatic cancer. Life was hard, but Winters women had learned to be survivors.

Genni tucked a dark chunk of hair behind her ear, an assumed gift from her nonexistent father, since her mother had been blonde, and tried to force the memories from her mind.

"I give all I have, my worldly possessions and half-ownership in the Boardwalk Manor, to my granddaughter and sole living relative, Genevieve Winters," Mr. Filchor said in a monotone voice.

Genni stiffened. "Excuse me?"

Mr. Filchor stopped and twitched his mustache. "I beg your pardon?"

"Would you read that last part again?" Genni's heart began to pound. Surely she had heard wrong. Or maybe the lawyer's mustache was interfering with his reading because that last sentence couldn't have been correct.

Mr. Filchor cleared his throat again and studied the paper, tilting his head back so he could see better through his bifocals. "I give all I have, my worldly—"

"The next part," Genni urged. A single bead of sweat ran down her spine, distracting her slightly. She sat back in her seat, pressing her shirt against her skin, hoping her blouse would soak it up so she could focus. She would worry about the dry cleaning bill later.

Mr. Filchor glared at her above his glasses. "I was getting to that."

She forced herself to nod, but not speak again. Genni's clasped hands became clammy and her foot wanted to tap impatiently, but she wrangled her body into submission.

"My worldly possessions and half-ownership in the Boardwalk Mansion, to my granddaughter and—"

"I think there's been a mistake," Genni interrupted.

Mr. Filchor humphed, his mustache wiggling, before straightening in his seat. "What do you mean?"

Genni took a deep breath, keeping her voice calm. "You said half-ownership. That can't be right."

Eyebrows almost as large as the mustache rose high on a wrinkled forehead. "It is."

"How can that be?" Genni leaned forward. "My grandmother owned that house. She owned it before I was born, and I grew up there. She always told me everything would belong to me. Who else would she leave anything to? I'm the only family she had."

Mr. Filchor sighed and took off his glasses, pinching the bridge of his nose. "I'm sorry to be the one to tell you this, Ms. Winters, but there is nothing incorrect in the will." He looked up, his dark eyes slightly sunken in his old age, but still as sharp as a man half his age. "Many years ago, when you were just a tiny thing, Maggie...Mrs. Winters, was struggling to pay her taxes. She reached out to an old friend, who paid off the amount in exchange for half-ownership of the home." He wiggled his nose. "I don't have to tell you that your home is right on the beach. It's prime property." He chuckled darkly. "It was a shrewd move on Mr. James' part."

"Mr. James?" Genni could barely breathe. Every dream she had held onto for the past ten years was slowly going up in smoke. All the sacrifices, the time, money and jobs, the lack of social life and loss of companionship in her life had been worth it, as long as Genni could one day open her bed and breakfast. It was a dream she'd had since a young teenage girl, and now it was all for naught. There was no way she could renovate the mansion and open a business if she only owned half of the home.

The air felt heavy and thick as yet another blow was dealt to the last remaining Winters woman. *When will I get a break? Am I just as doomed as Grandma to live from one tragedy to another?*

Mr. Filchor nodded. "Yes, a Mr. Verl James. He was friends with your grandfather back in the day." Mr. Filchor's eyes became unfocused as he recalled his memories. "He hasn't been back here since the day he paid off the taxes," Mr. Filchor mused. Dark eyes met Genni's once more. "In fact, at his age, he'd probably be just as happy to sell you his half. He hasn't made any move to use his ownership in any way."

A small beam of hope began to ease the weight on Genni's shoulders. "Do you really think so?"

Mr. Filchor nodded firmly. "I don't see why not. If he wanted any say in the building, he's waited an awfully long time to do anything about it." He cleared his throat and shuffled the papers. "I'm sure we can look up his information and send him an email or phone call." Mr. Filchor raised his eyebrows. "Would you like my office to check into it?" He smiled softly. "In memory of Maggie?"

Genni relaxed, grateful for loyalty that seemed so common among the older generation. "I would really appreciate that, Mr. Filchor. Thank you." *I've waited this long. I can wait a few more days.*

"IF YOU'LL JUST SIGN right here," the lawyer said smoothly, pointing to a line on the bottom of the document.

Cooper's hand was shaking slightly as he put his name down.

"There," the lawyer, Ms. Mendoza, cooed. She gathered the papers, shuffling them to make the pile even, and winked at him. "It's all legal now."

"So..." Cooper pinched his lips together for a moment, gathering his thoughts. "The other owner? The woman living in the house now...does she know my grandpa owned half the deed?"

Ms. Mendoza nodded primly. "Yes. It was a deal made between them years ago, from what I understand." She tapped a pen on the desktop. "I wasn't around at the signing of the contract—it happened before my time—but I heard he helped her out of a sticky situation. Something about taxes, I think."

Cooper nodded, his eyes falling to the floor. "Do you know if she wants to hang onto the house?"

Ms. Mendoza's eyebrows shot up. "You want to keep the house?"

He shrugged, not wanting to go into details. His plans were none of this woman's business. "I'm just looking at my options."

"If I were you, I'd look into selling." The lawyer grinned. "A small town on the coast of Oregon is a far cry from the city we live in now."

"Right." Cooper pushed a hand through his hair. "But if I was interested in speaking to her, what would I do?"

Ms. Mendoza tilted her head consideringly. "I suppose you could call or email. I have no idea what her status is with the house." She snorted delicately. "At her age, she might be willing to sell you the whole thing for cheap. Then you could turn around and flip it for a profit. I'm sure there are people who enjoy small communities."

Cooper tapped his fingers against his thigh, an idea forming in his head. It was a little crazy, but he'd spent most of his life running on the edge of sane. At least this plan wouldn't end with him spending time behind bars. "Thanks."

"You're serious!" Ms. Mendoza said in shock. She laughed. "You actually want to keep the home."

Cooper nodded, his fingers twitching with his desire to get out of the stuffy room. "So...I can go now?"

She raised an eyebrow at him. "I suppose so, yes."

Cooper nodded again and spun on his boot heel.

"Mr. James."

He paused and glanced back.

"I haven't eaten since breakfast," Ms. Mendoza said with a smirk. "I know a quiet little place not far from here." The invitation hung heavy in the air and Cooper swallowed hard. This was exactly the type of thing he was trying to get away from.

"I'm sorry," he said softly, hoping he wasn't hurting her feelings. "But I don't think that's a good idea."

The second eyebrow joined the first. "Oh, really? And why is that?"

Cooper straightened his shoulders. He hated it when they wouldn't take no for an answer. "I don't mix business with pleasure."

Her lips twitched. "Our business is concluded."

Cooper shook his head harder. "I'm sorry, Ms. Mendoza. I'm not interested." There. He'd made it plain and he shouldn't have to repeat himself. Women tended to look at the tattoo on his bicep and his overgrown curls bouncing around his head and assume that he was the type of man who regularly flaunted the rules.

Can you blame them? his inner voice asked. *You used to be exactly that man.*

Ms. Mendoza leaned back in her seat, a pen twirling through her fingers. "I see..."

Cooper nodded again, feeling like a Bobblehead doll. "If you'll excuse me."

She waved him away, an icy tone to her voice. "By all means."

Swallowing a retort, Cooper left. He shivered once he was outside the office. Women who were overly aggressive used to be attractive to him, but he'd learned his lesson...a little too well. As he walked down the hallway, his eyes strayed to the windows he passed. Night had fallen during his time with the lawyer, which had felt like an eternity.

When he'd been called last week, telling him that his grandfather had passed and left him an inheritance, Cooper hadn't believed it. He hadn't spoken to Grandpa Verl since he was a rebellious teenager, trying to find his path in life.

And what a path that was, he thought scornfully. His curls brushed his cheeks as he shook his head, the sensation soft against his skin, even as his heart pounded painfully within his ribcage. "I can't believe he's gone," Cooper muttered.

He marched straight to his bike, zipping up his leather jacket as he walked. Grabbing his helmet from the back, he slammed it onto his head, grumbling at the tight fit. "Need a haircut."

After revving the engine a couple of times, Cooper brought his feet up and began to move forward. Looking both ways at the end of the parking garage, he punched it, jumping into the nighttime traffic just as he'd done a thousand times.

Memories swirled through his head as he rode. Images of him playing with his grandfather, playing catch or building a treehouse. Grandpa Verl had been a wonderful man who always had time for his family.

Cooper's lips thinned. *So what the heck happened to my parents?*

He hit the gas after idling at a stop light, enjoying the rush of adrenaline that zipping through the streets brought him. His bike was the only part of his old life that Cooper had hung onto. *Well...that and the tattoo. Can't really get rid of that one.* He slowed as he passed the mechanics garage on Forty-second and Alder. The place meant that Cooper was reaching the edge of town, but it also was a reminder of everything he would be leaving behind if he took the road laid out in front of him.

Miguel, the head mechanic, had given Cooper a job when no one else would. He'd helped Cooper get back on his feet, get a roof over his head, fill his belly and keep his most precious possession...his bike. When everything else had been taken from him, Nova had been left behind, just waiting for Cooper to get his head on straight and come back to her. Nothing else in his life had ever been so loyal.

Pressing the accelerator, Cooper sped back up and headed toward his tiny apartment. It definitely wasn't much to look at, but it was his. He paid the rent faithfully every month, just like a good citizen would do. Every part of his life now was in line with the rules, but somehow, it wasn't quite enough.

A shadow seemed to hang over Cooper, following him no matter how hard he tried to prove himself. It was as if the city wasn't willing to forget his mistakes and would forever seek for ways to punish him for them.

Cooper parked, set his kickstand and swung his leg off the bike. Cradling the key in his palm, he tucked his helmet under his arm and marched up the steps to his room. After getting inside, he locked the door, dumped his gear on the couch and sat on the edge of his bed. His eyes drifted around the small studio, taking in the bare walls and second-hand furniture.

Would you be sad to leave it behind?

He let the thought percolate for a minute, but the answer came easier than he expected. "No." The words broke the thick silence. "There's nothing for me here." He sighed, sinking into the squeaky mattress. He squished his lips to one side as he thought of living on the coast. He hadn't been to the ocean in years, not since he was living under his parents' roof.

Cooper's resolve began to build and a smile played on his lips. "New town, new job, and hopefully new home." He nodded in satisfaction. "It's about time things started going in my favor."

CHAPTER 2

A bell above the door jangled as Genni walked into The Hidden Daffodil. She smiled when a sea of heads turned her way.

"Genni!"

"You came!"

"We're so excited to see you!"

The general chorus came from a large group of women, who immediately rushed to her side. Genni's heart warmed slightly at the reception, though she tried not to show it. Grandma Maggie had always taught her not to need or rely on others, but try as she might, having this group of women felt good. The members in the Bulbs, Blossoms and Bouquets club had been the emotional support that Genni had craved, even if she wasn't one to admit to such a thing. Even though they were standing closer than Genni was comfortable with, she couldn't help but appreciate how much they wanted to help.

A lithe redhead made her way through the crowd. "Genni," she said softly, compassion in her gaze.

"Hi, Rose." Genni sighed. She found herself leaning forward, knowing Rosalinda would hug her if Genni allowed it, but Genni forced herself back. Touching was something she stayed away from. It made it harder to stay strong. Though only a few years older than Genni, Rose's maternal personality made it difficult at times, but Genni worked hard to keep from getting too close.

"How are you?" Rose whispered.

Genni nodded and shrugged. "Okay. I miss her."

Rose nodded, a line forming between her furrowed eyebrows. "It's completely understandable. The whole town will miss her."

Genni nodded, swallowing hard.

"Here, honey." Caroline stepped between the two, poking her head into Genni's personal bubble. "I brought you a little something to help you feel better." Caro winked. "Nothing helps grief more than a good piece of fudge."

Genni laughed as intended, her eyes misting up as she accepted the small plastic container. A dark, rich fudge, the consistency of thick frosting sat inside, with a wrapping of twine and ribbon on top. A small spoon hung from the bow, tempting Genni to sit down and eat immediately, but she forced herself to save it for later. "You always know exactly how to make a body feel better," she said with a grin.

Caro fluffed her perfectly coiffed hair. Highlighted waves hung to her tiny waist and if Genni didn't enjoy the feisty candy maker so much, she'd have to hate her on principle. "Sugar makes everyone feel better. I can't take credit. I just pair God's creation with other flavors to create magic."

Charlize, another member of the club, laughed huskily, along with all the other women. "Caro, you're one of a kind," Charli teased, wrapping her arm around Caro's shoulders.

Genni snorted.

"Why, thank you, Charli. I take that as a compliment." Caro preened.

"As I'm sure it was meant to be." Rose clapped her hands. "All right, ladies!" she called loudly. "Time to get started. Let's get to our tables."

Genni wiped at her eyes and walked over to her spot. She shared a table with Melody, a perky woman who owned the smoothie shop in town. "Hey, Mel," Genni said softly.

Mel smiled, her eyes sympathetic. "Hey, yourself." She frowned. "Are you all right? We've been worried about you."

Genni shrugged. "As good as I can be, I guess." She looked down at the supplies in front of her. Every month, the women of the Buds,

Blossoms and Bouquets club met to create a new flower arrangement. Rose, who owned the shop, ran the class, teaching the women
about arranging along with the language of flowers.

This class was the sole luxury Genni had allowed herself. At first
she had only come because one of the few things Grandma enjoyed
was flowers, but soon Genni found herself coming for the camaraderie instead. Most of the women were in their twenties or thirties,
and the vast majority were single, giving them common ground that
helped create friendships among a group of women who were as different as the flowers Rose sold.

Genni's eyes snagged on a large white flower in her vase of supplies. She frowned and reached out, pulling the lily from the others.

"It means sympathy," Mel explained. She gave a sheepish grin
when Genni looked over. "I Googled it before you came over."

Genni huffed and nodded. "Rose must have left it."

Mel nodded. "Yeah...she's so good about looking out for all of
us."

Genni nodded and her eyes went to her friend. They met and
Genni nodded her thanks.

Rose nodded in return and put a hand to her heart.

Genni smiled, warmth swirling through her chest, helping to
warm the cold that had permeated her body for so long. It felt so
wonderful, but Genni knew it wouldn't last. Nothing ever did.

"Before we get started..." Charli called out, startling the room into silence, "I'd like to hear an update on Genni's situation."

The whole room turned to look at Genni and she cringed slightly
under the attention. "Well..." She turned to Rose, making sure it was
okay to share before continuing. "I met with the lawyer, signed the
papers and now..." Genni made a face. "Half the house is mine."

Several shocked gasps rang through the room.

"What do you mean, half the house?" Caro demanded. She put her hands on her curvy hips. "I thought Maggie was leaving you that house free and clear."

Genni nodded. "Yeah, well, the bank doesn't own any of it. But apparently some old guy across the country does."

Caro pursed her lips. "Spill it, girl. Who do we need to beat up?"

A chuckle of amusement rippled through the group and Genni couldn't help but smile as well. "No one," she assured her friends. "But I might need to approach the bank for a loan." She scrunched her nose. "I was hoping to not have to do that, but I want to try to buy out the other half of the deed."

"Can you explain a little more?" Charli asked, her brows furrowed. "I don't get why someone else got half of your house."

Genni picked up a fallen leaf and twirled it between her fingers. "Apparently Grandma got in trouble with her taxes back when I was a baby." She took in a heavy breath. The obstacle in her path still bothered her, but Genni was determined to overcome it. *I've overcome everything else. This should be a piece of cake.* "She asked for help from an old friend of my grandpa's." Genni shrugged. "I don't know the guy, a...Verl James, I think was the name. Anyway, he paid the taxes, but in exchange, got ownership of half the house."

The room erupted with cries of outrage and disbelief.

Rose put a hand in the air. "Ladies...let's let her finish."

When it was quiet again, Genni continued. "Mr. Filchor said Mr. James is quite a bit older, so my plan is to offer to buy him out. He's never been back here, so there's no reason for me to think he has any real interest in the house at all." She held up her right hand with her fingers crossed. "Here's hoping he'll listen to my offer."

"In that case..." Rose disappeared into the back room, coming back quickly with a bundle of green stems littered with small white blossoms. "I think we'll add these to our bouquets tonight."

"What are they?" Caro asked, adding a stem to her vase.

"Gardenias." Rose smiled at Genni. "They bring good luck."

COOPER SLOWED HIS SPEED to an almost crawl as he came into Seaside Bay's city limits. A grin tugged at his lips. The coastal highway went right down what appeared to be Main Street and it was every bit as picturesque as he'd expected. "It looks like a painting," he mused under the noise of his ride.

Several people walking along the sidewalk turned to look at him as he rode by. *Probably haven't seen many bikes like this,* he mused. In an attempt to be friendly, Cooper raised a hand in greeting. Most of the onlookers waved back, but a few frowned. He brought his hand back to the handle, feeling foolish. *Don't worry about it. They don't know who you are. All they know is your vehicle is louder than they're used to.*

A sign for a beach front motel caught his eye and Cooper pulled off the road. He chuckled at the small parking lot. There was only room for maybe twenty-five cars, a far cry from the soaring parking garages he was used to.

Standing up, Cooper groaned and stretched his legs. He'd been sitting for four days straight as he traveled to this destination. Whipping his helmet off, the first thing he noticed was the tang of salt in the air. He took in a long breath through his nose and immediately felt a lifting of the tension on his shoulders. "I'm going to have to take a walk later." His eyes dropped to his heavy motorcycle boots. "But maybe I'll change shoes first." Cooper grimaced. "Or maybe I'll buy new shoes first. Some flip flops or something."

"You coming in?"

Cooper's head shot up, moving immediately to the front door of the motel. "Uh..."

An elderly woman stood with her hands on her hips, giving him a considering look. "Well?"

His eyebrows shot high on his forehead. "I guess I am." *You'd never find this in the city.*

"Then get on in here." She turned, letting the glass door slam shut behind her.

Cooper grinned. There was something decidedly funny and enjoyable about a sassy grandma. Deciding he just might like it here, he tucked his helmet under his arm and walked inside. His leather outfit squeaked as he walked, but Cooper was used to it. Plus, it was helping with the cool breeze that was nipping at his cheeks and nose.

Once inside, he headed straight to the small front desk. "I need a room, please," he said politely.

The woman, whose name tag said "Grandma Nan", gave him a look. "I should think that would be obvious."

Cooper paused, then snorted a laugh. "Why do I get the feeling you don't mince words?"

"Because you have a brain between your ears," she snapped back, then winked. "I don't see much use in beating around the bush. By the time you get to be my age, you learn not to waste time."

"Mrs. Nan, I think we're going to get along just fine," Cooper said, leaning on the counter with a grin.

"That's Grandma Nan to you," she said, pointing a finger at his face. "Now...I need a credit card, your name and why you're in town and how long you're staying."

Cooper fished around in his jacket pocket for his wallet. "I'm Cooper James," he said as he handed it over.

"A good manly name," she said with a sniff. "And how long are you going to be here, Cooper?"

He shrugged. "I'm not sure. I'm here for a while, but I'm hoping to not necessarily be at the motel the whole time."

She narrowed her gaze. "That's suspicious, boy. Makes it sound like you're up to something nefarious."

Cooper chuckled. "Nefarious? That's not a word you hear very often."

She eyed his hair and stubbly chin. "You might hear it more than the average person," she grumbled before punching some numbers on the computer. A beep caught her attention and she frowned. Pulling her glasses from her hair, she put them on and tilted her head back. "Darn technology. My granddaughter assured me it was the only way to stay open, but heck if I can figure it out."

Cooper's smile grew. "Need some help?"

She waved him off. "No. I just need your reason for being in town."

Cooper's brow furrowed. "You need that for the computer?"

Grandma Nan shook her head. "Nope. Need that for my sewing circle. They'll want to know who the new hunk is in town."

Cooper choked on air. "Excuse me?" he asked as he coughed.

Grandma Nan peered at him over her glasses. "We're old," she scolded. "Not dead."

Cooper's laugh was deep and genuine.

Grandma Nan put a hand over her heart. "We're also not immune to heart attacks, so ease up on the cuteness, young man."

Cooper nodded and wiped at the corner of his eye as he got control of himself. "Grandma Nan, you're making me feel more at home than I have in a long time."

She laughed. "Honey, you just wait until the Fourth of July town festival. You'll be so smothered in grandmotherly goodness, you won't be able to breathe."

He chuckled and put his credit card back in his wallet.

"You still haven't answered the question, you know," she reminded him, writing out a slip with a number on it.

Cooper sighed. "It's a little complicated," he admitted. "I'm not sure I should say anything until I've spoken to some other people."

She paused, her hand in mid-air with the key. "Okay...now you've really got me worried." She leaned forward on the counter top. "Let me tell you something, hot stuff. I've lived here for over fifty years. There's nothing I haven't heard and no one I don't know. You coming in and making vague comments is only going to get everyone's dander up."

"So how do I avoid that?" he asked, feeling wary for the first time since he arrived.

Grandma Nan shrugged. "Tell me why you're here and I'll get you started in the right direction."

Cooper's brow furrowed and he pushed a hand through his unruly curls. "I'm here because I inherited something."

Grandma Nan's eyebrows shot up high. "And just what is that?"

He pinched his lips together, unsure if he should say anything. He really should talk to the woman who owned the house first, but on the other hand, Grandma Nan more than likely knew exactly who he needed to talk to. "Truth is, my grandfather just passed away, leaving me half of a house here."

"Half?"

Cooper nodded.

"That sounds fishy."

"I know, but it is what it is." He shrugged.

"And what are you hoping to do with half a house?" Grandma Nan asked, putting her hands on her rounded hips.

"I'm hoping to buy the other person out."

"And who is the other person?" she pressed.

"I don't actually know her. I just have a name and an address."

"Which is?"

"Fifty-seven, thirty-one Bridge View Court. The lady is Margaret Winters."

Grandma Nan's jaw dropped open. "Oh, dear."

"What?"

She shook her head and handed him the key. "You'll find out."

CHAPTER 3

Genni put her hands on her hips and sighed. "This is going to take forever," she muttered. Slowly, she walked through the old mansion. The paint was chipping, and the hardwood floor was scratched. The furniture looked as if it had come from a second hand store a hundred years ago.

A small smile tugged at her lips. Despite the run-down appearance of the home, there were many good memories here. Grandma Maggie had taught Genni how to knead bread on the peeling laminate. They'd baked so many casseroles in the ancient oven that Genni was positive anything that came out of its doors would taste like Tater Tots and cream of mushroom soup.

"I miss you," she sighed into the quiet space. Yet, even with the sadness that losing her only relative brought, there was a small shimmer of anticipation. Of finally having the chance to realize the dream Genni had been working on since she was young. "If only Mr. James will agree to it," she muttered as she walked into the dining room. "Until then, I'll have to restore this place on an even tighter budget."

Genni had hoped to wait to take out a loan for as long as possible, but there was no way her meager savings from waitressing in the diner could cover a renovation and a buy-out. Money would have to come from somewhere and it wouldn't be from her account.

Grabbing her sketchbook and pencils, she sat down at the dining room table and let her eyes wander. She pictured in her mind's eye what the space would have looked like when it was first built in the late 1800s. The home had been built in the Queen Anne style. It was two-and-a-half stories high with a full basement and four-story tower, creating a home with over ten thousand square feet. Having originally been built by a wealthy sea captain for his young bride, the home had once contained every modern luxury.

Genni grinned as she sketched, remembering the creaks and groans that used to frighten her as a child. The emptiness of such a large home with so few inhabitants still bothered her, and that's exactly why she planned to fill the spaces with joy and laughter. "Someday..." she mused, her pencil flying, "we'll bring this place back to its original glory, and every room will be filled with smiles."

Just as she leaned back to admire her design ideas, a sharp knock came on the front door. Genni jumped from her seat. *Maybe it's Mr. Filchor with news about the other owner.* She slid across the hardwood in her fuzzy socks and grasped the old, golden handle, jerking the door wide. "Hi..." Her words died in her throat. Standing on the front wraparound deck was a man Genni didn't know...and he was gorgeous.

Brown curls bounced around his head, coming down to chin level to meet up with a neatly trimmed beard. Or at least the start of a beard. It was quite short, just enough stubble to look filled in, but not yet long. The beard framed a strong jaw attached to a straight nose and deep-set, hazel eyes.

A slight aura of danger drifted from the stranger, despite his handsomeness, and Genni found herself taking a step backward before she caught the movement. She forced her eyes not to stare, but in moving away from his face, it only caused her to notice his thick biceps, one with a wraparound, barbwire tattoo, and his slightly intimidating height.

At five-foot-seven, Genni wasn't exactly short, but this man was definitely over six feet. The entire package was intoxicating, but frightening all at once. Not knowing what else to do, Genni tried to put the manners she'd been taught into practice. "Can I..." She swallowed, trying to bring moisture back to her mouth. "Can I help you?"

The stranger's brow was furrowed and his eyes drifted over her, causing Genni to lament the fact that she was wearing sweats and a raggedy T-shirt, rather than something nicer. *Wait a second! I don't even know this guy! I don't want to impress him.* Forcing herself to stand a little straighter, she tried again. "Excuse me, sir. But can you please tell me why you're here?"

He cleared his throat and scratched at his beard. "Sorry...I didn't expect..."

Genni raised her eyebrows. "Didn't expect what?"

"Uh..." He looked at a piece of paper in his palm then back at her. "I'm looking for Margaret Winters."

Pain slammed into Genni's chest, the same way it always did when someone brought up her grandmother. She rubbed the spot on her sternum and bit back the tears that usually accompanied the sensation. "She's not here," Genni snapped, her pain making her tone sharper than usual.

His eyebrows crept up. "When will she be back?"

Genni's jaw worked as she held back a rude retort. *He doesn't know. He's a stranger.* She tried to reason with herself. "Look, I'm sorry to have to tell you this, but Grandma Maggie passed away last week. She's not coming back."

Immediately the stranger's demeanor softened. "I'm sorry," he said softly.

Genni nodded once. "Yes, well...thank you. Now if you'll excuse me—" She stepped back to close the door.

"Wait!" The stranger put his hand out and stopped the door from latching.

Genni scowled and pulled it back open. "What?"

He shook his head and stepped forward a little. "If she's gone, then who do I talk to about this home?"

Genni froze. "Why do you need to talk to anyone about the home? It's not for sale." Her heart began to pound harder than normal as she waited for his answer. Once again, luck didn't seem to be on her side. Her grandmother had only been gone for a few days, and already the vultures were descending. *Please let it be a Realtor and not something else...*

He shook his head. "I'm not here to buy it," the man explained. "My name is Cooper James."

Black spots burst into Genni's vision.

"I own it."

The heavy thudding of boots was the last thing Genni heard as her knees collapsed, but instead of a hard landing, strong, warm arms caught her, and right before the world disappeared, Genni felt herself be pressed into a broad chest.

"NOW YOU'VE DONE IT," Cooper cursed at himself as he held up the unconscious beauty. He had pressed her against his chest, but with her legs still dangling, he couldn't exactly move her around. Shifting his hold, he held her upper body steady with one arm, then swept the other one under her knees. He grunted as he lifted her, then immediately walked inside the home.

He didn't bother to look around, only to search for a place to set her down. Spotting one of those couches with only one end on it, he hurried over and gently laid her on her back. Straightening, his eyes stayed glued to the woman. She hadn't said her name, but it had been obvious that his meant something to her.

"Just who are you?" he murmured, his hands going to his hips. She wasn't the type of woman that Cooper normally dated. He snorted. *If I've left that life behind, I suppose I don't have a type of woman I date at all, do I?* he thought sarcastically to himself.

Her thick, dark hair was in a messy bun on top of her head, but some of the strands had fallen on the back of her neck and along the side of her face, softening the severe look she had given him when he'd first arrived on the doorstep. Her eyes had been dark, nearly black, creating an exotic look against her lighter skin. Her dark pink lips were plump and her nose straight if not just a little longer than society deemed perfect.

But the biggest thing Cooper had noticed was the tightness in her face. Fine lines, despite her young age, sat at the edge of her eyes. She looked like a woman who had known hardship and had pulled herself through by her own bootstraps.

"Oooh..." she moaned, putting a hand to her forehead. "What the heck happened?"

Cooper's first impulse was to step forward and comfort her, but he held himself in check. He didn't know this chick and had no right to touch her. "You fainted," he explained.

The woman jerked her eyes open and looked over at him with her jaw hanging open. "Oh my gosh," she murmured, sitting up, then pausing to close her eyes. "Too fast," she rasped.

"Can I...get you something?" Cooper offered, feeling like an idiot as he just stood and watched.

She shook her head slowly. "No, thank you. Nothing except to leave."

His eyebrows shot up. "I think I explained at the door that I own this place."

Her jaw clenched and a twitching muscle was visible in her throat. "You do *not* own this home."

Cooper grinned and put his hands in the air. He wasn't trying to upset anybody, but he had come a long way to claim his inheritance, and he was going to do exactly that. "Look, I'm not here to cause trouble."

"Good. Then you can go." The woman stood and marched toward the front door.

"I might not want to cause trouble, but being the owner of this home means that I don't have to leave." He probably shouldn't be egging her on like this, but he wanted this settled. He still didn't know this woman's name for crying out loud! Just that she didn't want him there. *She's probably been living here since Ms. Winters died and doesn't want to lose her home.* "I'm sure you've grown attached to the place—"

"This is *my* home," she spat at him.

"I get that you've been staying here, but it's mine now." He gave her a sympathetic look. "I have the paperwork to prove it."

She shook her head adamantly. "No. You have paperwork to prove you own *half* of this home." Her shoulders straightened and she stuck her nose in the air. "I own the other half."

Shock hit Cooper in the gut. Really, he should have seen this coming. *If Grandpa passed his ownership onto me, it makes sense that someone else would inherit Mrs. Winter's half. I've been an idiot.* Putting out his hand, he stepped in her direction. "Good to meet you. I'm Cooper James."

Looking like she was facing a communicable disease, she brought a limp hand up to shake.

Cooper plastered his smile in place, ignoring her reaction. "And you are?"

Her lips were in a thin, white line and the words seemed difficult for her. "Genevieve Winters."

"Great." Cooper nodded his head and rocked back on his heels. "Are you Margaret's daughter?"

"Granddaughter."

He nodded again. He had expected the original owner to be as old as his grandfather, so that made sense. "I'm sorry for her passing."

She nodded. "Thank you." Her brows scrunched together. "I was told Verl James owned the other half of the house."

"My grandfather."

"So you..." She was obviously fishing for his story. Cooper wasn't ready to tell her everything, but he could give her the bare necessities.

"He died." Cooper shrugged. "I ended up with a surprise."

"Oh." Genevieve chewed on her bottom lip. "I'm sorry to hear that."

He nodded. "Thank you." This conversation was going in circles. *Time to get things settled.* "Okay, well, I can tell I caught you off guard with everything. Why don't I take you to dinner and we can get everything out in the open, and talk about where to go next."

Her eyes narrowed and she seemed to be considering his words.

Please, please, please, he begged. He already liked this quaint little town, and after getting a small glimpse of the large mansion, he wanted nothing more than to put down his roots here. *Roots that will be far better than where I came from.*

"I will, on one condition," she said cautiously.

"Name it."

"That you're willing to listen to my proposal."

Cooper paused. That was exactly what he was hoping she would do for him. Knowing she had some kind of plan made him nervous. If she had an agenda, it would be harder to get her to sell. *Money talks,* he reminded himself. *If I offer her more than this place is worth, it should go a long way in changing her mind.* His eyes scanned the room quickly. *Especially because I don't think money has been easy to come by for her.* "Deal," he said. "But you have to agree to do the same."

Her skin paled, but she nodded.

"Tonight? Seven?"

Once again, she nodded. "I'll be ready."

"Sounds good. Thank you." Cooper moved toward the door. "I'm afraid I'm going to need a suggestion on where to eat. I've never been here before." He paused with his hand on the doorknob.

"The Clam Pot has the best seafood, but we have a few of the normal chains like Seafood Galley and Denny's."

"What would you like?"

Her dark eyes were on the floor. "Uh...if it's all the same to you, Denny's is fine."

She refused to meet his gaze, making Cooper suspicious, but he didn't know what to accuse her of. "Okay. Can I pick you up?"

"Do you have something besides that death trap outside?" She looked at him with a challenging eyebrow.

Cooper chuckled. "Not yet."

"Then I'll meet you there, thank you. It's probably better that way anyway."

He nodded, a bit of disappointment hitting his stomach, but he brushed it aside. *She's the competition, nothing more.* "Thanks, I'll see you there."

CHAPTER 4

The first thing Genni did after Cooper left was run upstairs to change her clothes. She straightened her hair and brushed her teeth, jumped into a pair of walking sandals and rushed out to her car. "Mr. Filchor had better have a good explanation for this," she grumbled.

Her hands shook as she drove the couple of miles to the lawyer's office. Cooper James' visit had her completely rattled. His good looks had sent her senses for a loop, but then she'd discovered who he was, and it had knocked her back on the ground. Literally.

"Why can't I just catch a break?" she muttered, shoving the car into park. Her eyes were pooled with tears, but Genni bit her tongue until she could force them back.

She had come too far and fought too hard to let this set her back. *But how? That guy definitely didn't show up here because he was just planning to sell the place. How can I convince him to do that?*

"Ms. Winters," the secretary said with a surprised smile. "We weren't expecting you. If you'll just have a seat, I'll let Mr. Filchor know you're here."

"No thanks," she grumbled, storming around the desk to the office door.

"Ms. Winters!"

Genni was not usually one to flaunt the rules, but her emotions were running too high to listen to reason. She had no intention of sitting in a cold waiting room with her rear going numb, waiting for Mr. Filchor to fit her in. This situation needed *immediate* attention.

Genni shoved open the door, pausing dramatically in the doorway. The strong action gave her a small sense of satisfaction, but she held back a smile. "Mr. Filchor," she stated firmly. "I need to speak to you."

Those caterpillars rose high on his forehead and the mustache twitched a couple of times. "I'll have to call you back, Herb," he said into the phone, his eyes never leaving Genni. "Mm, hm. Yep. I'm on it. Thanks. Bye." The phone went gently back in the receiver. "Ms. Winters."

"Mr. Filchor."

"I tried to tell her you were busy, Mr. Filchor, but she wouldn't listen," the secretary said, glaring at Genni.

Genni ignored her. "I've got a problem."

Mr. Filchor stood and waved to an empty seat. "Come on in, Ms. Winters." He looked to the secretary. "Mrs. Munchkin, thank you, but I'll take it from here."

Genni heard the woman huff but leave the room, closing the door behind her.

"What's the problem, Ms. Winters?"

Genni walked toward the desk, but didn't sit. "A man showed up on my doorstep this morning," she began. "He claimed to be Verl James' grandson."

"I see."

"No..." Genni shook her head. "I don't think you do." Genni put her hands on her hips. "He's here. He says his grandpa died and left him the half-deed." She took a deep breath. "And he doesn't seem to have any intention of selling...or leaving."

Mr. Filchor cleared his throat, the mustache wiggling. "Well...that does seem a little uncomfortable."

"Uncomfortable? No...uncomfortable is having the seam of your sock rub against your toe. This isn't uncomfortable. This is insane!" She pushed her hands through her hair. Her stomach was churning and her anxiety soaring through the roof.

"What exactly do you want me to do about it, Ms. Winters?"

"You were supposed to contact this Verl guy about selling!"

He sighed. "I'm assuming my inquiry will come back with the information you just shared."

"Then what am I supposed to do?" she demanded. *Get control of yourself, Gen. You sound like a spoiled toddler.* She squeezed her eyes shut and pinched the bridge of her nose. "I'm sorry, Mr. Filchor. I didn't mean to snap at you. I'm flustered and not reacting well to the situation."

Mr. Filchor sighed and moved to sit back down in his cushy leather chair. "It sounds to me like you had quite a shock this morning, I suppose anyone would be struggling under the circumstances."

"Thanks," Genni mumbled. She plopped into a seat. "But that doesn't help me know what to do next."

"Have you offered to buy this young man's half?"

She shook her head. "We're having a meeting at dinner tonight. He did promise to listen to my proposal, but he didn't look happy about it." She slumped backward, the righteous anger draining from her body.

"Then I don't think anything can be done until you've spoken to him. He has a legal right to the house and you can't stop him from exercising it." Mr. Filchor tilted his head to the side and gave her a sympathetic look. "I'm sorry it came to this. I assure you, no one expected him to just show up and want to claim his property."

Those darn tears were threatening again. "Right." She sniffed and bit her tongue. It was going to bleed soon if she didn't stop with all this emotional slop. "Guess I'll figure it out on my own." *Just like I've been doing my whole life.*

"I'm sorry I'm not more help," Mr. Filchor said, standing with her. "If there was anything I could do legally, I would."

She nodded, not trusting her voice to be strong if she spoke. "Thank you for your time," she forced herself to mutter, then spun on her heel and strode out of the office. She held her shoulders straight and her chin slightly elevated, all things she had learned to do to exude confidence, even if she didn't necessarily feel it. *Fake it 'til you make it.* The mantra had gotten her through more hard times than Genni could count.

Slamming her car door shut, she paused, then let her forehead drop to the steering wheel. The tears that had threatened multiple times finally broke free and she began to sob. "Why? Why can't anything ever go right in my life? I haven't been wanted since the day I was born, and it still feels like I'm unwanted. Just when everything I've worked for was supposed to come to fruition, I'm still being blocked." She took in a shuddering breath. "As if I don't deserve any of my dreams."

Her shoulders shook as she let the tears flow. The insecurity she tried to hide was threatening to drown her and Genni found herself grasping for a solid hold on reality, but it was harder than it should have been. "No!" she growled, gritting her teeth. "No! I *can't* give up now." Sitting up, she sniffed and wiped at her face. "I've worked too hard. He has to see reason." She started the car, determination building within her. Her life might have been full of hardships and trials, but she was still here, she was still surviving. "I'll just have to make him an offer he can't refuse," she vowed. "He's not emotionally attached to the house. Yesterday was the first time he saw it." She sat up taller. "I'm sure he'll understand that he'll be happier somewhere else. Any sane person will understand where I'm coming from."

Now she just had to hope he was a sane person.

COOPER FORCED HIMSELF to put the cologne back on the counter. "This isn't a date," he reminded himself. *But you are trying to impress her. After all, you want something from her.*

Cooper glared at his reflection. Quickly grabbing the cologne, he sprayed a little on, then slammed it down. "There. Happy?" His inner voice chuckled in satisfaction. "I'm a complete idiot," he muttered, pushing his hand through his curls, messing up the work he'd put into trying to tame them.

He grabbed his gear and stormed out of his room.

Grandma Nan whistled low under her breath. "You clean up pretty good, hot stuff."

Cooper laughed, her teasing helping to break the tension he was carrying. "You're not so bad yourself," he tossed back. "Got a date tonight?"

"Only with the television." She grinned. "*Murder She Wrote* is on, didn't you know?" Grandma Nan shook her head. "They don't make 'em like Jessica Fletcher anymore."

Cooper chuckled and shook his head. "Have fun," he said, using his back to push open the front door of the motel.

"I think I should be saying that to you!" she shouted as the door closed.

Cooper took a calming breath and walked over to his bike. "I'm not sure anything about tonight is going to be...fun."

It only took him a few minutes to find Denny's. The neon yellow sign was brighter than the street lights and with so few large restaurants around, it stood out like a sore thumb. The parking lot was only half-full, making it easy to park and get inside.

"Good evening, sir," the young woman said from the hostess counter. "One tonight?"

"Two, please," he said, holding up two fingers.

She nodded, then grabbed a couple of menus. "Right this way, please."

The smell of pancakes and coffee permeated the air like a heavy fog as Cooper followed the hostess to a table.

"Is this one okay?" she asked, waving to a small table in the far corner of the room.

Cooper nodded. The hostess probably thought being tucked away would let him have a romantic moment with his date, but Cooper figured it would also help him keep their conversation private. "This is great. Thanks."

The young woman beamed and set the menus down. "Your waitress will be here shortly."

After she was gone, Cooper shrugged out of his jacket and sat down. He was surprised how chilly it was, being spring and all. *Must be the ocean. Speaking of which...* He made a mental note to take a run in the morning. He'd managed to catch a few glimpses today, but instead of taking time to really get a good look, he'd been busy working out the logistics of his plan.

"Hello."

Cooper jumped out of his chair when Genevieve arrived. "Sorry," he said, cursing himself for being too caught up in his mental wanderings. "I didn't see you come in." He tried to move and help with her chair, but she beat him to it.

"No worries," Genevieve said easily. "It's not like this is a date or something."

Any thought Cooper had that she found him the slightest bit attractive fizzled like a leaking balloon. *Okay...guess we're doing this the hard way.* "Thank you for being willing to meet me tonight."

She nodded, her eyes on the menu. "Why don't we order before we talk business?"

He nodded his agreement and they got the task out of the way. Once the waitress was gone, Cooper folded his hands on the table top. "So..."

A slim, dark brow taunted him. "So."

"You said you had a proposal. Would you like to go first?" He watched her throat move. The swallow was almost audible and it gave Cooper hope. It was the first sign of the evening that she was as nervous as he was.

"Mr. James," she began.

"Cooper."

Genevieve paused to blink, then shrugged. "Fine. Cooper."

"Or Coop if you prefer. I go by either one." *STOP talking!* He snapped his mouth shut.

"Coop," she repeated as if testing the word in her mouth. She shook her head, her luxurious hair spilling around her shoulders and distracting Cooper. "I need you to understand something."

He nodded.

"I have lived in that house my whole life."

Cooper's heart fell to his stomach. *How can I argue against that?*

"My mother died when I was young and I was raised by my grandmother there." She gave him a placating smile. "It's the only home I've ever known. Truth is, your grandfather only bought half of the house in order to help my grandparents out of a difficult situation. It's obvious he didn't truly want it, since he never came back after he gained it."

Cooper leaned back. At first he'd been feeling sorry for her, but she was now dangerously close to insulting his grandfather, and that made Cooper's temper begin to shift.

"I have plans for that home. Plans that you won't be interested in," she continued.

Cooper folded his arms over his chest and pursed his lips. "I wouldn't, huh?"

She shook her head, still smiling pleasantly. "No. I want to open a bed and breakfast, have for years. I've saved all my money and plan to restore the home to its original state, then rent out the guest rooms." She paused to take a sip of water.

"You don't even know me," Cooper interjected. "How do you know I wouldn't be interested in that plan?"

Genevieve snorted. "Are you telling me you want to cook?" Her eyes drifted to his leather jacket, then out the window where Cooper knew his motorcycle was waiting. When her eyes met his again, they were taunting. "I don't think so."

"Maybe I like to cook," he shot back, not appreciating her judgment of him before ever getting to know him. This chat was not going how he'd expected at all, but now he was getting angry and wasn't sure how to turn things around.

Her mouth firmed. "Look," she hissed, slapping her hands on the table and leaning forward. "The truth is, you don't belong here. You don't know the area, the people or the Boardwalk Manor."

"And you do?" he pressed.

"Yes, I do."

"You know everything that goes on around here, huh?"

"Of course!" she answered, scoffing at his supposed ignorance.

Cooper leaned in, ignoring the whiff of enticing perfume he got from her nearness. "Well, then, I suppose you already know that tomorrow I'm moving into the mansion."

She gasped.

"And I'll be helping make any decisions *before* any renovations are made. Half of that home is mine and you will either work with me, or I'll take you to court and take it all."

"You wouldn't dare," she said, her voice slightly wobbly.

"I've never been more serious," he declared. He hadn't come planning to make an enemy, but Genevieve's condescending attitude had pricked his pride, and he felt compelled to fight back.

Her nostrils flared and she slammed the white, cloth napkin down on the table. "Well, then, I guess we don't have anything left to say to each other." Shoving her chair back, she stood. "But good luck getting in. I'm the only person in town with a key."

Cooper smirked, knowing it would come across as arrogant, but not caring at the moment. She'd just declared war and he wanted to let her know who she was dealing with. "Actually, I already have one.

The kind woman at the title office made me a copy, once I proved my identity."

The blood drained from Genevieve's face and Cooper almost leapt to his feet, fearing she would faint again, but instead she whirled, her dark hair flying, and stormed out of the restaurant.

That went well, he thought sarcastically. Sighing, he hung his head backward. "How am I going to make this work?" he grumbled.

"The American Burger?"

Cooper looked up to see their meals being delivered. "That's for the lady," he said, pointing to her empty spot. "Actually, she's not coming back. Could you box it up, but leave me the other dinner?"

The waitress looked confused for a moment, but nodded. "Be right back."

Cooper tucked into his dinner, even though his appetite was gone. He'd pay for both dinners, just like he'd planned to from the beginning, though the gesture was useless now. Just because he'd gotten stiffed tonight didn't mean the waitress had to be.

CHAPTER 5

G enni's thumb pounded mercilessly against the steering wheel as she drove. Last night had been an absolute disaster. "What were you thinking?" she scolded herself. Sighing, she turned the radio off. The music was only adding to her anger.

She'd met him at a Denny's, of all places. *Because you're too poor to be able to afford anything else,* she lamented. "A business meeting at Denny's. Nice." Genni shook her head. "Whatever. But how are you going to keep him from moving into the house?"

She had called Mr. Filchor again last night, but he had said she had no legal leg to stand on. Half of the house was his and the man had every right to live there if he wanted to. "Why, Grandma?" Genni asked, her eyes stinging with withheld tears. "Why didn't you buy back the house once you got on your feet? Surely you had enough time to do it." Genni sniffed then wiped at her face and nose. "So stupid," she muttered. "Crying doesn't help anything."

It was a lesson she had learned too many times over her growing up years. Crying didn't keep Genni from losing her mom, or from not being able to keep friends during high school, or from having to have a job when she'd have rather been socializing. Crying had helped even less when Genni had started taking care of her grandmother, only to still lose her in the end. Worst of all, crying didn't help when she was lonely and knew she was completely alone in the world.

She clenched her jaw, forcing her emotions under control. "I can't do anything about Mr. Jerk Face right now, but I can do something about the dining room." She cleared her throat and straightened in her seat. She had left first thing this morning in order to drive to the next town over and buy paint and wallpaper supplies. She didn't care what Cooper James said. Genni had been planning this renovation in her head for years, and she was going to act on it. "And if he doesn't like it, he can just stuff it," she muttered as she parked in the large parking lot of the home improvement store.

Locking her door, she headed inside, aiming straight for the paint section. She immediately began to pick up paint samples. Her mind must have been wholly engaged in the project because she never heard anyone come up beside her.

"Looking to paint something?"

Genni jerked and looked over. "Uh..yep" she stuttered. "That's why I'm picking up paint samples."

He chuckled. "Sorry. I guess that wasn't the best opening line." He nodded toward her hands. "Perhaps you should just call me Captain Obvious."

Genni relaxed a little and laughed lightly. "It's not a big deal. Sorry, I wasn't trying to be snippy. I've just got a lot on my mind."

His grin softened. "Anything I can help with?"

She gave him a look. "Considering the fact that I don't know you, I'd say that's a no." Her eyes quickly took in his slick hair and pressed pants. There was something about this guy that made him look out of place in a store where people regularly walked around in paint-stained clothing. Still, he was attractive...in a big city type of way. *Not like the rugged handsomeness of Cooper James.* "Why are you here?" she asked, forcing herself away from long wavy hair and neatly trimmed beards.

The man raised his eyebrows at her. "Since I don't know you, I'm not sure I should tell you that."

Genni gave him a sheepish grin. "Sorry. Guess I'm the one putting my foot in it now, huh?"

He laughed and stuck out a hand. "Nope. I started it. I'm Hudson Baumgartner."

Gennis shook his hand, finally relaxing enough to enjoy their flirting. "Genevieve Winters."

"Genevieve...not a name you hear that often."

She shrugged. She knew full well it was an old-fashioned name. "I was raised by my grandmother, so..."

"Ah...well, if it helps, it's beautiful." His eyes warmed. "Just like you."

Genni scoffed. "Laying it on a bit thick, aren't you?"

Hudson shrugged, stuffing his hands in his pockets. The look was so boyish that it helped downplay the crispness of his outward appearance. "I think you could tell from the beginning that I'm not exactly the smoothest person when it comes to women." He looked up from under his eyelashes and Genni's heart fluttered. "Especially when I'm trying to ask her to dinner."

"Oh." Genni's mouth formed the word, but it was barely audible. *What in the world is going on here? I never get asked out.* She blinked rapidly, not sure how to answer such an invitation. In a small town where everyone knew everyone, Genni was more than aware that the single men of Seaside Bay were not for her. But she'd never exactly found herself attracted to men who spent more time in a salon than she did. *Motorcycle riding intruders, however...*

Once again, she slammed the lid on the train of thought. The guy was a jerk and Genni wanted nothing to do with him.

Hudson chuckled uncomfortably and rubbed the back of his neck. "Sorry. I guess that was too much too quickly." He pointed away. "I'm just going to go..."

"Wait!" Genni called out, forcing her worries to silence. She smiled and dropped her voice back to normal. "Dinner would be nice."

The beaming smile on Hudson's face instantly made Genni feel better. Just because he didn't appear to be her usual type didn't mean she couldn't get to know him. He was handsome enough, just a little more put together than she was usually drawn to. But could she really fault the guy for having good fashion sense?

"Fantastic. Can I pick you up tonight?"

Genni immediately shook her head. "I don't actually live in this town. I'm over in Seaside Bay."

Hudson's smile brightened. "Perfect! That's actually where I'm staying."

"Staying?"

He nodded. "I don't live around here. I'm just here for an extended visit."

Genni tilted her head, curiosity beginning to niggle at her. "Oh, are you visiting family? I probably know them."

He grinned. "No. No family. I'm here for work."

Genni leaned back. "What in the world would bring you to our podunk area for work?"

"I'm the legal counsel for a company," Hudson said smoothly. He shrugged. "It's not very exciting."

"So you're a lawyer?"

He nodded. "Yeah. That's probably the right term."

Genni frowned. It was a weird explanation, but she didn't really know quite else what to say. It wasn't like she knew anything about the legal world. *Except for Mr. Filchor...* Her mind began to spin. *Maybe Hudson can offer me some kind of advice that Mr. Filchor didn't think of!* Suddenly she was more than a little excited for this date. Hudson wouldn't be able to just brush her off or tell her she had no rights. They'd be stuck at dinner together, which should give her ample time to see if she had any way of keeping Cooper James from moving into her home. "I actually have another appointment tonight, but can I meet you somewhere tomorrow?"

"Where's good?" he asked, then leaned forward. "And I'm paying, so don't worry about that." He grinned.

Genni grinned back. "In that case, how about the Clam Pot. Six-thirty?"

He nodded. "I'll look forward to it."

Genni found herself being truthful when she said, "Me too."

"YOU'RE JUST GOING TO move in?" Grandma Nan screeched while Cooper was checking out the next morning.

Cooper gave her a look. "It's my house, too."

"Maybe so," she started, leaning forward. "But this town isn't very big. Do you really want to make your first impression by moving in with a girl?"

Cooper sighed and scratched his beard. "It's not like that," he argued.

"But others won't know that," Grandma Nan explained. "You'll make everyone think there's something sneaky going on."

Cooper chuckled. "Sneaky? Considering how much Genevieve loathes the sight of me, I don't think there will be any sneaking."

Grandma Nan clucked her tongue. "She doesn't loathe the sight of you." Grandma Nan pursed her lips. "She might loathe *you*, but not the *sight* of you."

Cooper made a face. "What makes you say that?"

"The girl has eyes in her head, doesn't she?"

Cooper laughed.

"On the other hand..." she mused, tapping her lips. "You might be exactly what this town needs for a little shake-up." She dropped her hand. "We've been stuck for too long. Maybe with a fresh handsome face like yours getting noticed, you'll kick the men in this town into action."

Cooper put up his hands. "I'm not here looking for anything but my inheritance," he explained. *Genevieve might be beautiful, but the only thing between us is business...and it's staying that way.*

"So says you," Grandma Nan quipped. She smiled. "But never you mind the ramblings of an old woman. Just come back and say hi once in awhile, okay?"

Cooper gave her a mock salute. "Will do."

She waved as he pushed open the front door and walked out to his bike. He stuffed his clothes in the compartments and slung his leg over, enjoying the feel of the rumbling engine beneath him. It only took minutes for him to get down to the house, which was just on the outskirts of town.

Cooper paused in the driveway, his legs supporting the bike on either side, as he looked at the house. It was older and definitely needed some fixing up, but it was large and beautiful. Three stories high, a wraparound porch...it was definitely an antique worth saving and the perfect place for him to start putting down his roots.

He could understand why Genni was interested in turning it into a bed and breakfast, but the idea didn't sit well with Cooper. He wasn't excited about the idea of having people in and out of his home all the time. It sounded intrusive and chaotic. When he settled down, he wanted peace and quiet, not a bustling hotel.

He turned off the engine, gathered his things and went to the door. His hand automatically raised to knock, but he stopped himself. "I don't have to knock, this is my place too," he reminded himself. "Not to mention, she'd probably slam the door in my face." He retrieved the key from his pocket and headed inside. It was dark and silent, bringing Cooper to the conclusion that she was gone.

"Perfect. I can get my stuff settled in without her ranting and raving about anything." Whistling a cheery tune, he began to walk around, inspecting the home as he went. The rooms were good-sized, but broken up, nothing like the modern great rooms that were so popular in today's new houses.

The furniture looked as old as the house. The wooden frames looked in good shape, but the fabrics were faded and holey, making the whole area appear drab and in neglect. In fact, most of the house looked like it hadn't been touched in ages, except the kitchen. Laminate countertops were definitely not original to the home, and the appliances of course were not one-hundred-plus years old.

Cooper walked over to the sink and ran the water for a moment. "Hopefully the plumbing has been updated as well," he grumbled. He marched through the kitchen, the butler's pantry, the dining room and back into the sitting room. "Bedrooms must be upstairs." Walking to the grand staircase, he let his hand test out the bannister, glad to see it appeared sturdy.

The hallway upstairs was lined with doorways and Cooper started on the left hand side, moving his way down the hallway, then back on the opposite. All in all, there were five bedrooms, two bathrooms and a storage room, which was filled with more dust than possessions.

Two of the rooms appeared to be in use and Cooper assumed one belonged to Genevieve and one had belonged to her grandmother. Moving to the room farthest away, he plopped his stuff on the bed, coughing at the dust that erupted, and put his hands on his hips. His eyes roamed the wooden walls and floors. The furniture was dark and the bedspread looked like it had once belonged to a little girl. *Ponies and stars aren't really my thing,* he thought with a chuckle. "I'll have to go grab some supplies," he murmured in order to make a mental note. "But first, let's find the vacuum."

He spent the next half-hour cleaning out the room, making the space livable again. With earbuds in and music blasting, he completely lost track of time as he worked.

"What do you think you're doing!"

Cooper paused and slowly turned around. He was pretty sure what he would see, but decided it was best not to make any sudden movements anyway. Genevieve stood in the doorway with her mouth gaping open. She looked pale and shaky as her eyes fell on his bundle of clothes. "You're moving in?"

Cooper dropped the rag and dust spray he'd been using, then folded his arms over his chest. "I told you I was."

"Yeah, but I didn't think you'd do it so quickly!" she shouted. Her hands went to her head. "This is crazy." Wild, dark eyes turned to his. "You know that, right? I don't even know you, and you're moving into my house."

"Our house," he corrected.

Genevieve shook her head. "This has to be some kind of nightmare." Her eyes were glassy and Cooper had a moment of compassion.

It really was an odd situation. How often did two people each own half of a house? Especially complete strangers. *I'm not leaving, but at least we can fix one of those problems.* "Look," he said, stepping in her direction. "I know this is awkward, but we're both adults. Surely we can work together, right? We just need to get to know each other a little better."

Genevieve's eyes widened and she stumbled backward. "No," she said, her voice softer than normal. "This isn't the way it's supposed to happen." She leaned forward, seeming to regain some of her anger. "This house should be mine. I've scrimped, saved and sacrificed most of my life in order to turn this into a bed and breakfast, and that dream doesn't include you. I work alone."

Ouch. Cooper knew she was upset, but wow...that had been a bit harsh. Her stubbornness made it easier for him to dig in his own heels. "Well, you'll just have to get used to it. I said it before and I'll say it again. I'm not going anywhere."

She pointed a shaking finger at him. "We'll just see about that. I'm going to find a way to get you out of here."

"Go ahead," he said, shrugging his shoulders. He hoped his nonchalant act was working. Truth was, he felt like a small boy who was constantly being pushed aside by his parents. Unwanted and unavailable. *But I haven't had a real place to call my own in a long time, and I'm not willing to go down without a fight.*

Genevieve nodded. "I will," she vowed, then turned and stormed down the hallway.

Cooper sighed. "This is going to be harder than I hoped."

CHAPTER 6

G enni took a deep, sweet air-filled breath as she walked into the flower shop later that day. Technically it wasn't quite time for another class, but it wasn't uncommon for the women to gather for an evening to chat and socialize, and Genni was more grateful than she could express that tonight was one of those nights.

"Genni!" Caro called out. She walked over, her hips swinging. "How was the fudge?"

Genni grinned and patted her stomach. "Amazing, as usual. Thank you for thinking of me."

"Always, sugar," Caro said, giving Genni's arm a squeeze. "We ladies have to watch out for each other." She leaned back. "It's not like any of us have a man to do it for us, now do we?"

Genni laughed uncomfortably. Caro was cute, petite and bubbly. She could probably have any man she wanted, but her Southern sass had scared more than one man away before anything got serious. "I suppose so."

Caro peered closer. "Wait a minute..." Her eyes grew large and round. "You met a man!"

Genni's mouth gaped open as the room's noise fell away. "I...I don't know what you're talking about," she said, but even she could hear the lie in her voice.

Caro put her hands on her hips. "Spill it, honey. We ain't got all day."

Rose walked over, her elegance showing in every step. "What's this?" She furrowed her brows. "Have you met someone, Genni?"

Genni shook her head adamantly. "Nope. No way."

"I can smell your fib as surely as I can smell burning sugar, Gen," Caro said smugly.

Genni rolled her eyes. "I haven't *met* a man the way you're implying," she explained, then sighed. "But there is a man living at the house."

"What?" Rose exclaimed over the top of everyone's gasps. "That's it." Rose started walking toward the back room. "In here, ladies. We need hot drinks and tasty treats."

"She means chocolate," Caro said in a loud aside, making Genni laugh.

"I never say no to chocolate," Charli said as she passed Genni. "And I definitely never say no to a story about a handsome man."

"Who said he's handsome?" Genni cried, throwing her arms in the air.

"Your red face!" Charli called over her shoulder.

"Come on, ladies," Rose called. "Lilly's in bed, so we can chat as late as we want."

Genni pouted for a split second. She loved Lilly. The tiny girl was such a sweetheart and the entire group of women fussed over her like a group of mothers, though Rose was the only one to actually hold that calling. Rose had shown up in town almost four years ago with the world's most beautiful baby attached to her hip. Genni had never heard Rose speak of a husband, so she assumed there was a divorce or death along the way.

Rose was a few years older than the other women, appearing to be in her early thirties, instead of mid-twenties like the rest of the group. The age difference and motherhood seemed to give her an air of maturity and elegance that Genni often envied. But Rose's sweet and giving demeanor didn't let those feelings linger for long. If there was a problem, Rose was the first one to help and the last one to leave. There were few women like her in existence, and if she felt the need to keep her past a secret...then Genni wasn't about to push for answers.

The Hidden Daffodil had opened three months after their arrival and the rest, as they say, was history. Women had flocked to the beautiful creations in the window and the classes had started not long after. The resulting friendships had only grown stronger the more time that passed.

"Mmmm..." Melody said, sniffing the air. "Between the flowers and the chocolate, I think I'm in heaven."

Caro chuckled. "There's just something about those olfactory senses, amiright?"

The women all murmured agreements as they grabbed cups and plates of goodies. Soon they were seated and munching to their heart's content.

"Spill," Caro said with a grin. "I haven't had a good man story in a long time."

Gennie sighed and rolled her eyes. "This isn't that kind of story."

"Wait, wait, wait..." Charli said, leaning forward. "Does this have anything to do with the new guy in town?"

"What new guy?" Melody asked.

"The one on the motorcycle," Charli said in a dramatic voice. "Mm-mmm, I've only seen him from a distance, but he looks more delicious than your salted caramel, Caro."

"You're joking," Rose said, setting down the bite she was about to take.

"Nope," Charli said smugly. "He was staying at the motel, according to Grandma Nan." Her gray eyes landed on Genni. "But it sounds like that's not the case now."

Genni swallowed and it felt as if a brick hit her stomach. "It's complicated," she whispered.

"You don't have to tell us," Rose said softly. Her understanding tone made Genni want to weep sometimes.

"No, it's okay." Genni straightened her shoulders. "Remember how I told you some guy named Verl James owned the other half of the house?"

The women nodded.

"The new guy is Cooper James." Genni paused a second as the women reacted. "He's Verl's grandson and apparently has inherited the deed."

"So, he what? Just moved in without your permission?" Charli asked, her mouth gaping open.

"Basically," Genni said with a shrug.

"Can't you call the police?" Mel asked, worry furrowing her brow.

Genni shook her head. "Mr. Filchor said Cooper has a right to be there. Since he owns half the house, I don't have any legal recourse."

"That's a load of bull wonky," Caro grumbled. "I thought the law was meant to protect us."

"Is he dangerous?" Rose asked, her voice low and serious. "Does he scare you in any way?"

Genni didn't answer right away. Instead, she searched the feelings she had had around him. His looks had stunned her senses, but his stubborn personality was driving her crazy. "No," she finally stated. "I haven't been scared at all, just frustrated." She stabbed her eclair with a fork. "I wanted to try to buy him out, but he won't listen to my offer. Says this is his inheritance, and he's staying." Genni scrunched her nose. "He also demanded I run any renovations by him before I do anything."

"Like he's going to care about wall colors and upholstery," Caro grumbled. "Why does he care if you make the place look nicer?"

Genni shrugged. "I don't know, but he's awfully determined to make sure he gets what he wants."

"What are you going to do about it?" Rose asked, her head tilted. "Will you consider leaving?"

Genni shook her head. "No. I've worked way too long for this. I can't let him just come in and steal it away." She sighed. "I don't really know what I *can* do, but I'm not ready to give up." She gave a sad grin. "My grandma always said the Winters women were survivors. That means I should be able to survive this...right?"

"Of course you can, honey," Caro said quickly. "No one said you can't survive it." An evil grin spread across her face. "But no one said you have to take this lying down either."

"Oh, here we go," Charli said, rolling her eyes.

"What do you mean?" Genni asked.

Caro shrugged. "You might not be able to make him leave..." Her grin grew. "But if he doesn't like living in that run-down old house, maybe he'll leave on his own. The *environment* might be more difficult than he expects." She pumped her eyebrows and Genni raised hers.

Rose snorted a laugh. "You're evil, Caro."

"Why, thank you," she said, preening.

Genni smiled. "And this, ladies, is why I came tonight. I knew you wouldn't let me down." The women cackled and the eating resumed. Genni wasn't sure she'd do what Caro was suggesting, but if she became desperate enough, it was nice to have something to fall back on. *Just in case...*

"I SHOULD PROBABLY BE looking for a job," Cooper muttered as he marched down the sandy path. The sun was just rising over the horizon and the air was crisp and cool. The salty spray from the ocean was growing stronger, as was the rushing roar of water.

Genni had made herself scarce the last few days, leaving Cooper without a chance to reconcile with her. While he had no intention of leaving, he also didn't want to live as enemies. There had to be a way to find common ground between them.

"Whoa..." He paused as he reached the top of a grassy rise. In front of him lay a large expanse of sand and a wide view of the ocean just beyond. The wild grasses brushed against his legs in the morning breeze, tickling his skin and forcing him to keep moving. The plants ended abruptly, leaving nothing but sand and driftwood in its wake.

Reaching down, Cooper pulled off his flip-flops, brand new from the day before, and stumbled down the hill. The sand was chilly, but when he reached the high tide line, it was flat-out cold. He was surprised to see so many people out and about, most of them marching in waders, carrying a bucket and long round tool. Cooper squinted, unsure what the people were doing. Every once in a while, someone would tap the ground with their boot, then jam the pipe into the ground and twist. After sifting through the upturned sand, they would dump something in their bucket and move on.

"You look lost."

Cooper turned and gave a sheepish grin. "I suppose I am a little."

The man smiled back. "Visiting?" He settled a shovel on his shoulder, his hand gripping a bucket. A golden retriever sat patiently at his master's feet.

Cooper shook his head. "Nope. Just moved here."

The man's eyebrows went up and his eyes seemed to take in every part of Cooper. Fine lines sat on the edge of his dark eyes and a baseball cap was tucked low on his head. "I'm guessing it was from somewhere outside of Oregon."

Cooper nodded, feeling awkward that he looked that out of place.

"What brought you here?"

Cooper barked a laugh. "It's kind of a long story."

The man grinned and stuck out a hand. "I'm Captain Felix Mendoza."

It was Cooper's turn to look surprised. "Captain?" he asked as he shook the offered palm.

Felix grinned. "I'm Captain of the *SunCatcher*."

"A boat?" Cooper laughed. "And here I thought I was in trouble with the law or something." *That would be nothing new.* His tension eased and he found himself feeling comfortable around the friendly native.

Felix chuckled. "Not yet." He tilted his head toward the water. "You ever been clamming before?"

Cooper shook his head. "Nope."

"If you're going to live in Seaside, you have to know how to go clamming," Felix announced. "Come on. Hermit and I'll show you what to do."

"Hermit?" Cooper looked down at the dog while they walked toward the waveline. "Interesting name."

"I found him abandoned on the beach, with several hermit crabs stuck in his fur." Felix shrugged. "It just kind of stuck."

Cooper nodded.

"Here's good." Felix stopped, dropped the bucket and put the shovel down on the wet sand. "Not that I'm into big long, feely chats, but you've got me curious." He peered up from under his heat brim. "What's this complicated story you were talking about?"

Cooper put his hands on his hips and watched the waves for a minute. "I'm not really into those chats either."

Felix shrugged. "Then keep it to yourself. Doesn't make a difference to me."

Cooper watched in fascination as Felix overturned a bunch of sand. He shivered, watching the man sort through and begin to throw shells into the bucket.

"If you're going to live here, you need a pair of rubber boots," Felix said, squinting up with a grin. "Doesn't matter what time of year it is, we Oregonians wear warm clothing."

Cooper nodded. "So noted." He tilted his head. "So...what exactly are those?"

Felix huffed a laugh. "You've never seen a clam?"

"Does watching *Planet Earth* count?"

Cooper's new friend laughed. "Not quite." He stood and slapped Cooper on the back. "The boys and I are having a cookout tonight. Come join us and I'll introduce you around." He grinned. "You can get your first taste of our local delicacies."

Cooper smiled. "I think I'll take you up on that." He stuffed his hands in his pockets. "And I think I'll take this afternoon to buy the gear I'm gonna need."

"Sweatshirts, hats, a good pair of hiking sandals and you'll mostly be set," Felix said and he stood and dusted off his hands. "If you really want to blend in, you'll wear socks with your sandals, but most of the guys our age try to stay away from that trend."

Cooper chuckled as he walked with the man to another spot a few feet away, rubbing Hermit's head as the dog came over to sniff him out. "And rubber boots."

"Right. And rubber boots," Felix said with a laugh.

Cooper would never admit it, but meeting Felix was just proving to be another sign that he was meant to come to the coast. Other than Miguel, Cooper hadn't had any real friends in a long time. The immediate, easy camaraderie between the two men was something Cooper hadn't known he needed. Leaving his old life hadn't been that hard, since he wasn't leaving anything precious behind. But Felix looked like he might make a good friend, and the possibility of meeting other men their age was enticing.

"You know, I think I might go take a run," Cooper said. "But I think I'll take you up on the invitation for this evening."

"Down here at six," Felix said. "We cook it right over the fire."

Cooper smiled and reached out to shake the Captain's hand again. "Thanks. I'll be there."

Felix nodded, then turned back to his work, leaving Cooper to head out. He couldn't help but smile as he left. Things with the house might be complicated, but the rest of his life was looking pretty darn good at the moment.

CHAPTER 7

Genni poked her head out of her bedroom. She held her breath, listening carefully for any sounds of life. *Just because he's living here doesn't mean I have to see or speak to him.* When nothing could be heard, she slipped out and began to hurry down the stairs toward the front door. She only had a few minutes until she was supposed to meet Hudson for dinner.

Once outside, she let out a long breath and grinned in triumph. *You do realize that skulking through your own home is childish?* The thought made her frown. *Shut up,* she told her inner voice. "It's not like he's a guest or something," she grumbled. "If he wanted the nice treatment, he should have taken my feelings into consideration."

Genni jumped in her car and pulled out into the street. She knew full well that at some point she was going to have to face reality and figure out what to do about her unwanted roommate, but right now, she had a date to get to. "And several legal questions to ask."

Friday nights in their small town tended to be a bit busier during the summer months, so it took Genni a little longer than usual to reach her destination, leaving her five minutes late. She grabbed her purse and rushed out of the car, practically running inside.

"You made it." Hudson's smooth tone caught her attention and Genni tried hard to hide how frantic her breathing was.

"Yep," she said, forcing her chest to slow down, rather than heaving as crazily as it wanted to.

He winked. "I was starting to think you might not show, so I'm glad you're here."

Genni gave him a stiff smile. *I wasn't THAT late.* "Sorry. Traffic was more than I expected."

He shook his head. "It's fine." His eyes went to the dining room. "They already assigned us a table. Shall we?"

"Sure." Genni held onto her purse with both hands as she followed him to a small booth in the back. She wanted to object, as the booth was definitely more intimate than she would have preferred with a stranger, but when she thought of the questions she wanted to ask, Genni decided it was better this way. *I don't need anyone overhearing my problems.*

Hudson stood at one side and waved an arm for her to enter. "Thank you," Genni said, sliding past him while doing her best not to brush up against him. He was handsome and all, but something about him was a little too...much. *I barely know the guy. Maybe I'll be more interested after we talk for awhile.*

"Oh." She blinked rapidly when he followed into her side of the booth. She hadn't expected his thigh and shoulder to brush up against hers. The touch made her a little uncomfortable, so she tried to subtly move further into the bench, creating space between them.

If Hudson noticed, he didn't say anything, just picked up his menu and began to peruse the offerings. "Wow. Everything here is seafood," he said with a chuckle.

She gave him an odd look. "Well, it is called the Clam Pot and we're right on the ocean..." Genni left the rest of the explanation hanging. Surely he could figure out why a restaurant would specialize in fish?

"Right." He laughed and rubbed the back of his neck. "I keep saying really obvious things around you." His hazel eyes slid her way. "You seem to make me lose my train of thought."

Genni felt a slight blush at his compliment and smiled shyly. "I'm not sure if I should say thanks or not."

He laughed quietly. "Just take it for the compliment it was meant to be."

"Then thank you," Genni said softly. She turned back to her menu.

A few minutes later, their waiter brought them water, took their orders and disappeared again.

"So..." Hudson smiled widely at her. "Tell me about yourself."

Genni laughed uncomfortably. "There's not a lot to tell. I, uh, have lived here my whole life."

"Wow..." Hudson raised his eyebrows and took a sip of water. "I can't imagine being in one place so long."

She shrugged. "It's not so bad. I mean, on one hand... you know everybody." She grinned. "On the other hand...you know everybody."

Hudson laughed as intended. "Well, there must be a lack of men in this town, or someone as beautiful as you wouldn't still be single then."

She raised an eyebrow. "I'm not easily taken in by flattery, Hudson."

He chuckled. "So noted. But it wasn't meant to be flattery. Just telling the truth."

That blush came back once more. "Then, again, I thank you."

He grinned. "What about your family? Brothers? Sisters? What exactly are you fixing up with that paint you were buying yesterday?"

Genni shook her head. "Actually, if it's okay with you, telling you that will lead me into a couple of questions I'd like to ask you, as a lawyer."

His eyes widened slightly, but he quickly schooled his face. "Great. Go for it."

Shoot. Now he thinks I only came in order to get free legal advice. "Sorry, we don't have to—"

Hudson put up a hand to stop her. "No. Really. It's okay. Go ahead."

Genni sighed and twisted her water glass in her hands. "Well, I actually don't have any family. No parents or siblings, and my grandmother, who raised me recently, passed away." She jumped slightly when his warm, slightly clammy hand landed on hers.

"I'm sorry for your loss," he said, his voice soft and sympathetic.

Genni slowly eased her hand away from his hold. "Thank you. It was expected, but it still hurt."

Hudson grunted in agreement.

"Anyway," she glanced at him from under her eyelashes, "I inherited half of her home."

"I thought you didn't have any other family?" he asked, leaning back.

"I don't." Genni pushed her water glass away. "That's where the story gets weird." She spent the next while explaining the split ownership of the home and ended with the arrival of her new housemate.

"Huh." Hudson frowned and scratched at his chin. "That's quite a story."

"The only lawyer we have in this town says I have no legal leg to stand on," Genni hedged. "So I was hoping..."

He grinned. "You were hoping someone from out of town might have a better idea of what you can do?"

"Yeah." Genni made a face. "But it's not the only reason I came out with you, just for the record."

His smile turned genuine. "That line intrigues me, so we can get to that later." He leaned forward, his arms folded over the table. "But I have to admit I'm not sure that I'm going to be any help to you. Unless you have some kind of proof the title company doesn't have, your lawyer is correct."

"What do you mean? What could I have?"

He shrugged. "I don't know. Some kind of document saying your grandmother bought him out, but they never made it official. A diary entry, a new will that never got notarized, that kind of thing." He took another sip of water. "I mean, there's no guarantee even those would work, but it would at least give you a starting point."

Genni chewed her bottom lip as she thought. *Surely Grandma didn't mean to leave me living with a stranger. The buy-out was so long ago, there has to be something in her stuff that addressed this situation.* A spark of hope began to grow inside her and Genni knew what she had to do. *But where will I find it? Grandma didn't keep any records that I'm aware of.*

Genni decided that as she renovated, she would also spend time searching for paperwork that might aid her in getting rid of one Cooper James. *He's handsome, and alluring, but there's no way I'm going to just let him take over my home without a fight. Hopefully I can find something in Grandma's things that'll help.*

"THIS IS BENNETT, JENSEN..." Felix grinned at the last guy sitting around the fire. "And the old man over there is Captain Ken Wamsley."

Geez, how many captains are there?

Ken raised an eyebrow. "Just because I'm more experienced and better-looking than you toddlers doesn't mean I'm old."

Cooper grinned as the men laughed. "Nice to meet you," he said, reaching out and shaking everyone's hands. "I'm Cooper James."

"Word on the street says you moved into the Boardwalk Manor."

Felix sputtered, spitting out his drink. "What?" He wiped his mouth with the back of his hand. "I thought Genni had inherited the house?"

Cooper stuffed his hands in his pockets and rocked back on his heels. This had gotten awkward really fast.

"She did." Ken tilted his head to the side and narrowed his gaze. A bottle of soda hung from his fingers. "But apparently she only owns half the house." The bottle swung in Cooper's direction. "Our main man here inherited the other half."

Felix smirked. "This one is the cop you were afraid I was. Watch out for him. He's a stickler for speed limits."

Cooper nodded, but didn't smile. He was starting to think that coming tonight wasn't as good of an idea as he had thought.

"There's a story here," the man introduced as Jensen said. "And I want to hear it."

"Let the man fill his stomach first, huh?" Bennett scolded. "The food is hot and ready, and I'm starving."

"You're always starving." Ken laughed.

"I'm on my feet all day," Bennett defended. "Can I help it if I need to keep up my caloric intake?"

Felix snorted. "You're not going to keep fitting in those tiny shorts if you eat like this all the time."

Bennett glared, but the rest of the man laughed, ignoring his anger. "You wish you could make those blue shorts look as good as I do," he shot back.

Cooper looked from one man to the other, trying to figure out what the heck was going on.

Felix looked over with a grin. "Bennett is our friendly neighborhood mailman."

"Ah, gotcha." Cooper nodded, though he still felt out of place and was a little nervous about sitting down.

"Here, man." Ken slapped the seat next to him. "Grab a plate, sit down and tell us why you're in town."

"Once a cop, always a cop," Jensen muttered with a grin.

"If you'd stop speeding in the school zone, we might actually be friends," Ken said with a smirk.

Jensen rolled his eyes.

Cooper hadn't felt this lost since he'd been a little boy.

Felix slapped him on the back. "Go ahead and listen to the cap, he orders everyone around." Felix pushed Cooper a little toward a pile of metal pie tins. "We're not fancy here," he explained.

"Plus the tins hold more food," Bennett added. He exclaimed in protest when Jensen slapped him across the back of his head.

Cautiously, Cooper took his food, eyeing all the shells on his plate, then sat down. He wasn't quite sure what to do with everything. He'd never been big into seafood and this stuff hadn't been plated for him in any way.

"Here." Two small Styrofoam bowls were handed to him.

"Uh, thanks."

The rest of the men chuckled. "Like this," Felix said. He picked up a clam and popped the shell open. "Grab it by the neck," he said, demonstrating.

Cooper set the bowls in the sand and followed Felix.

"Swirl it in the broth."

Cooper frowned but followed.

"It gets the rest of the sand off," Felix explained.

Sand? What the heck am I getting myself into?

"Now dip it in the butter and chow down."

Cooper tried to keep his wariness from his face, but from the laughter emanating from the other men, it didn't work very well. He put the clam on his tongue and instantly recoiled a little at the texture. It was much slimier than he would have preferred.

"Don't chew too much, just let it go down," Ken urged.

Cooper swallowed and paused. "I guess it's all right," he said slowly.

The men laughed. "Try a few more," Felix urged. "Once you know what to expect, they're better than you'd think."

Cooper snorted, but went ahead and ate several more, only to realize that Felix was right. They weren't bad when he knew what he was getting into.

Silence reigned for several minutes as the men ate their fill, but all too soon, each was leaning back in his seat, relaxed and warm.

"Okay," Jensen said, wiping his hands on his shorts. "I still want to hear about the house."

All eyes turned toward him and Cooper felt himself grow slightly warm at the attention. It was such a contrast for him. He used to not care, even used to seek it out, but now, with his new life, he wanted to blend in. He squirmed slightly in his seat. "It's kind of a weird story."

"We got nothing but time, man," Ken said, his eyes intense. "And even though I've been hearing all sorts of things through the precinct, I'd like a first-hand account, if you don't mind."

Cooper pursed his lips and nodded. "I guess my grandfather knew Genevieve's grandparents," he began. "Years ago, Mrs. Winters got in some tax trouble and called my grandfather. He bailed her out, but took half-ownership of the house in return."

Bennett's eyebrows went up and Jensen whistled low under his breath. "Geez, that seems pretty steep."

"Not as steep as losing the house over stupid government taxes," Felix muttered, putting a bottle to his lips.

Ken waved Felix off. "So, now what? You came to claim it?"

Cooper nodded, leaning forward to rest his elbows on his knees. "I guess you could say that. Grandpa died a few weeks ago and left it to me in the will."

"Just like Old Maggie died and did the same for Genni," Jensen said. "Crazy."

"I'm guessing Genni didn't take too kindly to you showing up," Bennett said with a grin. "She's a beautiful woman, but kind of cold."

Felix slapped Bennett's head, who rubbed the sore spot with a scowl. "Gen's had a hard life," Felix defended. "You might be a little difficult to get to know as well if you'd been through everything she has."

"Yeah, well..." Ken cleared his throat. "I'm curious how the house situation is going."

Cooper gave a long sigh. "So far, we've mostly avoided each other," he admitted.

"Just what exactly are you hoping to accomplish by coming here?" Ken took another swig.

Cooper shrugged. He was beginning to like these guys, but definitely wasn't ready to spill everything. "I guess you could call it a new start."

"Nothing wrong with that," Jensen responded.

"Hmm..." Ken hummed, his eyes still staring hard.

"Dude!" Felix yelled at Ken, then turned to Cooper. "Coop. Are you a criminal?"

Cooper sputtered, not wanting them to know just how close to the truth they were getting. "N-no."

Felix turned back to Ken. "Lay off with the cop eyes, man. Everyone needs a do-over now and again."

"Cop eyes?" Ken asked with a scowl.

"Yeah..." Bennett added. "You do this thing where you're, like, trying to see inside our sinning souls, or something." The men laughed. "It's worse than an old preacher screaming about fire and brimstone."

Cooper relaxed in his seat as the men began to shout insults and banter at each other. The fire was warm, the air was chilly and the company was growing on him. He took a deep drink of his soda. The men hadn't pressed him any more about his past and no one had given him grief about claiming his inheritance. The hope he'd formed earlier began to rise again and Cooper let himself relax. *Yeah...this was a good decision. Now if I could just get Genevieve to agree.*

CHAPTER 8

Genni wiped the back of her hand against her forehead. "Geez, it's hot in here," she grumbled. She'd opened the windows ages ago and at first the early morning air had made the room slightly too cool, but now she was sweating and wishing she had air-conditioning.

Her fingers skimmed the floorboards once more and she sighed when nothing stood out to her. Huffing, she sat back on her heels. "There's nothing here," she murmured.

Unable to sleep with ideas running around in her head, Genni had gotten up before the birds to try and search the house a little. She'd automatically looked through Grandma's study first, but no business papers or diaries had been there.

It's funny how I lived here my whole life and never once remember seeing Grandma deal with bills or anything.

Frankly, it had never occurred to Genni. Even while her grandmother was sick, Genni had spent all her time working or caring for the ailing woman and Grandma had continued to take care of the mail.

Genni blew a raspberry through her lips. "She had to have had some kind of system though. But what?"

Not knowing where else to start, and since the dining room was on today's agenda for painting, Genni had been looking through the room with a fine-toothed comb trying to find any secret compartments or loose floorboards that might be hiding something important, but so far she'd come up with nothing.

She squinted at the window, seeing that the sun was a decent height above the horizon. "Time to start painting," she urged, pushing herself to her feet. The door to the dining room was closed, as Genni was still doing her level best to avoid Cooper at all costs. No noise from the main part of the house was filtering through the thick walls, so Genni assumed it was safe to play herself a little work music.

Setting her phone on the table, she pulled up a playlist and kept the volume a little lower than she would like. "No need to disturb the intruder," she smirked. *And if that means he can't stop me from renovating, then too bad for him.*

She spent the next couple of hours dancing around as she painted from one corner to the other. Pausing, she stretched her neck. Her shoulders were screaming at the abuse and her arms felt heavy from moving the heavy roller around. Try as she might, Genni couldn't quite reach the top of the wall, so her strokes were about a foot short of the actual ceiling and she knew she'd have to go back and do edging after getting the bulk of the walls done.

Sighing, she put the brush in the bin. Putting her hands on her hips, she stepped backward and surveyed the room. "Nice," she murmured. The color was soft and earthy and was going to be the perfect foil for the wallpaper Genni had been eyeing online. Three walls in paint and one accent wall in paper would make a stunning dining area for her bed and breakfast.

"You've got to be kidding me."

Genni spun with a gasp. She hadn't heard Cooper open the door. "How long have you been standing there?" she demanded, pulling on her anger to keep from admiring his shirtless physique.

He must have been running somewhere because sweat glistened on his skin and his hair looked windblown and completely adorable. His tattoo was on full display, and though she'd never been drawn to ink before, Genni found the barbed wire look on his arm to be intriguing enough to touch.

She ruthlessly forced the thought away. There was no way she was going to admire someone who was trying to take her home away from her.

His hazel eyes met hers and the lines of his face hardened. "It's pink."

Genni swallowed, but put her chin in the air. "It's not pink. It's mauve. In fact, if you want to get technical, it's Verbena Sunrise." She smirked. "And it's beautiful."

His head shook slowly and he moved further into the room. Genni backed up as the smell of ocean and wind overpowered the paint odor in the room. "I thought we agreed you wouldn't do anything without consulting me first," he said, his voice low and hard.

Refusing to be afraid, she folded her arms over her chest. "No. You demanded it, but I never agreed." She raised an eyebrow. "I haven't agreed to anything. You've just barreled your way through without caring."

This time both eyebrows went up. "Barrelled my way through? You make it sound like I've left destruction in my path."

"Maybe you have."

"According to who?" he asked, leaning in her direction. "You? Funny. The title office and everybody else seems to understand that I have rights as well." He cocked his head. "You're the only one who feels like I'm stepping where I don't belong."

Genni felt her temperature rising in the already warm space and she clenched her fists. "You *don't* belong here," she said through her tight jaw. "You have no history here, no family memories." She brought a hand to her chest, the movement forceful and jerky. "I took my first steps in this place. My mother was born here." Blinking rapidly, Genni found herself mortified that her eyes were filling with tears, but was unable to stop it. How could he not understand her position? Everything she'd known and worked for was being taken from her all because of some stupid agreement years ago.

For just a moment, a look of compassion and longing crossed his face and it brought Genni up short. Just what was he thinking?

"I get it," he said, his voice softer, but still firm. "I really do, but if you want me to listen, then you have to do the same."

"Oh?" she asked archly. "Tell me why you're so intent on being here. What's in it for you?"

His muscles visibly loosened and he stepped back from her, taking the smell of the ocean with him. Genni had to catch herself from leaning forward for one more good whiff.

"Has it ever occurred to you that some of us might be looking to create the same history and foundation that you're talking about?" he asked.

Genni's breath left her in a great rush.

"I..." He dropped his chin and shook his head. "It doesn't matter," he grumbled, then looked up at her with his scowl back in place. "Point is, I have a right to be here, and you can't paint the house this...this..." his warm waved at the walls, "Pepto Bismol color and expect me to go along with it."

Genni gasped, then glared. "You want to be here? Then deal with it."

He turned and stormed toward the door, clenching the doorknob in his fist before turning to talk over his shoulder. "Fine, but you might not like the consequences."

Without another word, he slammed the door behind him and Genni had to catch herself on the edge of the table. She'd never been drawn to confrontation and the toll was more than she'd expected. Her knees were knocking and her heart racing, all while her mind spun with anger, regret, sympathy and even attraction. "What have I gotten myself into?" she moaned, putting a hand to her forehead.

Forcing herself to breathe deeply, Genni waited until her body had calmed down and she felt more in control of herself. Slowly, she stood upright and looked at her hard work. His words had hurt, but she'd heard hurtful things before and had never let them stop her. Even in small towns such as this, there was plenty of school bullying and with her family history and second-hand clothes, Genni had been a prime target.

"But I survived," she reminded herself. She stuck her chin in the air. "Because Winters women are survivors. It doesn't matter if he likes it or not. This is what the dining room is going to be, and he can just eat somewhere else." Nodding her head firmly, she walked over to pick up the wet roller, determined to finish what she'd started.

There was no stopping her now.

COOPER'S JAW WAS CLENCHED the whole way back to town. Normally Nova was his salvation. The breeze, the freedom...all of it usually helped calm him down, but after the argument with Genni, Cooper was too wound up even for his motorcycle to help.

"Stubborn woman," he muttered. "Who paints a dining room pink?" He scoffed and steered his bike into the parking lot at the grocery store. While he had a chunk tucked away, Cooper needed a job if he was going to stay in this town, and he was hoping there would be a community board or something he could look through.

Other than notices for summer celebrations and an extensive amount of fishing tours, Cooper didn't find anything of worth. He sighed and pushed a hand through his waves, knowing they were probably standing on end about now.

Fighting with Genni didn't settle right with him, no matter how insulting she'd been. It was clear that she held that home deeply in her heart and for a moment, Cooper had felt a longing so strong, he'd thought his knees would buckle. *What would it be like to have that kind of history? To be proud of where you came from and know exactly where you're going?*

Her defense of her actions had touched something deep inside Cooper and he had almost shared with her exactly why he was so desperate to stay. Luckily, he'd reached his senses in time and had shut the lid on those emotions. They weren't going to help him in the war currently waging. "Now if I can just get her to stop painting things weird colors," he grumbled.

"You all right over there?"

Cooper jerked at the feminine voice and turned to see a petite woman looking at him curiously. "Uh...yeah."

She pursed her shiny red lips. "Are ya sure? I don't think most healthy people stand around talking to themselves."

For a minute Cooper stared, then he barked a laugh. "Sorry," he said, putting up a hand. "I've got a lot on my mind."

"Hmph." Her Southern accent was perfect with the sass she was throwing his way. "I can see that. Trouble is, talking to air ain't gonna fix it."

Still smiling, Cooper walked over and offered his hand. "Cooper James."

She gasped. "*You're* Cooper James?"

He paused warily. "Yes?" he said, his voice coming up at the end.

"Well, are you or aren't you?" she demanded.

Sheesh. Are all the women in this town difficult? "I am," he stated firmly.

"You're the one pushing Genni out of her home?" The woman shook her head. "You should be ashamed of yourself."

"Hold on," Cooper said, starting to get angry. "I'm not pushing anyone out of their home." He stepped toward the woman. "Is that what she's been telling people?"

The woman put her hand on her curvy hip. "No. But any man who would just move into another's home without permission is doing exactly that in my opinion."

Cooper looked heavenward and said a quick prayer for patience. "It's not just her home," he said slowly, trying to make sure she understood. "I own half of it."

"And you'll own the whole sin when the good Lord sees what you're doing by moving in with her." She folded her arms. "Now what exactly were you looking for?"

Cooper scowled. What was going on? How could this lady go from one extreme to the other so quickly? Cooper had to admit, she was a pretty little thing. Small, but curvy, highlighted hair and perfect make-up. A picture perfect Southern doll. But even as he looked at the woman, Cooper found himself thinking of dark eyes and thick, satiny hair...He blinked and cleared his throat. *Nope, nope aaaaand nope. Not going there. Even if Genevieve wasn't trying to kill me, I don't mix business and pleasure.*

"Excuse me?"

Cooper's eyes came back into focus. "Sorry, drifted off. Uh...I don't think you told me your name."

She narrowed her blue eyes and didn't speak right away. "Caroline, but everyone calls me Caro."

"Nice to meet you, Caro," Cooper said politely.

"You still didn't answer my question."

His mind scrambled for what she'd asked. "Oh, yeah. Uh..." He rubbed the back of his head and looked at the board before turning back to her. "I was trying to see if there were any job postings," he finally admitted. *Nothing like humbling yourself by having to admit you're out of work. Nice.*

Some of the tightness of her face eased and a resigned look settled in its place. "So you're really here to stay?"

Cooper nodded.

Caro sighed. "What kind of work are you looking for? I'm assuming a seasonal job, isn't it?"

Cooper shook his head. "Not really. I mean, not unless I have to. I was a mechanic before I came here. Something along those lines would be perfect, but I'll do just about anything until I get settled."

Those red lips were pursed again as she flipped her hair over her shoulder. "Old Frank's been overworked for as long as I've known him," she said. "Head down Main, take a left on Aspen and you'll find him on the right." She rolled her eyes. "You can't miss the tower of tires and gas cans."

Cooper couldn't help but chuckle. "Good to know. Thank you."

Caro waved him off. "Just don't tell Gen that I helped you." She paused before leaving. "I'm still on her side, you understand. But you don't seem quite as horrible as I expected."

Cooper smiled and frowned at the same time. "Thank you? I think."

Nodding regally, Caro turned around and walked away, leaving Cooper chuckling. He pulled his helmet from under his arm and walked to the entrance of the store. "This town just keeps getting better and better."

It only took him ten minutes to find the place Caro had been referring to. She was right. It stood out like a sore thumb. While the rest of the town looked cutesy and coastal, this place looked like a dump heap that hadn't been cleaned up in fifty years.

He got off his bike and took a deep breath of grease-filled air. "Yep, this is it." Cooper looked down to put his helmet away when he heard a lot of high-pitched barking. He turned to see a full herd of dogs rushing toward him. "What the—?" He lifted his feet as the puppies began to jump and yelp at him.

"Dang things," an old man said, rushing as fast as his large body would let him. "They just don't know when to shut up." He began scooping up puppies in his arms and trying to pull them away from Cooper and his bike, but there were just too many of them.

Cooper laughed softly as he counted the dogs. "Wow. Ten puppies is pretty impressive. Where's their mama?"

The man squinted at Cooper, his jaw filled with gray stubble and his eyes slightly bloodshot. "She's in the shop, like the good thing she is." His face looked down at the squirming brood. "Probably rejoicing in a few minutes of peace from these hellions."

Cooper laughed again. "I'd say you've got your hands full, but I don't think it needs to be reiterated."

The man gave a grunt and a smile, then put out his hand. "I like a man who knows when to be quiet. Name's Frank. What can I do for ya?" His eyes drifted to the bike and he whistled low under his breath, taking his hat off to scratch his bald head before slapping it back on. "Nice ride, son. But it sure don't look like it needs fixin'."

Cooper shook his head. "It doesn't. I do." He grinned. "I'm looking for a job."

Large white eyebrows shot up high. "Are ya now? You ever worked in a garage before?"

Cooper nodded. "Yes, sir. I'm certified and have references if you want to see them."

Frank's smile widened and the lines of his cheeks nearly took over his eyes. "I'm not one to stand on ceremony, son. You come work for me a couple of days and I'll know if you're a good fit." His eyes went to the bike again. "But anyone who can keep that beauty running probably knows what he's doing."

Cooper didn't know what to say. It had been too easy. "Just like that?"

Frank nodded. "Just like that."

"I..." Cooper shook his head. "Thank you, sir." He reached out his hand. "Cooper James."

"Like I said, I'm Frank." He narrowed his gaze. "Not sir or anything else you might think up, ya understand?"

Cooper smiled and nodded.

"Good. Be here tomorrow at eight." Without another word, Frank turned and began herding the puppies back into the garage as best he could. It was a wild bunch, but eventually they were all gone.

Cooper turned back to the bike.

All except one.

Although they were definitely a mix, Cooper was sure he could see some Australian Shepherd in the long hair and shape of the body. A pretty little pup, about three different shades of brown, sat still, watching him carefully. Cooper squatted and reached out to pet its head. Bright green eyes greeted him seriously and Cooper felt a little tug on his heart.

"Sorry, miss," he said, after discerning it was a female. "I just got in town. Otherwise I might enjoy a companion just like you."

With a quiet snort, the puppy jumped to its feet and bounded after its siblings. Cooper watched her go, still feeling drawn to the furball. Shaking his head at his foolishness, he slammed his helmet on and mounted the bike. *Nothing a little ride won't fix*, he assured himself as he pulled out. *Highway 101...here we come.*

CHAPTER 9

G enni grinned even as glue slid down her arms. The wallpaper she wanted had miraculously been in stock in the next town over and yesterday afternoon while the paint dried, she'd driven down to get it. The golden luster and flowers were exquisite. Together with the paint, the room would look perfect and give a rich feel to the dark woods and fancy chandelier that Genni planned to buy.

"And won't Cooper just looove this," she murmured with a grin. After she had recovered from their confrontation, her rebellious streak had completely taken over and she found herself looking forward to his reaction to her add-on.

His flashing hazel eyes came to mind and Genni found herself pausing slightly in her work. He really was good-looking. A wild, rugged sort of handsome, but handsome nonetheless. When he had stalked toward her yesterday, his movements had been lithe and predatory. It was enough to shock Genni, but also to send a quick thrill down her spine.

"There's just something about a manly man," she whispered to herself with a giggle. *Oh, if Grandma could see me now.* "I'd probably get a lecture on how Winters women survive just fine on their own."

"I'm glad to see my opinions matter," Cooper said in a deadpan voice.

Genni squeaked and spun on her heel to turn toward him, but the wallpaper she was putting up hadn't quite stuck yet, so it floated down and settled over her head. "Crap!" Fumbling, she pushed at the limp paper until she was able to get it off her ponytail, only pulling out a handful of hairs in the process.

She grimaced at the long dark hairs now stuck on the flowers. "Look what you made me do," she snapped.

"Me? Since when is your clumsiness my fault?" Cooper retorted.

"I'm not clumsy," Genni argued. "Not usually anyway," she grumbled under her breath. She sighed, knowing she would have to figure out how to salvage the piece. It had been a little more than she'd planned on and she definitely didn't have enough money to buy extra. Turning back to the wall, she began pressing the paper back into place. "Did you need something?" He had looked far too delicious this morning. His hair was wet from a shower and looked curlier than normal. His face was freshly shaven and Genni had a moment's regret. The stubble had only emphasized his strong jawline. She shook her head. *Not happening! He's the enemy!*

"Oh nothing," he drawled. "I just enjoy having my thoughts and feelings stomped on, so I thought I'd come say hello this morning."

Genni bit her lip to keep from laughing. One quick moment to remember his refusal to give up his share of the house, however, had her easily scowling again. "Glad I could accommodate," she quipped. She stepped up a small ladder so she could reach the top corners.

"I won't be around today," he said carefully.

She glanced over her shoulder. "Oh? Tired of being insulted already?"

Cooper gave her a wry look. "I got a job yesterday. But I'll be back around dinnertime." He sighed heavily. "Don't you think we should talk this out, Genevieve? Both of us are going to be completely miserable if we keep going at it like this."

"Can't," she said, forcing some sunshine into her tone. "I've got a date." Genni hadn't been very excited about going out with Hudson again, but now she found herself extremely grateful for his persistence.

Cooper snorted. "Oh, really? Which guy is looking to be eaten alive tonight?"

Genni turned and glared at him. "I'm not a man-eater."

"You could have fooled me," he grumbled into his mug.

"I'm actually pretty sweet when I want to be," Genni pressed. Man, she was feeling bold. Something about Cooper just brought out her feisty side. She gave him a saccharine sweet smile. "I reserve the acid for you."

"Don't I feel lucky," he said, sarcasm dripping so heavily from his tone that Genni was sure she'd find a puddle on the floor.

"As you should," she snarked.

Cooper rolled his eyes. "Whatever. It doesn't have to be tonight, but one of these days we need to sit down and find a way to keep the peace." His eyes narrowed. "Without you painting any more rooms like bubblegum throwup."

Genni threw up her hands. "I have spent years planning this out, Cooper. I'm sorry you don't like turn of the century stuff, but I want this home to look like what it would have when it was originally built. Wallpapers were extremely popular. Either that or they used a lot of wall hangings and other art. Since I can't afford to buy a bunch of art, I'm settling for this."

His nose was wrinkled as if he smelled something rotten. "We'll definitely be discussing this when we sit down together. I get what you're trying to do, but we still have to live here."

"No one's forcing you to stay," Genni said with an inviting smile.

Cooper tipped his mug to her. "And it's that sweet invitation that just makes me want to stay all the more." He tipped his head back, downing whatever was in the mug. It couldn't have been coffee with the way he chugged it down. But before Genni could ask anything, he walked out of the room. "Until later," he called out, a lilt in his voice.

Genni stuck her tongue out after him. "Jerk."

"I heard that!"

"Double jerk," Genni muttered as she stepped down from the ladder.

"Heard that too."

"You were meant to!" she shouted back, then grinned. Talking with Cooper was exhilarating, even if most of their conversation consisted of insults. Genni could feel a flush in her cheeks and her heart was beating faster than normal. Her energy levels were stronger as well and she couldn't help but let her eyes trail to the window when the sound of a revving motorcycle engine rang through the air.

Hurrying, she moved to the window just in time to see him ride down the driveway. "Oh my word, that's hot," she muttered. She fanned herself and turned to put her back against the wall. "This can't be healthy," she said into the empty room. "Who in the world finds themselves attracted to their arch nemesis?"

The ringtone of her phone startled her from her daydreams and she hurried to answer it.

"Hello?" Disappointment slid through her at the voice on the other end. "Oh. Hey, Hudson." She listened for a minute and nodded before answering. "Yeah. Six-thirty's fine. Not a big deal." She paused. "Yeah. Okay. Mm, hm. See ya then. Bye."

She hung up and carefully set the phone back down. "And who in their right mind is *not* attracted to the normal man who actually seems interested?" She shook her head. "This whole thing is so messed up." With a heavy sigh, she went back to the wallpaper. "I've just got to find something in Grandma's papers. That'll take care of the whole situation. No more sharing the house, no more roommate, no more insulting banter. Life can go back to what it should have been in the first place."

For some unknown reason, a small part of Genni found itself disappointed at those words.

"YOU SURVIVED," FRANK said with a laugh, slapping Cooper on the back.

Cooper smiled back after righting himself. For a guy at least four or five inches shorter than himself, Frank sure could pack a punch. "I did," Cooper responded.

"Think you're willing to show up again tomorrow?"

Cooper's smile widened. "If you want me here."

"You know your way around an engine, that's for sure," Frank mused, scratching his stubbly chin. "And I haven't gotten this far through my orders in years."

Cooper chuckled. The man had a backup that was probably three months long. Tourists that were only here for a few days got the VIP treatment, but the poor residents of Seaside Bay were stuck. "You do seem to have plenty of work," he said.

Frank laughed. "That settles it." He stuck out his thick hand. "Welcome to the team."

Cooper took the proffered agreement. "I'm glad to be here. Thanks."

Raucous barking caught their attention and both Cooper and Frank turned to see the puppies stumbling in the side door of the garage, fighting over a length of rope. Mama looked resigned and tired as she led the way.

After everyone was inside, one last little furball walked in. It was the same female that had stuck around with Cooper yesterday. He squatted down and she daintily walked up to him, sitting and staring with those unblinking green eyes.

"Do you charm all the women? Or just pups?" Frank barked a laugh at his joke.

"I think I might be the one who's charmed," Cooper admitted, scratching the little lady behind her ear. With a yip, she ran off and joined her siblings, staying just out of the chaos. "She's a little different than the others," Cooper mused.

Frank grunted. "Yeah. Less inclined to trouble."

Cooper stood and Frank eyed him speculatively. "If I include her as a bonus, would you be willing to stick around for a three-year contract?"

Cooper's eyes widened and he laughed. "I don't think I'm in a position to take on a dog right now, but I'll admit it's tempting." He watched the puppy a moment longer before sighing. "I'd be happy to sign a contract, but I just can't take her. My, uh, living quarters need to be sorted out first."

Frank nodded. "I hear ya. You are new in town after all." Wiping his greasy hands on his coveralls, he started toward the office. "Well, let's make this official so I can go home and eat. Lunch was too many hours ago."

Cooper grinned as he followed Frank. The old man was loud, a little uncouth, but friendly and knowledgeable. It was an ideal situation for Cooper to start in as he built himself a new life.

Now if we could just get the rest of it all settled. His temper flared a little as he thought of Genevieve out on a date that evening. Despite their arguments, he found himself enjoying their banter for the most part. What would it be like to have a woman who was strong and successful at his side, rather than one who was sneaky and manipulative?

"Are you kidding me?" he asked himself with a scoff. "No mixing business and pleasure. Get it straight, man." Cooper growled quietly as he rode down the street. "In fact..." He looked over his shoulder and turned the bike around, heading to the edge of town. His attraction to Genevieve had to stop, as did her thoughts that she could just run over his opinions.

"If she's going to be difficult, I can be too." Revving the engine, he sped up, crossing the speed limit barrier and praying that Ken wasn't watching. The next town came up quickly and Cooper found the home improvement store without any trouble.

Marching inside, he headed to the paint aisle. It only took him fifteen minutes to know exactly what he was going to do. Walking out of the store with a gallon in each hand, he decided the loss of sleep would be worth putting Genevieve in her place.

"Starting a new life doesn't have to mean I became a pushover," he grumbled as he did his best to find a way to strap the paint cans to the bike. "But it might mean I need to get a car." He sighed. "I'll have to see what kind of winters they have here." The city he'd come from had been large enough that when there was snow on the ground, Cooper just took public transportation. But this area didn't seem to have that. "I guess I could always walk," he said as he straddled the bike.

A cool breeze from the ocean wrapped around him as he headed back to the highway. "Or not."

By the time Cooper had arrived back at the house, he'd decided that a car was going to be a necessity. So was showing Genevieve that she didn't get to make all the decisions. After checking the house to make sure all was quiet and she was gone on her date, he unloaded the paint cans and brought them into the dining room.

Cooper sighed and put his hands on his hips, wincing at the colors she had chosen. "It's going to be a long night." Not wanting to give her any chance to squawk her argument, he had bought his own brush and roller and other supplies. It took a few minutes to get everything ready to go and even longer to tape the trim, but Cooper was nothing if not efficient.

Running up to his room, he grabbed his head phones, popped them in, turned on a playlist and set to work. He'd made significant progress when headlights flashed through the window. Cooper froze. He tapped his headphones, pausing the music, and pulled out the one in his right ear.

Tiptoeing to the door, he listened carefully as the front door was unlocked and footsteps began to move through the house. *Please let her go upstairs. Please let her go upstairs.*

"Cooper?"

He stiffened. *What? Why is she calling me?*

Genevieve's footsteps began to move and Cooper panicked as they came in his direction. He practically dove around the table and folded himself as small as he could behind a dining chair. Holding his breath, he waited to see if she was going to discover him.

The steps, however, continued right past the door and toward the staircase.

Once she had ascended and he could hear her over his head, he allowed himself to breathe. "Dude, that was too close," he grumbled, shoving a paint-riddled hand through his hair.

Just as he was starting to get back to work, her steps overhead became quicker and came back toward the stairs.

"Crap, crap, crap," Cooper muttered, turning off the light and crouching down again. *Why am I crouching? The door is closed. It's not like she'll see me if I'm upright.*

His logical voice didn't seem to be enough to overcome the worried criminal inside of him as he prayed for deliverance from her upcoming wrath. It was one thing to let her discover the issue when he was gone. It was going to be another if he had to face it head on.

"Cooper!" she shouted.

What does she want? "For someone who doesn't like me, she sure is making an effort to find me," he grumbled, shifting his weight to keep from losing the feeling in his feet.

Grumbling could be heard through the door, but Cooper couldn't understand the words. He waited until once again, she went upstairs and a door slammed, letting him know she was more than likely in her room.

He let out a long breath of relief and flipped the light back on. He wasn't sure why she wanted to speak to him so badly, but there was no doubt it could wait. Right now...Cooper had a job to finish.

CHAPTER 10

Squeezing her eyes shut, Genni tried to force herself to go back to sleep, but it was no good. The sun was pouring in through her blinds and her mind was already moving too much in order to find dream land again.

Grumbling, she sat up and stepped out onto the cold hardwood. "Carpets. One of these days I'm going to buy carpets." Grabbing her clothes, she headed out into the hallway bathroom and used the shower to catch her body up with her mind.

Finally feeling more like herself, she dumped her pajamas in the hamper and headed downstairs, checking her cell for the time as she went. Last night she had had another semi-pleasant date with Hudson, but she wasn't sure she wanted to see him again.

Not only was there no spark between them, but most of his attention seemed to be on wanting to know about the house. He'd asked an insane number of questions to the point where Genni had been ready to get up and leave.

Hudson must have noticed her discomfort, because he'd smiled and backed off. The rest of the meal had been okay, but Genni just wasn't feeling it. "Besides, he's not here long-term," she reminded herself. "There's no point in starting something that already has an end date."

Yawning, she reached the bottom of the stairs. Movement came from the kitchen and Genni was reminded of her unwanted house-guest. *Guest.* She snorted. That wasn't really the right word for him. He was more like an annoying gnat or housefly. Unwelcome, but hard to get rid of.

She had looked for him last night after her date, thinking it was probably a good time to have that talk he was insistent about, but the man had been gone. His bike was out front when she got home, but he hadn't answered her calls and she hadn't been able to find him either. "I found him now," she murmured, throwing back her shoulders and preparing for an argument.

Sparks always seemed to fly when the two of them were together, and they weren't always good sparks. Genni would admit to herself that she found Cooper handsome, but no one else was going to ever know that. He was too stubborn, too obstinate, too...well, he was just too everything.

She pushed open the swinging door to the kitchen and marched inside.

Cooper looked up from the stove and gave her a sardonic grin. "Morning, sleepyhead. Have a good date?"

There was a slight sneer in his tone and Genni paused for a second. *Why does he sound jealous? It's not like there's anything between him and me.* "I did, thank you," she said. She would never admit to Cooper that her date was a bust. "And you? I couldn't find you when I got home."

Cooper turned and put his hand over his heart. "You were looking for me?" He made a mock sad face. "If I'd known, I'd have come running. I didn't quite have my fill of sharp barbs for the day."

Genni's lips twitched, but she held back her smile. "I thought maybe we could have that chat," she said, slipping onto a bar stool.

Cooper paused, his face losing the sarcastic look. "Really? You're willing to hear me out?"

Genni shrugged. "Maybe. I guess it depends on what you have to say."

Cooper studied her and Genni grew warm under his gaze. She could imagine getting lost in those hazel eyes. They seemed to change color depending on what shirt he was wearing. Yesterday, the brown had been almost nonexistent against his forest green shirt. To-day, however, he was wearing gray and it brought the brown tones to the forefront. Either way, Genni knew that a girl could stare into them for a long time. *As long as he's not spouting nonsense anyway.*

"Okay," he said cautiously. "That would be great." Turning back to the stove, he dished up a pile of eggs. "I have some extra. Would you like some scrambled eggs?"

Genni's eyebrows shot up. "That would be nice. Thank you." She hadn't had anyone serve her in a long time and a small part of her heart softened before Genni strengthened the wall again. She was about to tango with the devil. Being emotional was definitely not in the cards today.

"There you go," he said, sliding a plate toward her across the counter.

"Thanks." Genni grabbed the sides. "Would you like to eat in the dining room?" she teased, although it wouldn't be a bad idea. Something about being in the place of her rebellion kind of gave her strength. Their fights were a prime example. Genni had never stood up for herself as loudly as she did when surrounded by her hopes and dreams.

Cooper smirked and his eyebrow twitched. "If you're sure that's what you want." He leaned back against the counter and shoveled a large bite in his mouth. "I'm fine in here though."

Genni twisted her head and glared at him. "Why do you sound suspicious?"

"Suspicious? I don't know what you're talking about." Cooper straightened. "You know what? The dining room would be great. Maybe we shouldn't talk where you can get your hands on sharp objects."

Ignoring his taunt, Genni turned and stormed out of the kitchen. Dread pooled in her stomach as she drew closer to the dining room. Something about his smug face told her she wouldn't like what she found in there. *Please say he didn't take down the wallpaper. I can't afford to replace it!*

She pushed open the door and her knees almost buckled. "No..." she said breathlessly. Her breathing grew ragged and her chest began to heave. Black spots entered the sides of her vision and Genni forced herself to slow down. She was *not* going to faint again. She wouldn't give Cooper the satisfaction. "What. Did. You. Do?" she rasped.

"Fixed it," Cooper said.

She spun from the blue monstrosity in the dining room and tried to fry Cooper where he stood. "How could you?" Her vision blurred. "I came to you...willing to listen, and this is how you repay that?"

Cooper straightened from his relaxed position on the wall. "Are you kidding me right now? You have done nothing but make me feel unwelcome and throw insults ever since I got here."

Genni shook her head. "Yeah, well, that's not changing now," she said, her voice thick. "I don't know how to make you understand how much this means to me," she cried.

"Maybe you should be willing to see why this means so much to me," he shot back. Cooper shook his head, his waves flying into disarray. "I've got to get to work."

"Not until you change it back!"

He sneered at her. "Do it yourself. You seem to be good at that."

Genni reared back as if she'd been slapped. "You know what?" she snapped. "You're right. I am good at doing it myself. Because I'm a Winters. Winters women are survivors. We don't need anyone else."

"Good luck with that," Cooper muttered as he walked to the door. "You might think it's great, but to me it just sounds lonely."

The slamming of the front door echoed through the front entry as Genni stood frozen to the spot. The weight of the situation seemed to grow heavier and heavier until she fell to her knees and burst into tears. "What do I do?" she sobbed into her hands. "It wasn't supposed to be this way." Her tears were streaming steadily, but slowly her innate determination built back up. "I've got to take time to go back through Grandma's things. There has to be something about this stupid sale."

COOPER SLAMMED HIS kickstand into place before straddling the bike and racing down the driveway. It was a good thing no one was near the entrance because he tore out of there without looking for oncoming traffic. He had meant to start the morning being polite, knowing she would eventually be upset at him, but as soon as he'd begun to ask about her date, he'd felt a sliver of jealousy crawl up his spine. The emotion had surprised him, and he'd ended up starting the morning on the wrong foot, rather than buttering Genevieve up like he should have.

It wasn't until he was five minutes down the road that Cooper began to pull back on the gas. *Killing yourself isn't the answer,* he grumbled internally.

A flash of a siren caught his attention and Cooper glanced in his mirror, then groaned. "Just what I needed," he muttered. Putting on his signal, he pulled over and stopped, then pushed up the visor on his helmet. *Please don't let him pull my record. I'm just starting to make friends in this town.*

The police car behind him came up close and Ken got out, sauntering up to Cooper's side. "What do we have here?" he asked with a grin, his eyes hidden behind sunglasses.

Cooper made a face even as relief went through him. Ken might be willing to let things go since it was Cooper's first offense. "Nice to see you, Captain Wamsley."

Ken laughed and pushed his glasses up onto his head. "I'm sure it is," he drawled. "Most of my buddies don't like meeting me like this."

Cooper chuckled. "I'll bet not." He pursed his lips. "Just out of curiosity, how often do they see you in this position?"

"More than they'd like," Ken said with a grin. He put his hands on his hips. "Care to tell me why you were going over the limit?"

Cooper huffed. "Not really."

Ken's eyebrows shot up. "Wow. That's not usually the response I get. Most people are dying to give me every excuse under the sun."

Cooper shrugged. "I was frustrated," he said.

"From?"

Cooper didn't answer. He didn't think his argument with Genevieve was any of Ken's business, no matter how nice the guy was.

"I see..." Ken muttered. "Well, I'll give you the same spiel I give everyone new in this town."

Cooper nodded, waiting to hear how bad the ticket was going to be and bracing himself for when Ken found out about his past. *It's gonna come out sooner or later. Hopefully he'll let me explain before things go crazy.*

"I try to keep this town as safe as possible. We're a tourist area, which means we have tons of families and little kids running around. Follow the signs, and we'll get along great. Break them? And I'll be renovating the precinct with your retirement. Got it?"

Cooper couldn't help but grin even with the fear clawing at his throat. "I'm pretty sure that's not how tickets work."

Ken winked. "So you say."

Both men laughed. "All right, I got it." Cooper looked down at his watch. "I really don't want to say this, but I've got a job to be at in five minutes. Is it possible to get the ticket taken care of?" *And find out if we're still going to be friends?*

Ken popped his glasses back on his nose. "You're an interesting one, Coop. Even the boys argue with me now and again."

Again, Cooper shrugged. He'd fought the law before, and had no desire to do it again. Oregon was a clean slate for him. *Hopefully...*

Ken grunted. "First one is a warning," he said. Leaning forward, he pulled the glasses down just enough to make his eyes visible. "Second one is full price, no matter how good of friends we are."

Relief flooded Cooper, so strongly he nearly laughed out loud, but instead of giving into the sensation, he swallowed it. "Thanks, Captain," he said with a grateful smile. "I think I owe you one."

"Don't tempt me," Ken grumbled good-naturedly. "I've always had a thing for motorcycles." He laughed hard when Cooper stiffened. "I was kidding," Ken explained, still laughing. "I know what happens between a man and his bike."

Cooper sagged in the seat. "Thanks."

Ken nodded, still grinning like crazy. "See ya around."

With a nod, Cooper dropped his visor and got back on the road. By now he was late, but he figured Frank wouldn't mind. The man hadn't seemed like the type to obsess over a couple of missed minutes. Cooper did, however, keep himself to the speed limit. After that close call, he definitely didn't want to tempt fate and have everyone learn about the mess he'd left behind. For the most part, the future was looking bright and Cooper wanted to keep it that way.

Barking greeted him as he parked behind the garage, and soon his boots were surrounded by fur and baby teeth. "No biting," Cooper grumbled, moving the brood aside as best he could so he didn't step on any tiny paws. He managed to make it inside without hurting anyone and was met with his favorite little puff of fluff.

After waiting for the rest of the puppies to charge back outside, Cooper got down on his haunches and scratched behind her ears. "Hey, girl," he said softly. "Miss me?"

"You gonna name her?" Frank shouted from across the garage.

Cooper straightened. "Why would I do that? Won't the family who takes her want to name her?"

Frank gave him a wry look. "Do I look stupid to you?"

Cooper grinned. "Why do I feel like that's a trick question?"

Frank laughed, coughed and then spit, making Cooper gag a little. "We both know she's not going home with anyone else," Frank said after wiping his mouth on the back of his hand.

Cooper huffed a soft laugh. "I can't take her, Frank. No matter how cute she is."

Frank just shook his head. "You'll see."

Ignoring the insinuation, Cooper headed to the office to grab his coveralls.

"You're on the Altima," Frank hollered when Cooper emerged. "Guy said it rattles when he hits the freeway."

"Got it." Cooper went to the car in question and popped the hood. Walking to the side table, he grabbed a light and attached it above his head so he could see better. A small yip caught his attention and Cooper looked down to see the female waiting patiently at his feet.

Her green eyes were wide and her tail moved quickly from side to side as she watched him.

"You're killing me, Smalls," Cooper whispered. "You know I can't take you home. I just moved here."

The puppy said nothing, just continued to sit and watch.

Cooper shook his head and determined he was going to have to ignore her. But by the time he clocked out at the end of the day, that had proved to be impossible. "You're a determined little bugger," he said, petting her soft head.

She wagged her tail and panted at his attention.

"Told ya," Frank said with a grin.

Cooper started to shake his head again, but stopped. *Why does it matter? Why can't I take her home? She's well-behaved and it would certainly be nice to have at least one female in the house who actually wanted me there.* He stared down at the bundle of fur, and the longer he let the idea ruminate in his head, the stronger his desire became.

"Hey, Frank?"

"Yep?"

"I think I might take you up on that sign-on bonus."

CHAPTER 11

Genni sat sipping a cup of tea at the kitchen counter when Cooper's motorcycle roared into the driveway. She smiled a little to herself. *He has no idea what's coming.* This past week had been a crazy mix of ups and downs with her emotions feeling completely out of control.

She was still in mourning for her grandmother, and so to have this...stranger leaping into her life had sent Genni into a tailspin. She'd cried more since Cooper arrived than she had when Grandma Maggie passed away. *Nothing like having someone strip you of your dreams to turn on the waterworks,* she thought sarcastically.

But no more. After she and Cooper had fought that morning, Genni had pulled on her big girl panties and decided that enough was enough. She wasn't going to let this man take over her life. And she certainly wasn't going to let him take over the house.

After carefully going through her bank account numbers, Genni figured she could take another two weeks off work before she'd have to go back, which was plenty of time to get a real head start on the renovations. *Even fixing the one he ruined.* "I suppose I should be grateful he didn't ruin the wallpaper, at least," she mumbled into her mug. Painting back over the blue color had been easy enough, but horribly annoying. All that taping and prepping was tediousness at its best, but she'd done it.

And now that she was feeling better, she was feeling magnanimous enough to hear what he had to say. Her hope was that if they could have a civil conversation, she could find a way to convince him to sell out. "It's not like he's attached to this house already," she said to herself. "He just got here."

The front door opened and heavy boots could be heard on the hardwood, followed by tiny scratching noises. Genni frowned. *What in the world is that?* She listened harder and her eyes widened. "Oh, no he didn't." Jumping off her stool, Genni rushed out of the kitchen only to come to a screeching halt. "What?" She gaped like a fish out of water. "What is that doing here?"

Cooper grinned like a proud papa. "Genevieve. Meet Butterscotch. Scottie for short." Cooper looked down at the fluffy little thing. "Scottie, meet Genevieve." He leaned closer to the puppy. "She's a little cranky, but maybe you can soften her up."

His tone was teasing, but Genni couldn't process what he was saying. "You can't just bring a dog in here!" she cried, her voice becoming shrill.

"Why not?" Cooper tilted his head and raised his eyebrows.

"Well...because..." Genni tried frantically to gather her thoughts, but she was so shocked by the situation that she couldn't seem to form a full sentence. "Because I live here too and should have a say in whether or not there are pets." *There. That sounded logical.*

Cooper snorted. "Oh...you mean like how I had a say in you painting the dining room pink?"

"You painted it blue," she pointed out with a frown.

"Yes, but did you leave it that way?" His smirk told her he knew exactly what she'd spent the day doing, and it irked Genni.

"How did you know I repainted it?" she asked, her eyes narrow.

Cooper shrugged. "Lucky guess." He smiled and Genni melted a little against her will. "Not to mention you seem dead set on having your way with everything, so I figured you'd retaliate."

Some of her anticipated elation at having bested him ebbed away. For some reason, his words made it seem less like a victory and more like she was some spoiled child demanding her way. *But I've never been spoiled,* she reassured herself. *People who have to scrape through life with their fingernails are anything but spoiled.* "Still...a dog is a lot different than a paint job." She jumped when the puffball yipped.

"Scottie," Cooper said firmly. "We're quiet in the house."

The puppy seemed to grumble, then put her nose to the floor and began to sniff around, following some imaginary trail into the sitting room. "We can't have a dog," Genni said, eyeing the animal like some weird creature. She had zero experience with animals, but if her grandmother was to be believed, all they did was ruin furniture and wreak havoc, both of which were things Genni couldn't afford right now.

"*We* don't have a dog." Cooper walked past her toward the stairs. "I do."

"But I live here!" she called after him, hurrying to the bottom of the stairs.

"I know," he called back. "Me too."

"Which means I'll have to deal with the beast." Genni was starting to feel frantic. She really couldn't have an animal tearing things up and going to the bathroom on the floors. Movement at her feet had Genni looking down and she backed up quickly. The dog had come to the stairs and was practically sitting on her foot, staring up at Genni with dark green eyes. "Just...go away," Genni said.

Cooper gave her a weird look as he came back down the steps. "You're acting like she's some kind of monster," he scoffed, swooping down to pick the puppy up.

"Isn't it?"

He stood still for a moment, the dog cradled in his arms as he scratched its ears. If she was being honest with herself, Genni would have to admit that the picture they created was intriguing. Despite her reservations and even a little fear, the animal looked soft to touch. And Cooper's big arms holding the small thing made an interesting contrast, causing Genni's heart to flutter just a little.

"Didn't you ever have a dog growing up?" he asked softly.

Genni shook her head. "Grandma said they were mangy mutts that ruined furniture."

That same sympathy she had seen from him several times flashed through his eyes. It simultaneously made Genni want to share her feelings and scream in frustration. No one liked being pitied, but having someone look at you with any type of softness was addictive.

Cooper stepped forward slowly, as if unsure of his reception. "Would you like to pet her?"

Genni blinked several times. "I..." She swallowed. A small part of her did. She was curious as to what she'd missed out on all those years. Her grandmother had taken care of every necessity in Genni's life. She'd never been hungry for food or water, but she had been hungry for something else. *Life.* All the little experiences that gave joy and built memories to bring a smile to a person's face. Things like petting a puppy or drinking milkshakes at midnight with your friends. Other than her friends at the flower shop, Genni's memory box was embarrassingly empty.

"She's really soft," Cooper urged, coming a little closer.

Genni's fingers twitched, so she clenched them into fists. "Maybe another time," she forced out. She wanted to touch that dog, but an unexpected fear held her back. Touching the puppy felt suspiciously like giving in, and that made Genni feel weak, something she had vowed never to be. "You better make sure it doesn't urinate all over the house or chew the furniture," she snapped, her anger helping keep the soft feelings at bay.

Cooper's softness disappeared and he stiffened.

The loss hurt Genni more than she would have expected.

"Don't worry," he said with a sarcastic grin. "Scottie'll be the best-behaved female in the house."

WITH THAT PARTING SHOT, which Cooper immediately regretted, he stormed up the stairs to his room. For just a moment, he'd thought Genni was going to lower her wall, but apparently that hope had been too much.

After setting Scottie down, he slammed around in his room, gathering stuff for a quick shower. "She's the most stubborn woman I've ever met," Cooper grumbled. He walked to the door, then turned to look at the dog. "Stay here," he commanded. "Who knows what she'd do if she found you wandering around while I was indisposed." Huffing in annoyance, Cooper made sure to close his door, then made his way down the hall to his think tank.

Some people found happiness in flowers or the beach, but Cooper did all his best relaxing and thinking under a hot spray. While he scrubbed the grease from his skin, his mind went back to Genni's face as she looked at the dog. A fierce longing had been easily seen in her dark gaze.

"Has she really never pet a dog?" he muttered. "Who hasn't pet a dog before?" But the more Cooper pulled up what he knew about the cold woman, the more he figured that had to be correct.

Genni herself had said she'd struggled for years to be ready to turn this house into a business. Felix mentioned that she'd been through a difficult childhood. A mother had never been mentioned, nor a father. And judging by the lack of personal items in the house, the grandmother hadn't been the warm fuzzy type. The only family picture Cooper had found in the entire mansion was a small frame on the mantel. It showed a young girl, he was pretty sure was Genevieve, and an older, stone-faced woman. They weren't touching, just standing side by side. Genevieve was giving a shy smile, but the older woman was not.

He pursed his lips as thoughts whirled. His own childhood had been less than ideal, with over-indulgent parents, leading to an early adulthood where he started down a dangerous path, but there were good memories there as well. He'd never forget trips to Disneyland or Paris, along with weeks spent on the prettiest beaches or hiking through the mountains. His parents had been more like buddies than actual parents, but at least Cooper knew what it was like to have a pet.

Sadness began as a slow churning in his belly. He'd been so dead set on making this place his home and taking advantage of the opportunity for a fresh start that he hadn't thought about how something like this would affect someone like Genni. She put on a brave front, complete with a viper's tongue, but Cooper was starting to see that there was a soft, vulnerable little girl behind the brick wall.

His attraction to her simmered at the thought of breaking down her barriers. Some of their bantering was fun, like a quick jolt of caffeine that sent him off for the day feeling energetic. Some of it dug at his insecurities and he usually ended up fighting back. But seeing that glimpse of her needs tonight brought up the question... *Is she just covering her own insecurities when we argue? How do I find out for sure?*

Cooper shook his head, wiping the droplets out of his eyes. "I'd need to be a stupid psychiatrist to figure this thing out," he grumbled. Still, he found himself growing more intrigued as time went on, rather than uninterested.

He finally turned off the water and got himself dried off and dressed. Stuffing his dirty clothes into the crook of his arm, Cooper headed back to his room. "Ready to go get some dinner?" he asked as he came inside. Cooper paused, listening for movement, but there was none. He frowned, stepping further through the threshold. "Scottie?"

When there was still no answer, Cooper dropped his clothes and frantically began to search the room. "Come on, Scottie. She'll cook ya alive if she finds you. Where did you go?"

Cooper got down on his hands and knees to look under the bed just as a dark spot darted toward the open door. "No, no, no, no!" he shouted, rushing after the puppy. "Scottie! Come back here!"

To his horror, the dog yipped and rushed into an open door, which Cooper was positive was Genni's.

"Crap," he grumbled, slowing down in the doorway. "Scottie?" Cooper got down on his knees. "Hey, come on, punk, get out of there." He could hear little growling sounds, so Cooper glanced over his shoulder, noting that the hallway was empty. "I'm gonna regret this," he grumbled, crawling forward on his hands and knees to the bed. Getting on his belly, he lifted the covers and looked under it. "Scottie," he hissed. "Get out here!"

The danged pup yipped, and went back to making growly noises.

"You're gonna get the cops called down on my head," Cooper argued. "And I already used my 'get out of jail free' card this afternoon. Now, come here!"

When the puppy only backed further under the bed, Cooper grimaced, and then he began to pull himself forward on his stomach, squishing his body beneath the bed frame.

"If I get stuck, I'm gonna wring your neck," he complained.

When Scottie whined, finally starting to understand that her master was angry, Cooper felt immediate contrition.

"I don't mean that," he said softly. "But we do need to get out of here." He pushed with his toes and reached forward, stretching himself as far as he could go in order to grab the dog's scruff. "Gotcha!"

"Good catch."

Cooper dropped his forehead to the dusty hardwood and groaned. "I don't suppose we could just forget this ever happened?" he called out.

A low chuckle sent a tremor of awareness through his body and Cooper worked to back himself out from under the bed. Being under

the furniture gave him a distinct disadvantage, and he was too attracted to Genni to let his guard down like that.

"You know...this isn't helping your case with that dog," she stated
as he got his head out from under the metal frame. "It just leads me
to think that Grandma was right."

Cooper gave her his best smile from his place on the floor. "She
didn't chew up your furniture or urinate anywhere, so obviously
there were flaws in Grandma's story." He finished pulling out the dog
and nearly groaned again when he found a piece of clothing in her
mouth.

"Is that my scarf?" Genni gasped.

Cooper sat back, put Scottie on his lap and wrangled the cloth
from the puppy's jaws. "Uh...it was?" he said, handing it to her.

Genni snatched it, her jaw hanging loose.

"I'll get you a new one," he assured her, then glared at the puppy.
*I'm already on her list. I didn't need any help making it worse, thank
you very much.*

"This was my mother's," she said softly. Even without looking,
Cooper could hear the tears in her voice.

Now you've done it. "Genni, I'm so sorry." He scrambled to his
feet. "Is there someone in town who can fix it? How bad is it? Can I
see—" He stopped when she put a hand in the air.

"Go," she rasped. "Just...go."

Cooper paused for a moment, but not knowing how to make it
all better, he finally nodded and skulked away like a scolded child.
"That was *not* a way to make a first impression," he whispered harshly
to Scottie as he walked down the stairs to the kitchen. Cooper
sighed, shoving his hair out of his eyes. "I need food. I can't think
straight."

He wasn't sure what he was going to do, but somehow, he was
going to fix this. Genni was a puzzle that Cooper was growing more

and more anxious to solve. But his gut told him it wasn't to be easy or quick. *I guess the real question is...will it be worth it?*

CHAPTER 12

Genni coughed and waved a hand in front of her face. She had decided to take a break from her renovations today and tackle the attic in search of paperwork about the house. With the arrival of the puppy and Genni's subsequently ruined scarf, she was feeling more eager than ever to see if there was a way she could kick Cooper out of the house.

A short, sharp pang hit her in the sternum at the thought of sending him packing. "Stop it," she scolded herself. "He doesn't belong here."

The words didn't feel as true as they used to. Last night he had acted...nice, at least until she had snapped at him. But more than once Genni had realized that most of his difficult moments had been in response to her own anger. *If I quit fighting, would he?*

She sighed, then coughed when it caused her to inhale more dust. "Who knows," she grumbled, walking further into the dark space. "What I do know is this home should be mine. He's keeping me from my dreams of opening the house for a bed and breakfast." She grimaced. "And his dog is going to be a problem."

Last night when her scarf had been chewed up, Genni had been shocked and sad, but later when she'd revisited the picture of big, brawny Cooper crawling out from under her bed, she'd had to fight the desire to laugh. *Not that I'll ever admit that to Cooper.* She was still sad about her mother's scarf, but not as much as she had expected to be. The thing had already been quite ratty, and Genni never actually wore it. She usually kept it draped over her nightstand, adding a bit of color and reminding her of the woman she didn't remember.

Despite the scarf's connection to her past, Genni had found little satisfaction in the article of clothing. It didn't smell like perfume or bring back any memories. It was simply a piece of cloth. Nice, but not something that brought her a lot of comfort.

"Still shouldn't have chewed on it though," she grumbled. Finding a stack of boxes, she pulled down the top one and began to dig through the contents. "You've got to be kidding me," she said with a huff. "Who needs this many doilies?"

The entire box seemed to be filled with old, yellowing doilies. Genni had no idea where they'd come from or if a family member had made them. All she knew was that they weren't going to help her get rid of her pesky housemate problem.

With a heave and grunt, she picked up the box and set it aside. "Next." She lifted the lid on box number two, finding a few children's toys. "I wonder if these are worth anything..."

Box number three was filled with canning lids and Genni had to laugh. "What the heck?" She moved them around, their metal pinging loudly in the quiet attic. "Why would someone keep all these rings, like this?"

Sighing, she set that box aside as well.

A half-hour later, she'd been through another dozen boxes, but still found nothing but junk. "I'm going to have to make a trip to Goodwill."

A series of tiny sneezes sounded, catching Genni's attention. She spun. "What are you doing here?"

The tiny ball of fluff that was intent on ruining Genni's possessions stood at the top of the stairs, panting and sneezing from the dust. The sneezes were so cute and dainty and followed up by equally cute snorts that Genni found herself smiling, instead of being frustrated like she should have been. Slowly, she crouched near the ground. "You're not so bad...right?"

Scottie padded her way across the hardwood floor with a grin on her face, tongue lolling out. Pausing directly in front of Genni, she sat down, her green eyes wide with innocence.

"I didn't know dogs could have green eyes," Genni murmured. Slowly, she reached out a shaking hand to touch the dog's head. Without Cooper around to watch her, Genni found herself feeling much braver than the night before when touching felt like capitulation. "Oooh..." she breathed. "You're so soft."

Scottie whimpered and tilted her head around until she had Genni's hand right where she wanted it.

Genni laughed softly. "You like that, do you? Right there?" Her smile grew when the puppy fell over, exposing her belly to Genni's growing attention.

"You're a natural."

Gennis squeaked and landed on her backside. "Ouch."

"Are you okay?" Cooper rushed up the rest of the stairs and came to a halt right in front of her. He looked like he wanted to reach out, but wasn't quite sure if he should.

That same sharp pang Genni had felt multiple times in the last week hit her chest. "Yeah, I'm fine," she assured him. She pushed her way to her feet and brushed off her seat and pants. "I'm more embarrassed than anything else. The 'ouch' was an automatic response." She looked up and her breathing stalled slightly. Those eyes of his were intense and deep enough to hold all sorts of knowledge or secrets. She had a random thought that this man would know how to love someone, if given the chance.

Her eyes widened and she stumbled back. *What the heck am I thinking? I barely know the guy!* The small voice in the back of her brain chose that moment to enter the conversation. *Well, whose fault is that? He's tried to open a conversation with you multiple times.* Genni scowled. *Shut it,* she commanded.

Cooper put his hands up. "Sorry. I wasn't trying to intrude." He backed up and Genni realized he thought she was mad at him.

"No, I'm sorry," she said quickly, then bit her tongue when he looked surprised at her outburst. *Wow, I'm a mess.* "I, uh, I was just caught off guard. You didn't do anything...I think," she added, hoping to break the tension of the moment.

It must have worked because a slow, delicious smile crept across his face. "I'll take that as a victory." He grinned.

Genni rolled her eyes. "You would."

He laughed, which tugged at Genni's heartstrings, but she tried to keep herself in check. One moment of peace did not mean anything.

His eyes traveled around the room. "This place is crazy."

Genni nodded, feeling slightly unsure of herself.

"Are you looking for something in particular?"

Her mouth dropped open before Genni snapped it shut quickly. "Uh..." *I can't tell him what I'm doing!* "N-not really," she hedged. "I've never looked through any of this stuff, so I figured it was time." She shrugged weakly. "You know, see if there's anything I can use to put the house together."

Cooper nodded, seeming to buy her explanation.

Genni let out a relieved breath. They both turned as a crashing sound occurred in the far corner of the room. "What was that?"

"Scottie!" Cooper lunged toward the fallen boxes with Genni on his heels.

She had forgotten all about the puppy during her stilted conversation with Cooper. "Is she okay?" Genni asked, squinting into the dark corner. Paper appeared to be everywhere and Genni gasped. A notebook was open with dates and writing, looking very much like the diaries Genni was trying to find.

"Scottie, you punk." Cooper straightened with the pup in his arms. "Now look what you've done."

Genni cleared her throat and stuffed her hands in her pockets. She wanted to pick up that notebook, but wasn't about to with Cooper standing right there. What if it held the information he was looking for?

"This is gonna take me forever to clean up," he grumbled, looking at the mess surrounding his feet.

"No!" she cried, then forced her voice down. "I mean, no worries. I'll, uh, take care of it."

Cooper's eyes widened. "Really? You're not mad?"

She winced a little at his surprise. *I guess I really have been* that *woman, so I can't really blame him for his shock.* "No. I know the puppy, I mean Scottie, didn't mean to do it." She tried to smile, hoping it looked genuine. "I needed to go through all this junk anyway." She kept her eyes from the notebook, praying he wouldn't notice it.

Cooper looked at her suspiciously, then slowly nodded. "Okay. Thanks," he said slowly. Looking at his feet, he took a giant step out of the mess, but his back leg got caught on a box edge and he stumbled forward...right into Genni.

HOLDING SCOTTIE CLOSE to his chest in one arm, Cooper flailed and grabbed Genni around the waist with his other to keep her from falling as he rammed straight into her. "Oh my gosh, I'm so sorry," he said, his voice lower than normal.

Her body was pressed up against his, her hands on his chest as she leaned backward. Both of them were looking at each other with wide eyes and nobody was moving, except for Cooper's pulse, which had taken off like a racehorse from the near fall. His hand flexed involuntarily against her back and he couldn't help but noticed just how nicely she fit up against him.

Those alluring eyes were searching his wordlessly, but Cooper wasn't quite sure what they were asking. The longer they stared at each other, the thicker and more charged the air grew. His eyes began darting down to her lips, and when she gasped ever so softly, all logical thoughts ran from his brain.

The only thing left was want and desire, leaving Cooper no choice but to close the few inches between them and press his lips to hers. She sucked in a surprised breath at his touch and Cooper pulled back just enough to separate their mouths, waiting for some kind of sign that she was going to slap him. Fire was burning through his chest at the moment from that small, simple touch, and he was dying to try it again.

"Cooper," she breathed, then pressed upward to bring them back together.

He needed no further encouragement and quickly took control of their exchange. And it was an exchange. Genni's hands latched behind his neck and she pulled herself upright, steadying herself on her feet and leaning into the kiss. Cooper's hand slid up her back and neck, sliding into that heavy hair which had tempted him ever since he'd first seen her sprawled on the couch after her fainting episode.

He tilted his head, changing the angle and deepening the kiss, reveling in the sensations building inside of him. His head cloudy and his thoughts completely gone, all he could do at the moment was feel. The fire and passion in Genni was about to burn him alive and Cooper was jumping in with both feet.

Scottie whimpered and wiggled against his hold, breaking the intoxicating moment and bringing Cooper back to his senses. "Genevieve," he said hoarsely, backing up a little. "I..." He stopped, having no idea what to say.

Her eyes were slightly glazed and her breaths came in rapid pants. After Cooper spoke, she blinked several times and seemed to clear her mind, suddenly breaking free of his hold. "What...I..." Genni's eyes grew wild and she looked everywhere around the room except at him.

"Genni," Cooper said gently. "That was...completely unexpected. Why don't we go downstairs and try to figure things out?" The irony of his situation wasn't lost on him. In most situations, the women were the ones begging to speak about their situations and feelings, but in this house, Genni was the one who played things closest to the vest. They'd crossed a line today, one he hadn't expected, but didn't regret quite as much as he would have expected.

His experience in mixing a business relationship with a romantic one should have had him running for the hills, but Genni was so unlike the other woman that Cooper was struggling to remember why it had been a bad idea in the first place.

Her head shook quickly and he felt a cold trickle move down his spine. "We shouldn't have...I mean, I can't..." She backed up toward the stairs when her eyes got stuck on something to his side.

Cooper looked over, but only saw a bunch of papers and notebooks.

Lunging forward, Genni grasped one of the notebooks and hugged it to her chest. "I have to go," she whispered, then turned and darted down the stairs.

Scottie whimpered again, wiggling hard against his chest, but Cooper didn't move. All the heat and excitement that had rushed through him during the kiss was slowly leaching out of his body and into a puddle at his feet. He looked down, expecting the feeling to be visible, but only dusty wood and old papers met his gaze.

"Come on, punk," Cooper whispered. Slowly he started toward the stairs, his footsteps heavy and his heart heavier. Those few moments with Genni had given Cooper a vision of hope, but then it had been cruelly ripped away.

You barely know her, his logical side reminded him. "Maybe not, but I was trying." He sighed. "This is crap. So, she's not interested. That's not the worst thing in the world. I'm sure there are plenty more women in town that I haven't had a chance to meet yet."

Forcing himself to set aside the depression of the rejection, he took Scottie outside for some play time. The little squirt was much more active now that she was away from her family. "You fooled me good," Cooper grumbled as he watched her race around the yard. He couldn't stop his gaze from going back to the house. "Just like someone else I know."

"Dude, you sound like a woman!" Cooper scolded himself. Straightening his shoulders, he grabbed the dog and headed back inside. A good hard run on the beach was just what he needed in order to get rid of the restless energy and excess emotions plaguing his system. Hopefully by the time he got back, he would be better in control of himself.

He tore off his clothes and got into running shorts. Grabbing his earphones and strapping his phone to his arm, he took off. "Stay here," he said over his shoulder, ignoring Scottie's whimper. "You won't be able to keep up."

His strides grew longer and longer until at the bottom of the porch steps, Cooper took off into a sprint. The beach was only a few yards over the grassy rise and he knew without a doubt that the waves and sand would be exactly what he needed to get his head back in the game.

Remember Ciana, he reminded himself. *You should never have kissed Genni. It's Blackman Inc. all over again.* His breathing sped up as he upped his pace. *Last time landed you in jail. Never again.*

CHAPTER 13

Genni roughly wiped her tears, sniffing hard as she stormed out the back door. Sparse green grass met her gaze and beyond that, the distant roar of the ocean could be heard. Gulls squawked as they swooped over tourists and fish, keeping an eye out for any tasty morsels they could steal.

It all seemed so normal, yet Genni felt as if she was anything but. That kiss had turned her world upside down. The air had fairly sparked with chemistry as Cooper stumbled into her, grabbing her waist with his large hand, while still protecting the small dog with his other.

His eyes had been so green, yet as close as they'd been, she'd found the hidden flecks of brown that sometimes came to the forefront. The two colors were swirled in the most interesting arrangement, sucking her in until Genni's logical brain had taken a hiatus. The place where his hand rested had been warm, almost too warm, searing into her core and causing her body to react to the masculine figure in front of her.

"It would be just my luck," she said, her lips barely moving. "The man who finally makes me feel whole is the one who's trying to ruin my dream." Her face crumpled. "How is that even possible? It sounds like an oxymoron."

She plopped down on the top step of the porch and tucked her head into her knees. For a few minutes, Genni allowed herself to feel. She let the warmth and attraction she'd felt for Cooper consume her, followed by the heat of the kiss and the physical need to let someone hold her. But those feelings were fleeting, quickly followed by the coldness she'd grown up perfecting, the desire to make it on her own, the lack of desire for help or support of any kind. The war of her emotions created chaos within her mind and heart, and for the first time ever...Genni felt lost.

She'd learned young to always have a goal. She knew how to set aside distractions, how to get things done and how to do it herself. No one needed her and she didn't need anyone. The one exception had been when her grandmother was sick, but even the time that Grandma had finally taken to her bed had only been a few days before she'd passed. Winters women were survivors.

But Cooper had broken something inside of her. He'd shifted her icy core and allowed room for something different. It felt soft, fuzzy and invitingly feminine. Basically, it was the complete opposite of everything Grandma had raised her to be.

So why does it feel so good?

Her eyes drifted to her lap, where the notebook from the attic sat. Her heart began to pound heavily again as she considered what could be inside. A small part of her didn't want to know. It wanted to explore her feelings for Cooper and see if they could come to some kind of agreement, but the other part was driven to understand why Grandma had left her with only half an inheritance.

Cautiously, with shaking hands, Genni opened the first page. She sucked in a harsh breath at the dates. The diary started only a month before Grandma's death.

"Life goes on," Genni began to softly read. "Genevieve works herself to the bone, a product of my raising, I suppose." Genni swallowed, tears blurring her vision. "I have taught her everything I know, but it isn't enough. As I approach the end of my mortal existence, I realize that there was a part of life I haven't given her and it may be my greatest regret."

Genni paused, scared to go on. She didn't like seeing Grandma Maggie lament about regrets, especially in regards to Genni. Margaret Winters had lived a good life. A hard one, perhaps, as seemed the curse for the Winters family, but a good one. She gave to charity, went to church and raised her daughter's daughter. No one could look at those accomplishments and mark Maggie as a failure.

"I fear that in my old, tired mind, I have not taught her how to love. I should have learned when Esther's behavior became wild that there was something wrong with the way I was raising her. Instead, when I took Genevieve in, I grew harder, laid down firmer rules, and refused to give my own granddaughter the attention she needed."

A tear splashed onto the paper and Genni wiped it away, then used her sleeve to clean her face.

"Now my time is almost up and I cannot fix those wrongs. I have wondered, however, if I should take Verl up on the clause in our agreement to buy back our house. Perhaps it would be enough of a gift to Genevieve for her to forgive me."

Genni's eyes widened and her breathing stuttered to a stop. This was it, the answer she'd been looking for the whole time. "Oh, Grandma," Genni whispered through her tears. "What now?"

A buzzing from her back pocket caught her attention and Genni hurriedly wiped her face and cleared her throat. She glanced at the number and almost didn't answer, but decided that getting out of her own head might actually be a good thing at the moment. "Hello?"

"Genevieve!" Hudson said, the smile audible in his voice. "How are you today?"

She gave a watery chuckle at the irony of the statement. *I'm a crying mess, I just found out my grandmother thought she ruined me, plus there's a clause in an agreement that will let me buy back my house, but I have no idea where the agreement is!* "I'm, uh, good, thanks. How's your day been?"

"Could be better," Hudson replied. "I could be having dinner with a beautiful woman tonight."

Despite everything going on, Genni smiled. Hudson might not be for her, but he was definitely good for her ego. "That sounds like the kind of thing all men want."

Hudson chuckled low. "I suppose that's true. Which probably means we just need to man up and make it happen. So...are you free?"

She hesitated. "I..."

"You don't sound very excited," he pressed. "Is something wrong?"

Genni's eyes went back to the notebook. "Not really, but I've kind of had a big revelation and I'm not sure where to go from here."

"Anything I can help with?"

She chewed on her lip. "I don't know...maybe? There might be some legal ramifications, I suppose."

"A working dinner, huh?" He sighed. "Well, if it gets me your lovely company, I suppose I'll take what I can get."

She smiled softly. "That's very generous of you, but I don't want to take advantage."

"You're not. I'm offering."

She laughed and scrubbed at her face with her free hand. "In that case, I'll take you up on it. Thank you."

"Perfect. Meet me on the boardwalk at six? I'm thinking some comfort food might be good tonight."

"Great." She sighed again. "And thank you."

"No thanks needed. See you tonight."

Genni hung up and set the phone on the wooden slats next to her. One of these days she would have to tell Hudson she wasn't attracted to him *that way*, but right now, his advice might be useful. Setting the notebook aside as well, Genni put her elbows on her knees and her chin in her hands. She was too confused about everything to make any decisions. Hopefully Hudson could help her break it down and by tomorrow morning, she'd be back to her old self, ready to move forward.

COOPER'S CHEST WAS heaving as he jumped up the front porch steps. The run had been exactly what he needed to get his mind back on track. No more flirting with Genni. No more kisses. Only business and finding a way to work together. He was going to have to find a way to speak to her without just staring at her lips the whole time.

Cooper wiped his forehead on the back of his forearm. "Off limits," he reminded himself. Bracing himself, he pushed open the front door and went inside. The house was quiet except for a bit of scuffling upstairs that Cooper assumed was Scottie. "Shoot," he muttered. "I hope she didn't get into the bathroom."

He hurried up the steps, ignoring the burning in his thighs. "Scottie?" Cooper jerked the door open and relaxed against the frame. No unwanted smell met him, letting him know he wasn't too late. "Where ya at, Scottie?" He walked further in, then paused and grinned. "I really need to get to town and buy some supplies." Cooper walked to the corner where Scottie had built herself a nest of sorts.

Every article of clothing Cooper had left on the ground was now wadded into a ball and Scottie was sleeping peacefully on top of it. Cooper reached out and scratched her head. Scottie's eyes immediately burst open and she yipped at him.

"Let's go take a potty break, huh?" he asked, standing back up. "Come on, girl. Outside."

Scottie slid her way across the floor, nails clicking against the hardwood, and ran out of the room, nipping at his heels. "No biting," Cooper said firmly. He grabbed the dog so they could go down the stairs, then put her back on the floor and pointed toward the back door. "Outside."

He didn't want her leaving surprises in the front, so they walked through the sitting room and into the kitchen, which had a back entrance. Cooper held the door open and used his foot to give Scottie a little push. "Come on, girl. Outside."

Scottie looked up at him imploringly, then back at the door.

"Nope. Let's get your business done and burn off a little energy."

The puppy seemed to sigh before walking out onto the grass. The kitchen door came out at the corner of the home, just down from the extra wide back deck. As Scottie began to sniff around, Cooper headed to the deck in order to find a chair while he waited. He paused a few feet from the steps.

Genni was seated, her face red and blotchy, toying with her phone.

"Hey." Cooper closed his eyes and mentally smacked himself. *Good one. Very suave.*

"Hey," she returned, watching him cautiously.

He put his hands in the air. "I just came to bring the dog out. I promise not to attack." *But I don't promise not to think about it.*

A small grin played on her lips and she nodded.

Moving to the far edge of the steps, Cooper carefully walked up to the deck and found a chair a good distance from Genni that still allowed him to see the pup. Scottie appeared to be stalking a bird at the moment and Cooper chuckled at the puppy's antics.

"She's cute."

His head whipped around. Genni speaking to him was unexpected. He thought they'd go back to the silent treatment, at least until he worked up his courage to approach her again. "Thanks." He grunted.

She nodded, never looking his way. "I'm...sorry...that I got mad when you brought her home."

Her choice of words resonated harder inside Cooper than it should have and his resolve to keep his distance faltered. He knew what she meant, but using the word "home" touched that part of him that was still longing for a place to call his own. *Remember Ciana.* The thought worked and he was able to push aside all the warm fuzzies that were building. "It's okay," he assured Genni. "I should've spoken to you first."

She nodded again, but her eyes continued to remain on the yard. Silence came between them again, but this time it was awkward and heavy. They'd been ignoring each other for weeks without it being a big deal, but now it was weird. It felt like there were words being left unsaid, hanging between them, but Cooper had no desire to open that can of worms. Giving into the desire to hear her soft voice or see the fire in her eyes would only weaken his determination to keep their relationship strictly business.

Her phone buzzed and she glanced at it, then stood with a sigh, brushing off her jeans. "I should go shower."

Cooper smirked. "Hot date tonight?"

She eyed him sideways for a split second. "Uh...sort of, I guess."

"Oh." His heart fell. The question had been a joke, and he wasn't planning to pursue anything between them anyway, but hearing her blatantly say she was going out with someone else hurt...a lot.

Genni stuffed her phone in her back pocket and picked up the old notebook from the attic. "It's just that same guy from the other night." She faced the house and climbed the few steps to the flat of the deck.

Cooper nodded. "Things going well that way, then?" *This has to be, like, the third time she's gone out with that guy. If that's not a signal, I don't know what is.*

She shrugged. "I don't know. I agreed to go tonight, but I think this might be it."

Cooper frowned. "Why's that?" His lungs stuttered when her bloodshot eyes finally met his. Her usual spark and fire was missing, but there was definitely an intensity behind her dark eyes. She studied him, as if trying to figure out the secrets of the universe, and Cooper kept his face purposefully blank.

He clenched his fingers as they considered each other. Flashes of their kiss went unbidden through his head and he felt himself try to lean toward her, only being held back by stiff, disciplined muscles.

"He's not my type," she finally answered.

What is your type? The words were on repeat in Cooper's head. "Good to know." Neither said anything else as Genni went inside and he stared at the door she disappeared through. He was able to keep himself from going after her, but the roar of jealousy churning in his stomach wasn't willing to listen to reason.

Cooper knew it was wrong. He shouldn't feel intrigued by her. He shouldn't want to kiss her again and see if their chemistry was a fluke. He shouldn't want to make her part of the life he was building in this town. If they were going to be roommates, and maybe eventually business partners, then he needed to keep his distance.

It was good that she was going on a date tonight. She needed to be taken by some other guy who wasn't living with her. Someone who wouldn't be blinded by a relationship if she proved to be less than honorable in her business practices. He still wasn't set on the bed and breakfast idea, but maybe...down the road...they could come up with something that would make use of the large home. Which was just another reason there could be no other relationship between them.

Cooper had been that man once and he'd learned his lesson. Let some other guy get first-hand experience. It was no skin off Cooper's nose. *Business and pleasure don't mix. It's a cliche for a reason. Always has been, always will be.*

CHAPTER 14

Much to her disappointment, the new morning sun didn't bring the clarity that Genni had hoped for. Her mind still spun with problems, from wanting another kiss, to the seemingly semi-truce with Cooper yesterday evening, to fulfilling her dream of opening her bed and breakfast on her own. And the nasty little detail of possibly having a way to get Cooper out of her life didn't help either. In fact, it dominated the other problems, since solving that one would have consequences on the rest.

She sat on the edge of her bed and stared at the notebook. It looked innocent on her nightstand, as if it was incapable of the inner turmoil it caused. Two weeks ago, Genni would have jumped at the chance to find a way to get rid of Cooper. Yet, miraculously, his persistent presence was growing on her, and after that kiss...what woman in her right mind would throw a man out for that?

She shook her head. "I don't even know where the paperwork is, if it even exists." Standing up, she threw on a hoodie and headed to the kitchen. Maybe a full stomach would help her know what to do.

In the middle of flipping pancakes, she heard footsteps behind her. Genni glanced over her shoulder and had to bite her lip to keep from laughing out loud. Cooper's waves were like a rat's nest, wadded up all over his head, and he looked barely awake, which was unusual for him, though the bouncing puppy at his side was wide awake. When he stretched and his rising T-shirt showed her the edge of his low-slung pajama pants, however, laughter was the last thing on Genni's mind.

She spun back to the stove, ignoring her elevated pulse and how warm the room had suddenly become. "Good morning," she forced out. "I'm making pancakes."

Cooper grunted and she heard the back door open, followed by Scottie's skidding steps as the dog worked to gain traction in order to run outside.

"Rough night?" she asked, keeping her eyes trained on the pancakes.

"You could say that," came the gravelly reply.

"Was it the puppy?" Genni dared another look in his direction, just in time to see Cooper rub his eyes like a small boy.

"Mostly." He didn't look her way, keeping his eyes trained out the decorative window on the top half of the door.

"Anything I can help with?" *Oh my gosh, Gen. Shut up! You're not friends with him. He's still the enemy...sort of.*

His eyes moved to glance at her sideways, then went back to the yard as he grunted. "No."

"Ookay," she mouthed, her eyes wide. The pancakes were slapped onto a plate and she turned to set it on the counter. "Might as well eat while they're hot."

Cooper was scowling as he turned to her. "What?"

Genni's lips turned down at the edges. "Aren't you hungry? Pancakes are never as good after they get cold."

"You want me to eat your pancakes?"

A blush stole up her neck and Genni suddenly felt decidedly awkward. "I guess we haven't really done that, have we?"

Cooper shook his head, the curls waving with the movement.

Gen sighed and poured more batter into the hot pan. She waited until the initial sizzling was done before speaking. "Look, I know we got off to a horrible start. And truthfully, I'm not exactly sure where we stand at the moment, but you were right when you said we need to learn to at least get along." She turned to face him again, feeling some of her usual courage rebuilding. It didn't matter if they'd had a moment. She could be strong enough to face him without remembering the feel of his hard chest and soft lips. "I'm still set on opening a bed and breakfast, and that means we need to at least be able to work together as business partners."

His eyes were narrowed as he studied her until a knock came on the front door.

Genni frowned. "Who the heck would be coming over this early?"

Just as Cooper moved to walk toward the front door, scratching came from the back.

"Take care of the dog, I'll get it," Gen said. She turned off the stove and wiped her hands on the towel as she walked. A dark silhouette could be seen through the front window and Genni picked up her steps. "Oh! Hudson!" Her heart fell a little. She wasn't sure whom she was expecting it to be, but it definitely wasn't him. "I..." she paused and cocked her head. "How did you know where I lived?"

Hudson's smile was wide, as usual. It had always been just a little too big for Genni's liking. "Good morning. I'm here in my official capacity." His grin turned more smirk-like.

"Huh?"

"Who is it?" Cooper walked up behind her shoulder.

"I'm Hudson Baumgartner," Hudson said, reaching forward with the hand that wasn't holding his briefcase.

It was then that Genni noticed the sharp suit, flashy cufflinks, shiny shoes and expensive leather briefcase. "You're here for work?" she asked, starting to bring her mind back in hand. Cooper's presence at her shoulder was more than a little distracting.

Hudson nodded. "May I come in?"

"Oh, of course. Sorry." Genni backed up, which forced Cooper to do the same and let Hudson in. "What business does a lawyer have with either of us?" she asked after closing the front door. "You said you work for the government, right?"

Hudson ignored her and put his briefcase on a decorative table in the entryway. "My employer isn't exactly the government, though we have ties with them." He pulled a large manila folder out, then snapped the lid shut and closed the clasps. Turning, he presented the envelope with a flourish. "You have thirty days to become current, or I'm afraid the home will be repossessed."

"I beg your pardon?" Genni felt her eyebrows go nearly high enough to reach her hairline. Coldness seeped into her chest and her body slowly stiffened.

"What the he—" Cooper started to shout, startling Scottie, who was in his arms. He glanced at Genni, then back to Hudson. "Do you mind telling us what you're talking about?"

Hudson put his hands in his pockets, completely at ease, though the air was alive with anxiety. "Taxes." One side of his mouth pulled up into a crooked smirk as he looked at Genni. "Your grandmother, Margaret Winters, didn't pay property tax for nearly ten years before she died."

Genni gasped and Cooper growled. "No. That can't be true."

"I'm afraid it is, dear Genni," Hudson calmly explained. He sighed as if bored. "You owe slightly short of two-hundred and fifty-thousand dollars to my employer, who collects back taxes such as yours. If they remain unpaid, in thirty days, the home will revert to us." His eyes darted down to the envelope in Genni's shaking hand. "It's all in the document." Hudson smiled, but it looked more predatory than kind. "I'll let you two look it over. When you're ready to clean up your accounts, let me know."

Genni's whole body was shaking by this point. Just as she and Cooper were finally starting to speak, another monkeywrench was thrown into the pile. How many could one person take before they broke? *There's no way Grandma wasn't current on her taxes, is there?*

Wouldn't Mr. Filchor have said something? She shook her head. This wasn't his area of expertise. There was probably no way for him to know the undercurrents of the home, only what was said in the will. *She got behind once before...* Genni's eyes drifted to Cooper, tangible proof that her grandmother could indeed have gotten behind. *Last time it cost me half of the house. What if this time it costs it all?*

COOPER WAS SEEING RED. He didn't believe a bit of the bull this guy was peddling. If there were back taxes on the house, it should have come up with the title company. "Who did you say you were?" he asked, stepping toward the man. He was dressed slick, like one of the businessmen Cooper had left behind in his old city. Every part of the outfit screamed wealth and power, and Cooper despised it all.

"Hudson Baumgartner," he said, putting his hands in the air. "I'm only the messenger here." He smiled, and Cooper's stomach churned. "If you have questions or concerns, you're welcome to call my employer. The information is in the packet." His eyes went to Genni. "I'm sorry to do this to you," he said softly. "But you know how business is."

Cooper looked to see wet trails down Genni's cheeks and his protective instincts flared to life. He might not be willing to start a relationship with her himself, but that didn't make it all right for another man to walk all over her either.

Before he could speak up, her chin jerked into the air and Cooper felt a swell of pride. She was a strong one, sometimes too strong, but right now it was good to see she wasn't going to take this lying down.

"No...I don't know," she said boldly. "I can't say I've ever met a man who wined and dined a woman only to butter her up before serving papers." Her beautiful eyes narrowed and her lips pinched into a white line. "Some might call what you did a conflict of interest. Perhaps your employer would be interested in hearing about it."

Niiiice... Cooper thought, a small smile tugging at his lips. Seeing her throw it back in the lawyer's face was much too attractive. He turned back to Hudson, who was turning red. "I think you've out-worn your welcome." Cooper's voice was low and cold, exactly how he wanted it, and to his triumph, it had the right effect.

Hudson's eyes widened and he cleared his throat. "Well, thank you for your time." With a regal nod, he went back to the door and let himself out.

The silence was deafening until Scottie, obviously feeling the heightened emotions, began to whimper. "Shh...girl," Cooper said, putting her down on the floor. "Go play."

Scottie sat down and stared up at him, still whimpering.

"Go play," he urged, but the dog wouldn't listen. Cooper let out a harsh breath and pinched the bridge of his nose. "This is a curveball I didn't see coming."

A barking laugh, slightly wild, burst from Genni. "That's funny," she said, throwing her free arm in the air. "You think I'd expect things like this. My whole life has been one obstacle after another. Why not just one more?" Her voice died at the end and she began to cry in earnest.

"Oh man, come on, Gen," Cooper begged. "Don't cry." Forgetting the vow he had made only yesterday, he stepped forward and wrapped his arms around her. "We'll figure this out," he said into her hair. A slight citrusy scent caused his nostrils to flare. *Ah, geez. I'm in such trouble.*

When she leaned into his chest and allowed him to take some of her weight, Cooper gritted his teeth and tightened his hold. His own desires didn't matter right now. What did was helping Genni get a hold of herself so they could figure out their next steps. "I'm sorry," she blubbered. "I'm just so tired..."

Cooper nodded. "I get it. Life's been hard, but remember what you already told me. Winters women are survivors. And this time, you don't have to do it alone."

She stiffened slightly and raised her head. "I've never had help before."

His eyebrows rose up. "Not even with your grandma?"

She shrugged and relaxed again, her head resting in the crook of his neck. "She taught me what I needed to know and we did our own things. I...I don't think she wanted to get very attached."

Harsh. Except that Cooper knew exactly what she meant. His own parents had been distant, just not in the same way. They slathered him in gifts and freedom, but didn't teach him anything, other than how to look for a good time. He cleared his throat and gave her a small squeeze. "We're part-owners of this home. That means that anything about taxes is about both of us. You're not alone."

Genni straightened and stepped away from him, wiping her face. Cooper immediately felt the loss, but pushed the feelings aside. The whimpering pup caught both their attention and Genni laughed quietly through her tears. Bending down, Genni scooped her up and brought Scottie to her chest. "It's okay, girl. Your daddy's right. We'll figure this out."

Cooper held out his hand. "First thing we need to do is look at those papers."

She handed the envelope over. "I don't know how this could have happened," she whispered. "I mean, obviously Grandma got behind before, which is why you're here, but it's hard to believe it happened again and for such a high amount." Her hand began to absently stroke Scottie's ears. "I thought we had enough to get by, if only just."

Cooper didn't respond, just opened the paperwork and began to scan the papers. He still had a suspicious feeling that something wasn't quite right. With two recent deaths, something should have come up. It seemed odd that a problem this big had been so neglected. "Hmm..."

"What?" Genni moved around to look over his shoulder.

"I don't know," Cooper said. "Something just seems off." His eyes scanned the declaration. It looked very official. Large lettering at the top and a bunch of legalese stating about the tax problem.

"You think this is a scam?" she asked with a gasp. "How can you tell? It all looks legit to me."

Cooper nodded. "It does. But don't you find it odd that neither of us were informed of the back taxes when we inherited the house?" He pushed a hand through his snarls. "I mean, I'm not a lawyer and definitely not an expert, but it seems like that should have come up at some point in the process."

"That would make sense," Genni murmured. "But maybe this is just a separate situation? I mean, the lawyer who read Grandma's will doesn't deal in taxes, so who would have told him about it?"

"What about the title company?"

She made a face. "You're right. It does seem off." Her eyes glazed over for a moment before coming back to his. "But how can we prove it?"

"I would think if we can find your grandma's tax records, we can clear it all up." Cooper gave a tired grin. "And then your little boyfriend can go back to where he came from."

She hissed. "Don't call him that. I had already decided I wasn't going out with him again. This is just icing on a rotten cake."

Cooper chuckled. "Good to know." He'd never admit to the relief that flooded his veins. "Do you know where your grandmother kept her books?"

Genni blew out a breath and didn't answer while she took the time to let Scottie go. "No." Her face paled for a moment before she rallied. "But I'm sure we can find it somewhere. Grandma didn't throw away cottage cheese containers. There's no way she didn't keep her tax records."

Cooper nodded. "Okay. Then we start there." He glanced at the document again. "We have thirty days to either prove them wrong or pay them off. Hopefully that's enough time to get it all settled." He turned to face her and stuck out his hand. "Partners?" Cooper waited patiently while she stared at his hand. When her hand finally met his, it was cold and still shaking slightly.

"Partners."

And once again, we'll keep it strictly professional. No funny business.

CHAPTER 15

G enni blew a stray hair out of her face. "This is a wild goose chase," she grumbled.

Cooper grunted from across the room. "I have to say I'm surprised that your grandmother's paperwork is so disorganized, considering how you describe her. She sounded like a militant-type woman, and so I would expect her records to be the same way."

"You'd think," Genni muttered in return. She sighed. "I suppose this is part of why I worry that Hudson's claims are true. I mean, we know your grandfather had to bail her out once. Who's to say she didn't get behind again?"

"True," Cooper said, sounding distracted.

Genni looked over to see him reading a paper. His curls were framing his face and that stubble on his jaw was growing thicker again, just the way Genni preferred it. The initial attraction she'd had for him came slamming to the forefront and it took a quick stiffening of her knees to keep herself from walking over to ask for another earth-shattering kiss.

She would never in a million years have expected that the man she was constantly at odds with would be able to kiss her in a way that gave her hope that her broken pieces could be put back together.

The feeling of comfort, protection and rightness were a totally new experience to Genni. She'd gone on dates before, she'd kissed a few men, but never had she been affected this strongly.

The thought that Cooper might be more than a passing fancy or irritating housemate simultaneously frightened and excited her. She found herself craving more of the feeling, but being terrified of what it would bring. *Pursuing a relationship would mean letting him in.*

There's no way we would be able to just have something casual between us, not with that type of chemistry. But can I do that? I've never let anyone get that close, not even the women at the flower shop. The only people who know my story are those who grew up here, and luckily they don't talk about it. None of us do. She groaned quietly. Why was it that life was so hard?

"Find something?"

Genni snapped out of her thoughts. "Um...nope. You?"

Cooper shook his head, disgust on his face. "Not a thing." He huffed a laugh. "Unless you count grocery store receipts from the seventies."

"Niiice." Genni nodded slowly. "That's much more helpful than actual tax records."

He laughed and pushed a hand through his enticing hair. "Maybe we need to approach this from another angle."

Genni frowned. "What do you mean?"

"Well, we don't even know if this guy is legit," Cooper explained. "Maybe we should spend a little time looking him up rather than worrying about finding the records."

"You honestly believe he's lying?" Genni dropped her eyes to the floor. The idea that she was being conned or had been taken out by a criminal made her feel dirty somehow, like she was at fault for not recognizing the slimeball for what he was.

"Like I said before, I just think something smells fishy." Cooper dropped what he was looking at and walked to Genni's side. "I'd like to do a little research on him, if that's okay with you?"

A tiny bit of relief filtered through Genni. When Cooper had first suggested they search for the tax records together, she had been alarmed that they would accidentally discover the contract between their grandparents. Cooper had been so sweet about wanting them to work together to solve this problem and Genni was slowly losing her desire to kick him out. Having a partner was helping keep her together right now and she wasn't sure what would happen if she was left on her own again.

"Gen?"

"Of course!" she called out, too loudly. Her face flushed and she turned away from him. "I mean, go ahead. I don't care how we solve it, I just want it gone."

"You're sure you don't mind?"

Genni turned back to look at him. He was so earnest and it only served to continue to tug on that brick wall she'd built around her heart. *Remember that he has something to gain here too. If you lose the house, so does he. This isn't about any possible feelings between the two of you.* "I don't mind at all," she said, her voice a little cooler than it had been. *Good. Back to nothing but business.* "In fact, I think I'll try running those papers over to Mr. Filchor." She dusted her hands and began walking to the dining room table where they'd left them. "Even if he doesn't know about the lien, he might have some advice."

"That sounds like a good idea." Cooper headed toward the door. "I need to take the squirt out, then I'll grab my laptop."

Genni nodded and grabbed the manila envelope, then her keys. She marched outside with her head high and hopped in her car. Before she could back out, her eyes went to the side yard where Cooper was playing with Scottie. The joy in that moment sent tears to her eyes, shocking Genni.

She blinked rapidly and fanned her face. "What in the world is wrong with me?" Frantically searching her car, she found an old napkin and captured the few tears that had managed to break free. "I'm acting like a hormonal mess."

After checking her reflection in the mirror, she forced herself to leave without looking back again. This whole thing with Cooper was messing with her equilibrium. How was she supposed to stay independent and not rely on others when he made life seem so wonderful the other way?

Grandma had taught her time and again that the only person Genni would rely on was herself. But Cooper was teaching her the exact opposite. And she had to admit that his way looked much less lonely and stressful than her grandmother's way. The words of the journal came back to Genni and her vision grew blurry once again.

"Do I not know how to love?" she whispered thickly as she drove. "Have I grown into some kind of ice queen that will never let anyone in?"

Depression, anxiety, and longing were unwelcome bedfellows that seemed as if they were settling in for the long haul as Genni pulled into the lawyer's parking lot. With heavy feet and sagging shoulders, she walked inside.

"Good morning, Ms. Winters," the secretary said with a tight smile. "What can I do for you today?"

"I'd like to see Mr. Filchor, please," Genni added, knowing she hadn't left a very good impression the last time she'd been at the office.

"I'm afraid he's in meetings all day," the secretary snipped, her eyes going back to her computer.

Genni pinched her lips together. "Can you tell me when he'll have a free moment?"

"I'm afraid the schedule is busy for weeks."

Genni's temper began to flare. This lady was going too far. Just as she opened her mouth, the door to Mr. Filchor's office opened.

"I've got five minutes now, Ms. Winters," he said cooly, raising an eyebrow at his secretary.

To her credit, the employee just stuck her chin in the air, not at all embarrassed at having been caught being rude to a client.

Genni held back the desire to stick her tongue out at the cranky woman, but only just. Her heightened emotions were turning her into a tantruming child and Genni figured Mr. Filchor wouldn't take kindly to such behavior.

"Now, Genevieve, what can I do for you?" Mr. Filchor asked, his mustache twitching as he sat behind his desk.

Genni walked forward and handed him the envelope. "This was served to me and Cooper earlier. I'm hoping you can help me figure it out."

He raised his eyebrows and opened it up, pulling out the paperwork. "What in the world?" he grumbled as he started to read.

Genni waited, her heart pounding against her ribcage.

After a minute, he put down the papers and pinched the bridge of his nose.

"So...what do you think?" she asked, her knees shaking slightly.

"What I think, Ms. Winters," he said, his eyes coming up to meet hers, "is that you're in trouble."

COOPER SQUEEZED HIS eyes tight and laid his head back. His eyes were burning and tired from looking at a computer screen for so long.

Scottie whined from his side.

"Just a sec, girl," Cooper whispered. Water leaked out the side of one of his eyes and he wiped it away. "I hate it when that happens," he grumbled.

Scottie whined again.

"Okay, okay." Cooper sighed and set the laptop aside. "I need a break anyway." He stood from the chair and groaned, stretching his back, then rubbed his eyes again. "Here we go." Cooper walked carefully, Scottie practically dancing between his feet as they headed toward the back door.

He let her out, then moved to sit in one of the deck chairs. Leaning forward, he put his face in his hands. His head was pounding, but he wasn't sure if it was from the computer or stress.

Cooper's long search online had been a complete dud. He'd looked up the tax company and their website looked completely normal. He couldn't find anything that looked out of place. Social media showed the same thing for Mr. Stupid Hudson Face. The guy's slimy profile looked perfect. In fact, that was the only thing that Cooper could find itchy about the situation. It was all a little too perfect.

He scrubbed his face and searched for Scottie, making sure she wasn't getting into too much trouble. The tiny dog was torturing a squirrel, so Cooper let her be.

The door opened behind him. "Did you make any headway?"

Cooper looked over his shoulder. "Not a thing. You?"

She didn't have to say anything. The despair in her dark blue gaze said it all. "Mr. Filchor couldn't find anything wrong with the document, but he said he'd never heard any rumors that Grandma was in trouble again." She sighed and sat down in the chair next to his.

Cooper could smell her perfume and he forced his body to relax as he leaned back. "So where does that leave us?"

"He seems to think finding the papers is the best way," Genni said with a shrug.

"So back to square one?"

"I guess so." She wouldn't meet his gaze and picked at a loose thread in her jeans. It didn't take a genius to see she was struggling. Cooper felt her pain and it brought his protective instincts to the forefront. He wanted to hold her like he had earlier and tell her everything was going to be all right, but he couldn't. He didn't know if they would be all right and he respected the strong woman next to him too much to lie to her.

"Want to talk about it?" he choked out. *Those are never words that should come out of a man's mouth.*

Genni laughed harshly. "What's there to talk about? Either we prove there's been a mistake or we pay a ton of money."

Cooper rubbed the back of his neck. "And if we have to pay the money?"

Genni's shoulders sank. "I don't know your situation, Cooper. But I can't get that kind of cash. I've saved from my waitressing job for years, but it would only be a drop in the bucket for something this big." She shook her head. "And I don't know if I can get a loan in time to make it work. Plus, do they even give loans for back taxes?"

"You can get a loan for just about anything, but I doubt it would be very favorable terms," he admitted.

She nodded, her eyes going to the backyard.

They didn't speak for a bit, but Cooper's mind wouldn't shut down. He wanted to figure this out. He had a few options, but wasn't sure it was the right time to say them. His parents would have the money. But offering it to Genni felt wrong. He was sure she would be insulted and fling it back in his face, declaring she didn't need his help.

He scrunched his nose. There was one other option, but it was even less desirable than the first. Genni's small town lawyer probably didn't deal in problems like this very often, but Cooper had access to a guy who would know in a heartbeat if this thing was a scam. The problem was, he couldn't tell Genni about him without revealing why he knew this lawyer so well, which would bring up things in Cooper's past he wasn't prepared to share.

He respected Gen, he was attracted to her and was even beginning to like her more than he should. But telling a woman you had spent a few days in jail wasn't going to win him any favors, especially as their truce was still fairly tentative. He was under no delusions that she felt something for him beyond politeness. They were being brought together by a common cause, and right now that trumped their little property war.

Maybe I'll just send it to Carl and not tell her. If he doesn't find anything, we're not out any false hope, and if he does, well...I'll deal with it, I guess.

Genni turned to him with a frown. "Why aren't you at work?"

Copper chuckled. "I've been home all day and you're just now asking me that?"

She shrugged. "I was so caught up in everything that was happening with Hudson that I didn't think about it." She tilted her head. "I know that Frank's open just about every day, so how'd you manage to get time off?"

Cooper smirked. "I told him I only wanted forty hours a week. So that means I'm going to have a day off here and there." He shrugged. "It won't necessarily be the same day every week, but I'll be off some."

She nodded. "Good to know, I guess."

"Looking forward to having me around?"

"Only if it means we can get through all that junk faster," she shot back with a grin.

Cooper's smile was genuine as he bantered with her. He missed that little spark in her eye. Stupid Hudson Face had taken it away this morning and Cooper didn't like it. "So you only want me for my body? Wow. Way to admit it out loud."

Genni's face flushed and her eyes went to his arms and chest. Oooh, he wanted to flex so badly he could taste it, but Cooper forced himself to stay calm. They were already pushing boundaries they shouldn't be pushing.

"If that's why I wanted you, I'd be asking you to move the furniture, not sort grocery receipts." She gave him a triumphant look and turned away, but her blush remained.

Cooper chuckled again, but let it sit. He wasn't sure he could keep from going after another kiss if they kept flirting. He slapped the arms of his chair. "I guess it's time to get back to the grindstone."

Genni nodded. "You're right. The harder we work, the faster we can get this figured out."

"Scottie!" Cooper called, then cursed under his breath when the dog looked up, only to dart into some bushes.

Genni laughed. "Good luck," she called over her shoulder as she headed inside.

Cooper marched down the deck steps, but paused to wait until Gen disappeared inside. *Luck? Oh yeah...I'm definitely going to need it.*

CHAPTER 16

"You found papers where?"

Genni grimaced and tucked her hair behind her ear. "Under her bathroom sink."

Cooper barked an incredulous laugh, his jaw open as he stared at her. He'd just arrived home from work and had asked for an update on the search. "You're kidding...right?"

Genni shook her head. "I wish I was." She sighed. "I noticed I was out of, uh..." she eyed him, unsure if she should offer so much information.

He raised a curious eyebrow at her.

Genni gave him a look. "I needed a razor, okay? I was out and figured Grandma still had some so I didn't have to run to the store!"

Cooper cleared his throat and looked like he was holding back a laugh, making Genni all the more flustered.

"Anywaaaay...I looked under her sink and found a folder tucked in the back."

"How the heck are we supposed to find what we need if she stored them in all the weirdest places in the house?" He paced back and forth a little.

"Your guess is as good as mine," Genni said. She squished her lips to one side. "Maybe we start with the weird places? Look where papers don't belong?"

"In an eleven-thousand square-foot house?" Cooper scoffed.

"Sorry." Genni slunk back a little, feeling slightly attacked but not up to fighting back. The weight of their situation was getting heavier by the day. Thirty days wasn't very long and their first few searches had resulted in absolutely nothing of worth. With each evening, her heart grew heavier and heavier. It seemed as if the entire universe was combining against her.

"I'm sorry."

Her head snapped up. "What?"

Cooper walked toward her with a tired smile. "Did you really not hear me, or are you just trying to make me repeat myself?"

When she made a face, he laughed.

"I said I'm sorry," Cooper repeated. "I shouldn't have lashed out at you." He pushed a greasy hand through his hair. "I'm just tired and took it out on you."

She nodded. "Yeah. I know the feeling."

"What do you say we grab some dinner and then pick another room?"

Genni eyed him. Despite their truce, they really hadn't spent a lot of time together. They often split up when searching and their meal times were haphazard as each tried to find a way to get them out of this mess. "I think that might be nice," she finally admitted.

Cooper held her gaze, his hazel eyes intense as he nodded slowly. "I'm not much of a cook, but I make a mean fettuccine."

She smiled, feeling slightly shy. No man had ever cooked for her before. Or even offered to. "I know how to toss a salad."

"Salad...a woman's specialty," Cooper quipped.

Genni put her hands on her hips and glared. "And we wonder why women live longer than men."

Cooper turned to walk to the kitchen. "You keep your rabbit food. I'll take the fat any day."

Genni laughed softly and followed him.

To her surprise, dinner only took twenty minutes and soon they were seated at the kitchen bar. "Mmm..." she hummed, her mouth full. "This is delicious."

Cooper grunted, his own mouth too full to answer.

"Where did you learn to cook?" she asked, attempting an easy conversation. However, when Cooper stiffened, Genni felt as if she'd asked something wrong. "I...sorry, I didn't mean to—"

Cooper quickly shook his head, his curls flying. "No, no, no. It's okay. I shouldn't have..." He sighed. "An old friend taught me."

Genni nodded, not quite getting what was so weird about that, but assuming he wasn't quite telling her the whole truth. "So where do you want to search after dinner?"

"I think we should head back up to the attic."

"Oh?" She twirled her fork. "Why up there?"

"Remember all those papers that Scottie knocked over?" He took a drink of his soda. "Did you ever go through them all?"

Genni shook her head, feeling slightly ill. She had meant to get through them before Cooper could take a closer look. The contract between their grandparents might very well have been with the journals, and Genni was still torn about what to do with it. *One problem at a time,* she reminded herself. She needed to make sure the house wasn't repossessed before she worried about whether or not to try and buy out Cooper's portion.

"Does that sound all right with you?" he asked, giving her an odd look.

"Yep. Just dandy." Genni dropped a noodle on the ground for Scottie to lap up. The pup yipped and wagged her tail. "I think she swallowed it whole," Genni said with a laugh.

"You're gonna spoil her," Cooper said wryly.

Genni grinned. "Lucky you."

He rolled his eyes. "You're living with her just as much as I am."

"But she's not technically mine, so if she's being naughty I can just hand her back to you."

Cooper chuckled. "It sounds like she's a grandkid or something."

Genni laughed out loud. "I'm not quite ready for that. I think I might want a husband and child of my own first." Her eyes met his, and the humor of the moment stalled. Genni swallowed the rest of her laugh and felt her heartbeat begin to pick up. The air crackled with growing intensity and Genni found herself wanting to lean forward ever so slightly. The pull between her and Cooper only seemed to grow with time and it was getting harder and harder to resist.

Cooper was the first to break their staredown. He cleared his throat and stood up, taking his plate with him. "Ready to search, then?"

Genni blinked and felt herself blush all the way to her toes. Apparently a mixture of attraction and embarrassment was enough to make her feel like she was a blazing fire. "Yep," she croaked. "Search time sounds good."

Making sure she didn't meet his eyes, she darted to the sink, and then toward the attic stairs.

"Genni," he said softly from behind her.

Nope. I don't need him to make an excuse for rejecting me, she told herself. Ignoring his call, she practically leapt up the stairs. "You take the left, I'll take the right," she shouted, and hurried away from the small doorway.

She heard a heavy sigh, but then only the sound of his footsteps growing closer up the stairs, and farther away as he went to his assigned corner of the room. *Thank you,* she prayed. *I don't need another complication right now.*

COOPER'S BODY WAS THRUMMING with awareness as he listened to Genni rummage through the junk on the other side of the room. Every grunt, scoff or shuffle had his ears perking up, wanting to know what was going on. *I've got to get a hold of this attraction,* he scolded himself.

Shaking his head, he tried to put his focus back on the boxes in front of him. He lifted a lid and coughed at the amount of dust that puffed up. "Geez, vacuum much?"

"What was that?" Genni called out.

Cooper glanced over his shoulder. "Nothing. Just talking to myself."

She grinned, a smear of dirt across her forehead. "Yeah...a place like this does that to a person."

Cooper raised an eyebrow. "Are you saying I'm going crazy?"

Genni widened her eyes. "I would never."

He grinned. "You've been here longer than me. Isn't that like the pot calling the kettle black?"

Genni laughed. "Then I suppose it doesn't really matter at this point, does it? If we're both crazy, who's to say what crazy actually is?"

"Good point." After a moment, he turned back to his work, disappointed that their conversation had ended. *No. Not disappointed. I'm not disappointed about anything except the idea of losing this house. That's it.*

The thoughts were a bitter lie even in his mind, but Cooper refused to take them back. He didn't think he could risk it again. The first time he gave in was almost his last.

Clenching his jaw, he threw himself into his work. After the box full of dusty knicknacks, he found one filled with coffee tins. "What the heck were those for?" Cooper shook his head and set the box aside.

"What? Did you find something?"

"Just a bunch of junk," Cooper called back.

"Sounds about right," he heard her mutter.

Cooper scratched at an itch on his neck, then started to lift the lid of the next box. The itch came again and he slapped at the spot before scratching. However, when the tickle moved across his skin and away from his hand, he froze. The movement slowed down, but the chills racing down Cooper's back were fast and furious. "Genni," he said, his voice barely audible.

She didn't answer.

"Genni," he tried again, but his voice wasn't cooperating. It was raspy and stuck in his frozen vocal chords.

"Did you say something?"

"Yes!" Cooper managed a little louder. The movement came just under his ear and he squeezed his eyes shut. "Genni, get. Over. Here. Now."

"I can't hear you very well," she said, her voice muffled. "Can you talk a little louder?"

He started to shake his head, but immediately stopped. "No," he whispered. "Just come here."

"Geez," she said with an exasperated sigh. "Why are you being so weird?"

Much to his relief, Cooper heard her footsteps come his way.

"What?" she demanded.

Cooper could see her in his mind's eyes with her hands on her curvy hips and that expectant look on her face, the one where her dark brown eyes flashed with impatience. "Can you..." He swallowed, trying to bring moisture to his cottonmouth. "Can you please lift my hair up on the right side of my neck?"

"What? Lift your hair?" Genni scoffed. "What in the world is up with you?"

"Please," he said a little too forcefully. He made himself pull back in volume and strength. "Please, Genni. I need some help."

"Fine," she snapped.

He could tell she was still upset about earlier in the kitchen and hoped he wasn't going to regret asking for her help. The picture of her waiting for his kiss would be forever burned in his brain, but the memory of his past had given him strength to walk away. Right now, however, he needed her help and they hadn't cleared the air between them. *Please let her have a little mercy at the moment.*

His hair lifted and Genni immediately gasped and dropped the curls.

"Ah, geez," Cooper said through gritted teeth when he felt the eight-legged fiend head into his hairline. More appropriate words came to mind, but he was already on Genni's list.

"It's a spider," she hissed.

"I know," Cooper said tightly. "I need you to brush it off my neck." He suppressed a shiver. "Although, it's trying to climb into my hair now, so it's going to be a little harder than before."

"Why can't you do it?" she asked, stepping back.

"Because I can't see it," he shot back.

"But you can feel it!"

"Genni! Are you or are you not going to help me?" He felt a cold sweat break out on his forehead. It was taking every ounce of strength he possessed to not fall to the floor and cry like a little child. Spiders had been a fear of his since he was a little boy, and for some reason, not even becoming a motorcycle riding bad boy had taken that phobia away from him.

She came around so she could look him in the eye. "Are you...scared?" she asked, genuine concern in her eyes.

"No," Cooper snapped.

Genni raised an eyebrow at him. "Really? Then why are you not moving? You look like a statue. And you could barely speak a minute ago."

"Please, Gen," he said, his anger fading.

His words must have done the trick, because she relaxed and nodded. "Hold still."

Cooper bit back a retort.

She lifted his hair again and he could feel her shudder. "Eeww...it's a big one too."

He closed his eyes again. If she didn't get rid of it soon, Cooper was sure he would faint and never recover...from the situation and from embarrassment.

Her delicate fingers parted his hair. "Hold on. I'm gonna use a piece of paper." She reached to the side and grabbed a folder. She took a deep breath and then Cooper felt a scrape along his scalp as the corner of the folder flipped at something. "GOT IT!" she screamed, jumping around and stamping her foot on the ground.

Cooper scrambled back, his chest heaving.

"I got it!" she cried, looking at the floor. "I got it!" With a squeal of triumph, she lunged at him, wrapping her arms around his torso and shivering. "I hate spiders."

Cooper was still breathing heavy, but it grew much more shallow when she jumped into his arms. "Me too," he said breathlessly.

"Yeah...from the paleness of your face, I figured you had it worse than me," Genni said with a nod. "Which meant I had to be the one to step up."

Cooper wrapped his clammy hands tighter around her and buried his face in her neck. He kissed the soft skin there, unable to help himself. "Thank you," he whispered. "You saved me." The words hung in the air, feeling much heavier than they were meant to.

Gently, Genni leaned back, forcing Cooper to raise his head up until they were looking at each other, only inches apart. "You're welcome," she breathed, her eyes wide and filled with longing.

He was too close, too attracted, too shook up. Cooper knew without a doubt that at the moment he did not have the strength to resist a second invitation. Forcing all thoughts of bad consequences out of his head, he slowly brought his face down to hers. He moved carefully, making sure she had plenty of time to refuse him, but refusal was apparently the last thing on her mind.

With a little jerk, she came up to meet him and their mouths met fully.

It wasn't a fluke. Those were the only coherent words in Cooper's brain as sensations overtook him. Nothing in his life could have prepared him for the overwhelming rightness he felt at having Genni in his arms.

He twisted her slightly, pulling her into his shoulder and changing the angle of his kiss so he could deepen their connection. The thrill that shot through him at her sigh was nearly enough to have him losing his head.

Instead of giving in, however, Cooper allowed them another minute or two, then slowly brought them back down to Earth. "I think we need a break from the attic," he said between soft kisses to her cheeks and mouth.

"Mmm..." she hummed, her eyes staying closed as a small smile played on her bright red lips.

"Maybe some air?" Cooper kissed the tip of her nose. "Want to take a walk on the beach with me?"

"No, but I think we should," Genni said, stepping out of his embrace.

He felt her loss immediately, but knew they needed to keep their heads. Forcing a bravery he didn't feel, he held out his hand. "Let's put Scottie away and go."

Her smile was shy and utterly adorable as she slipped her fingers into his. "Sounds good."

CHAPTER 17

Genni's insides were still jumping as she and Cooper walked outside. Even though it was summer, the salty sea air held a touch of chill to it, but for the first time ever, Genni didn't feel it.

In fact, the air helped to cool her heated cheeks and flushed skin. Absolutely no part of her upbringing could have prepared her for what it felt like to be in Cooper's arms. She had felt warm, protected, special and even cherished. His touch ignited sparks, but was also as gentle as if she were made of glass. It made Genni want to curl up next to him and never leave, and she knew that was dangerous territory to be in, but at the moment, with her hand in his, and the roaring ocean in their path...she didn't care.

"Are you okay?" His question was spoken softly and the trepidation in his voice was audible.

It was a loaded question and Genni wasn't sure how to answer it. "In what way exactly?" she asked. "With the house? With the fact that I go back to work next week?" She eyed him sideways. "With...us?"

Cooper chuckled. "Wow. I didn't realize I was seeking the answers to the universe." His gaze dropped to the sand and he grew somber. "I suppose I was asking first about the house...and us." His grin was sheepish. "They're kind of intertwined."

Genni nodded. "Yeah...in a weird way, they are." She sighed. "And I'll be honest, I don't know what to think about us. I mean, your kiss is..." Her cheeks grew heated again. "What I'm trying to say is...I mean..." She slapped Cooper's arm when he started laughing at her. "Stop!" she cried, starting to laugh herself. "It's not an easy thing to say out loud."

"It's all right," Cooper teased. "You can say I'm an amazing kisser. I don't mind at all."

"I'm sure you don't," she grumbled, only making him laugh more.

Cooper pulled them to a stop and took her free hand, so he was holding both of them. "Just so we're clear," he said, still smiling wide, "I feel the same way." With a wink, he let go of one hand and they continued walking down the beach.

Genni couldn't seem to stop the smile from spreading across her face. She had no idea what this made her and Cooper, but to know he'd been just as affected as her made her feel less foolish for being curious about pursuing their obvious chemistry.

"But that doesn't help us with the house," Cooper continued. "There's got to be a way to stop this guy...but how?" He pushed a hand through his curls and Genni's fingers twitched.

She knew what it was like to touch that hair, and the new, girly side of her wanted to forget all about the house and go back to enjoying the texture of his glorious hair. Her more logical side, however, won out and she forced herself to focus. "I don't know. I feel like I'm going in circles. It can't be real, yet we can't prove it's not. Grandma should have records, but we can't find them. We could just pay them off, but we don't have the money." She blew a raspberry through her lips. "So where does that leave us? Should we just go ahead and try to split the amount and take out loans?"

Cooper shook his head. "Not unless it's a last resort. I really think there's a better way."

"But how?"

"COOP!" a deep voice called out enthusiastically.

Genni and Cooper both looked forward to see a couple and a dog walking in their direction. Genni squinted and finally realized Felix and his sister Charli were walking Hermit.

"Wassup, Captain!" Cooper answered with a grin.

"How do you know Felix?" Genni asked with a frown.

Cooper glanced down. "I met him on the beach when I first arrived. He invited me to a clam...uh, bake? Boil? I forget what term he used." Cooper shrugged.

Genni snorted. "I'll bet that was a load of fun. Those things are nasty."

Cooper raised his eyebrows. "Someone who was raised here doesn't like seafood?"

"Oh, I like seafood," Genni clarified. "Just not boiled pieces of slime."

Cooper burst out laughing just as Felix and Charlize arrived.

"Hey, Coop." Felix grinned wide. "Heya, Gen."

Charli's eyes dropped to Genni's hand, which was still attached to Cooper's. With a smirk, she folded her arms over her chest. "How's my favorite bed and breakfast owner?"

Genni gave her a soft smile, her cheeks heating up yet again at the knowing look. "Just plugging along...as always."

Cooper shook Felix's hand. "How's the water been treating you?" he asked with a grin.

Felix beamed. "It's been a good summer. Lots of tourism means lots of fishing trips." He laughed. "Who's going to complain about that?"

"Our freezer is so well-stocked, I think we'll be living off it for the next twelve years," Charli said wryly.

She eyed Cooper with interest, and Genni found herself struggling to contain an unwanted trickle of jealousy. Taking a deep breath, she forced it back where it belonged.

"I haven't met you yet." Charli leaned forward with an outstretched hand. "Charli Mendez."

Cooper nodded and shook her hand. "Siblings?" he asked, waving a finger between Charli and Felix.

She grinned and walked back to her brother, elbowing him in the ribs. "Unfortunately."

"Whatever. Complain much more and I won't let you mooch off my hard-earned food anymore." Felix laughed when she began to punch his side. "Easy, easy. I'm getting too old for you to beat up like this."

Genni watched with a mixture of amusement and longing. What would it be like to have a familial relationship like that? The loneliness she often felt when she remembered she was all alone came roaring back with a vengeance.

A squeeze on her hand had Genni sharply looking up, straight into Cooper's hazel eyes. He gave her a small smile before turning back to the siblings. That same warmth from their kisses began to penetrate the coldness inside her and wash it away. She wasn't sure how he knew she needed a reminder, but at that moment, Genni felt a little piece of her heart begin to slip away. Cooper was proving to be things she never knew she needed.

"Hey, man, I've got a question for you," Cooper said to Felix. "Have you ever heard of a guy called Hudson Baumgartner? Or The Tax Mitigation Company?"

Genni stilled. She hadn't planned to share their problems with the Mendez siblings. Talking about her personal life always made her uncomfortable and left her feeling vulnerable. Not to mention, Grandma had taught her that complaining was useless.

Felix frowned and looked at Charli, who shook her head. "Nah, man. Not familiar to me. What's going on? A tourist being stubborn or something?"

"Or something..." Cooper pinched his lips together.

Please leave it alone, don't say anything more. She squeezed Cooper's hand, praying he understood the subtle message.

Cooper looked at her. "Maybe they can help?"

"But how?" Genni asked back in a whisper.

"Okay, now you have to share," Charli said firmly. She put her hands on her hips and gave Genni a look. "Sounds like you're holding out on us."

Genni shook her head. "No, but—"

"But nothing," Felix interjected. "Come on, Gen. We've been friends a long time." His smile was kind, the kind Genni imagined he gave to his sister. "Let us help you."

She worried her lip for a moment before looking back to Cooper, who raised his eyebrows. He definitely wanted to share their problem, but it looked like he was waiting for her permission. Knowing that he would respect her privacy enough to ask proved to be all she needed. "Okay," she squeaked. "But I don't see what good it will do."

COOPER COULD SEE THE worry in Genni's eyes even as she agreed to tell Felix and his sister what was going on. He recognized that opening up to others was a big step for her. Although Cooper didn't have her whole story, he knew enough to understand she didn't rely on others...ever.

Pride warmed him as he watched her push past her fears and embrace something new. It was at that moment that he knew his earlier caution about mixing business with pleasure was coming too late. He was already beginning to lose his heart to the feisty homeowner and it didn't look like he'd be able to stop it at this point.

Cooper turned back to Felix. "We were served papers a few days ago saying that the late Mrs. Winters owed a large amount in back taxes. We have thirty days to pay them off or the house will be taken."

Charli gasped.

"I smell a rotten carcass," Felix said with a scowl.

Cooper nodded. "My first thought too," he admitted. "We've asked the local lawyer—"

"Mr. Filchor," Genni added.

Cooper acknowledged her comment with a nod. "And I've tried to do some online research, but nothing weird is coming up. All we have are our own suspicions and they won't help us in a court of law." *That and my lawyer back East, but I still haven't heard back from him.*

"Do you think Maggie could have really been behind?" Charli asked. "How much are we talking here?"

Cooper grimaced. "Quarter of a million."

Charli gasped again and Felix whistled low. "That's a lot of clams," he said.

Genni shrank back and Cooper knew she was growing embarrassed at admitting to a family weakness. "It is," Cooper admitted, shifting his weight so Genni was just slightly behind his shoulder.

"What are you going to do about it?" Charli asked. "I don't know anyone who keeps that kind of money lying around."

Cooper opened his mouth, but Genni beat him to it. He shifted out of her way as she spoke.

"We're trying to find Grandma's tax records so we can prove this whole thing is a big mistake," she said, her voice growing slightly stronger. Her shoulders dropped from their hunched position and her chin rose. Cooper could see the physical transformation come over her as she mentally decided not to give in to the desire to hide.

"Sounds smart...so what's the hold-up?" Felix tilted his head.

Cooper grinned when Genni snorted. "The hold-up is that Grandma apparently didn't have any kind of system when it came to any of her records. We've been finding them all over the house."

"Even under the bathroom sink," Cooper added.

"No way," Charli gushed. She tsked her tongue and shook her head. "This just keeps getting worse and worse."

"Thanks, sis, that was helpful," Felix said sarcastically.

"Watch it," she warned, elbowing him again before turning back to Cooper and Gen. "Have you tried to contact the tax company? Like the one she did her taxes through?"

Cooper raised his eyebrows. He hadn't thought of that. *I'm a complete idiot. I've been too twitterpated to realize we could solve this within minutes.*

"Do you really think Grandma hired someone to do her taxes?" Genni asked.

Cooper's heart fell. *So much for that solution.*

"I just don't see Old Lady Winters getting backed up that far and then leaving you to deal with it," Felix said, then he ducked his head. "Sorry, Gen. I shouldn't have called her that."

Genni shrugged. "It's not like I didn't know you guys said it."

Cooper felt a little pang of hurt for the fact that not only had she grown up in difficult circumstances, but obviously the other kids hadn't made things easy either.

"I know," Felix added, "but still, as your friend, I should do better."

Genni's smile was slow and a little unsure, but it was still glorious.

Hermit, who had been lying down during the conversation, suddenly jumped to his feet and tugged on the leash, barking out at the ocean.

It wasn't until his attention was pulled away from the conversation that Cooper realized it was starting to get dark. "Looks like we better head back," he said to Genni, who nodded. "Hey, it was good to see you," Cooper said, raising a hand to Felix and Charli. "I'm sure we'll see you around."

"Hang on a sec," Charli said. "I think we need to make some kind of plan."

"Plan?" Genni frowned. "What do you mean?"

"To save the house, of course," Charli said with a laugh. "What else would I mean?"

Genni's mouth flopped open. "You...you want to help me, I mean *us,* save the house?"

"That's what friends do," Charli said, leaning in to emphasize her words. "If you think anyone from around here is going to be okay with some company taking away the Boardwalk Manor, you've got another thing coming." She smiled to soften her words. "And it's not just about the house, Gen. We want to help you." Her nearly black gaze darted to Cooper, then back. Charli tipped her head in his direction. "We'll help Cooper by default."

Cooper laughed, not the least bit offended. "I'm glad to be included in such a noble effort." He looked over to see Genni's eyes swimming. "What did you have in mind?" he asked, turning back to Charli and trying to ignore his desire to pull Genni back into his arms to comfort her.

"I don't know..." Felix said, scratching his chin. "I can't think of anything off the top of my head." He looked to his sister.

Charli shrugged. "Me either. Maybe we should set up a meeting with everyone."

Felix nodded thoughtfully. "Sounds good." He looked to Cooper. "Let me talk to the boys and we'll get back to you two." A little smirk played on his lips as he looked at Genni, then Cooper again. "We'll figure out a time that works for everyone and then do some brainstorming."

"That would be amazing," Genni breathed out. "Thank you."

Felix and Charli both nodded. Charli gave Genni a wave and then the siblings left, Hermit trotting at their side.

Cooper tugged on Genni's hand and they headed back to the house. "You've got some good friends," Cooper said, eyeing her from the corner of his vision.

"Yeah..." she said, sounding lost in thought. "I guess I do."

CHAPTER 18

G enni studied her phone. "Tomorrow," she called to Cooper.
"What?"

She heard his footsteps coming down the hallway.

"Did you say something?" he asked, poking his head into the
guest bedroom Genni was working in.

She smiled, feeling slightly shy. They'd spent the last two days
searching through the house and getting to know each other better.
Genni found that with each moment that passed, she was enjoying
his company more and more. Her fears of giving up her independence for a relationship were fading to the background the more she
grew accustomed to his presence. *No...it's more than that. I actually
enjoy having him here.*

Each and every wall that she'd built up over the years was slowly
crumbling and Genni found that she didn't care. Her grandmother
wasn't a bad woman, but maybe, just maybe, she was wrong about
needing to go through life alone.

"Gen?" Cooper asked again, his eyebrows high. His hair was
pulled back in a ponytail and Genni wished he would let it down,
but she shook herself out of her wandering thoughts.

"Sorry. Charli texted and said that everyone will be at the flower
shop tomorrow night."

Cooper nodded. "The flower shop? Seems like a weird place to
meet."

Genni shrugged and put her phone back in her pocket. "Rose
owns it and we meet there a lot. At least us girls do. We're all part of a
monthly arranging class, which is where we became friends. Now we
meet there all the time."

He chuckled. "Okay, then. I guess I still have a lot to learn about this place."

Gennis smiled back. "Us small town folks can be a little quirky, but you'll get used to us."

Cooper's eyes began to smolder. "I find I'm definitely getting used to it."

Genni felt that now familiar heat climb up her neck and into her cheeks. "Have you, uh, had any luck finding anything?" she asked, hoping to break the thick tension in the air. As much as she wanted to kiss him again, their thirty-day mark was quickly approaching and Genni was feeling the pressure. She couldn't lose this home, she just couldn't!

Cooper rubbed the back of his neck. "No." He sighed. "This feels like a wild goose chase." His eyes went around the room. "Half the time I'm not even sure what I'm looking for."

Genni nodded. "Yeah. Me neither."

"You can't think of anything that might help us hone in a little on the proper target?"

Unwanted tears pricked her eyes and Genni immediately turned away, not wanting him to see her emotion. Truth was, she felt completely idiotic that she didn't know where Grandma kept her records. She'd lived with the woman for almost twenty-five years! How did Genni never think to ask such a thing?

"Hey, hey..." Cooper said soothingly.

She felt his presence behind her and stiffened until his warm hands began to rub up and down her upper arms. Like always, his touch helped calm her in a way she didn't understand. "Sorry," she whispered, wiping at her eyes. "I don't know why I'm such a watering pot. It's not like me."

Slowly, Cooper pulled her back into his chest and wrapped his arms around her. He brought his head down, his lips resting near her ear. "We're both under a lot of pressure right now. It's a wonder we have any tissues left in the house."

Genni gave a watery chuckle. "Then why don't I see you crying?"

Cooper snorted. "I am...on the inside."

Genni laughed again. "You're ridiculous."

His hold tightened. "You're right," he said, his voice having dropped in tone and volume.

Genni stilled, waiting to hear what he would say next.

"I'm ridiculously in like with you."

She swallowed hard. They hadn't talked about their feelings yet. The kisses hung heavy between them and the air often heated when their eyes met, but for the most part, they'd both just kept pushing forward with the tax issue, letting words and explanations go unsaid. Her heart slammed into her ribcage as Genni realized she needed to make a decision. Whatever she said right now would determine their situation going forward. "I..." *Why is this so hard?* She squeezed her eyes shut and slowly turned in his arms, letting her hands rest against his chest. In her mind's eyes, she could see her grandmother. Strong, determined, quiet, but most of all...alone. Genni had had enough alone time to last for eternity. Opening her eyes, she allowed her body to relax against his. Leaning forward, she brought their mouths within centimeters of each other. "I'm ridiculously in like with you too," she admitted.

Before she had the chance to regret or be embarrassed by her vulnerability, Cooper's lips claimed hers and Genni knew she'd made the right choice. Being strong on her own had never felt as good as being with Cooper did. Once the back taxes were paid, they'd have to decide what exactly they were going to do with each other, but right now, Genni just wanted to enjoy the ride.

"It wasn't supposed to be like this," Cooper whispered against her neck as he nuzzled it, leaving a trail of kisses in his wake.

"Hmm?" Genni hummed, not truly listening to his words.

"How did we go from wanting to kill each other to me not getting enough of you?"

His voice was husky, and it made Genni's stomach flutter. She pulled back to look him in the eye. "Honestly? I'm not sure, but as long as we're throwing things out there, I thought you were the handsomest guy I'd ever seen when you pulled up in front of the house on that motorcycle of yours."

Cooper's smile was slow and delectable. "You did, huh?"

She laughed and dropped her eyes to his T-shirt. Meeting his gaze right now felt just a little too intense. "I've never been one to go for the bad boy look, but you pull it off pretty well." She glanced up from under her eyelashes to see his smile falter slightly. Panic fluttered in her chest. *Crud. What did I say?*

When she lifted her face to look at him fully, his smile came back. "It sounds like we had similar experiences," he teased. "I was expecting an elderly lady to show up at the door, but instead I got a beautiful woman." He chuckled. "Totally threw me for a loop. And then you fainted in my arms, and I thought I'd died and gone to heaven."

"I'll bet you didn't feel that way when I woke up," she countered, enjoying their banter.

Cooper shrugged. "I hate to say it, but I kind of enjoyed our bickering." He pumped his eyebrows. "Something about that fire in your eyes always left me feeling energized and even more attracted than I already was."

Genni scoffed and stepped away from him, walking back to the stack of papers she had been going through. "So you're saying I need to keep biting your head off about every little thing?"

"Only if it makes you happy."

Genni spun back to look at him. Nobody had ever said that to her before. In fact, she wasn't sure anyone had ever *cared* about her happiness. "I..." She paused, really thinking about her answer. She wanted to get this right. "I don't want to fight with you," she whispered. "But I do like teasing you."

He smirked. "Got it. You're a teaser, not a fighter."

"Does that make you the lover, then?" she tossed back before she thought about how it sounded. As soon as she realized her mistake, Genni slapped her hands over her mouth. "Sorry. I didn't mean it like that. I'm not actually...I mean, I'm not that type of girl..."

Cooper's face was serious as he slowly stalked her way. His body movements were feline, like a predator, and it excited Genni more than she wanted to admit. He came up close, bringing them nose to nose. "The type of girl you are is exactly the type of girl I want you to be," Cooper whispered. "And while I'd be happy to be a lover, right now I'm just starving. So unless you want me to devour you, we'd probably better get me something to eat."

GENNI'S EYES HAD GROWN wide with every word he spoke, until he said he was hungry. As if on cue, his stomach grumbled in the heavy silence and Genni burst out laughing.

"I can't decide if that was romantic or not," she said through her chuckles.

Cooper grinned. "It wasn't either. It was the truth. I'm about to keel over."

"I can tell." She pointed to his stomach. "Come on. Let's go grab something on the boardwalk. I definitely don't feel like cooking tonight."

Cooper nodded. "Sounds good to me." He took her hand and they began to walk out of the room.

"Wait." Genni stopped walking and cocked her head. "Where's Scottie?"

"Crap," Cooper grumbled. "I left her downstairs."

Genni threw her head back and groaned. "All the furniture is down there!"

Cooper began walking, tugging her with him. "I've really got to get her some chew toys."

"Seriously," Genni agreed, thundering behind him. "Maybe I can grab some tomorrow while you're at work."

Every time they spoke, Genni opened up a little more, and while it was fantastic to see her coming out of her shell, it only added to the guilt sitting on Cooper's shoulders. He had yet to share any of his past life with her and still didn't feel ready to do so either. But some of the things he'd done, the things he'd been accused of...they could easily be deal breakers for Genni.

You've changed, he assured himself as they rushed down the stairs. *She'll see that...I hope.*

Cooper ran to the sitting room, where he could hear grunting noises from the puppy. "Scottie!" Cooper shouted as he skidded into the room. Genni was right behind him and nearly knocked into him as her socks slid across the wood floor.

When Cooper spotted Scottie, his eyes widened for a moment before his shoulders drooped. "Again?"

Genni was snickering behind him.

"I'm not going to have any shirts left at this point," Cooper grumbled. He stormed over to Scottie, who whimpered, then yipped and dove under a chair. "Come back here, you little punk," Cooper growled. He got down on his hands and knees, searching for the tiny dog.

Genni's laughter grew louder, the sound warming his chest. Not very long ago, she would never have felt free enough to make such a noise. In fact...Cooper couldn't help but smile when he heard her snort when laughing so hard. Finally, he sat back on his seat and looked at her, then grimaced.

Genni was nearly bent in half as she scratched behind Scottie's ears. The mongrel must have run around the side of the room, looking for protection from him. Pretending to still be upset about the torn up T-shirt, he pointed a finger at the dog. "You're gonna pay for those clothes."

Genni's laughter continued, though it calmed some as Cooper got to his feet and drew closer. "Don't blame her," she said between giggles. "A girl would have to be an idiot not to want to snuggle into you at any opportunity."

Cooper lost his fight to stay stern. "Genevieve, I do believe you do my ego good," he teased.

Genni's laughter stuttered to a stop, the puppy the only thing still moving in the room. "And you're good for me too, in more ways than one."

Once again, the air began to crackle around them. Their chemistry was growing stronger every day, and Cooper hoped he could stay in control. Maybe he needed to think about moving to the carriage house. There was a small apartment, probably old servant quarters, in a loft. If they couldn't save the house, moving out would be a moot point, but the idea lingered in his mind anway.

"Come on, ladies, let's grab dinner. Then we can get back to another search." The words were like tossing a gallon of ice water on a fire. All the fatigue and weariness of the past week landed right back on her face, and Cooper felt horrible about it. "She's a little young for a leash," he ventured, "but maybe we can try bringing her with us anyway?" He tilted his head toward the dog. If Scottie made Genni feel better, he wouldn't argue about it.

Genni put a small smile on. "As fun as that sounds, I think she might be more work than it's worth."

Cooper nodded. "Yeah...we might not actually get to eat if she's with us." He reached out and took the puppy. "Now, squirt. I'm going to put you away, and you better not cause any more trouble. My stomach is already trying to eat its way out of my body."

Cooper started to walk away when Genni stopped him. "Here," she said, running up to where he stood at the foot of the stairs. She held out a bundle of fabric. Genni winked. "She might behave better if you give her this."

Cooper growled and snatched the shredded shirt, then stomped up the stairs. His frown shifted into a smile as Genni laughed quietly behind him. He wasn't sure how he was going to do it, but some way, somehow, Cooper was going to help Genni save this house. It wasn't just about his own desire for solid roots anymore. Somewhere along the weird journey he'd taken to get here, he'd started to lose his heart to the beautiful woman waiting to eat dinner with him.

And now, he found himself wanting her dream to come true, as much as his. She wanted a bed and breakfast? He was going to see she got a bed and breakfast. Even if it meant breaking his own cardinal rule and speaking to his parents...something he had vowed never to do again.

CHAPTER 19

Genni wasn't sure why she was nervous, but her hand that was cradled in Cooper's was feeling awfully clammy at the moment. These were her friends. During the little chat on the beach, Genni had come to realize that her friends extended far beyond the women in the arranging class.

Felix's little speech and Charli's determination to help had been almost as good at breaking down Genni's barriers as Cooper's patience had. Her life had shifted in so many ways since Grandma died, and Genni was finding more and more that she liked it this way.

"Ready?" Cooper whispered as they approached the front door.

Genni wanted to say no. She wanted to keep her troubles to herself. She wanted to turn and not look back, just pretending that everything was fine. She pinched her lips together. *But it's not fine. And there's no point in pretending that it is.* "Sure."

Cooper chuckled. "Such enthusiasm." His eyes sparkled when they met hers, looking more brown today against his dark red shirt.

Genni automatically smiled back. The movement was becoming second nature. "I'm working on it," she said with a grin.

His smile continued as he pushed open the glass door and led her inside. "Whoa..." Cooper's eyes widened as he took in the room.

Genni's smile grew. Rose's shop was like the Garden of Eden. Vines and flowers were *everywhere*. Add in the humidity and smells and it was easy to see how it would be slightly overwhelming to new people. "It's pretty great, isn't it?"

"It's something, all right," he murmured, his eyes still wide.

Genni laughed softly just as Rose burst in from the back.

"Gen!" she cried, holding out her arms. "I can't believe this is happening to you." As she approached, Rose shifted and gave Genni a side hug.

For the first time ever, Genni found it wasn't quite enough. Letting go of Cooper, she turned and full-hugged Rose.

"Oh, Gen," Rose whispered, squeezing tight.

Genni's closed eyes couldn't stop a tear from leaking down her cheek. Rose always seemed to carry such a matronly vibe about her and right now, it was exactly what Genni needed. Though she wasn't quite ready to be done, Genni leaned back and gave a watery laugh. "Sorry."

Rose shook her head, her own eyes slightly misty. "Nothing to be sorry for. We're just glad for the chance to help." Her blue eyes drifted and a little smirk played on Rose's full lips. "You must be Cooper."

Genni wiped at her eyes. "Oh, yeah. Sorry. This is Cooper James."

Rose shook his hand, then looked back to Genni, intentionally widening her eyes. "I'm glad to see you two getting along."

Cooper laughed as Genni flushed. He took her hand again. "Me too. The paint wars were getting out of hand."

Rose's eyebrows shot up. "I hadn't heard about those. It sounds interesting."

"A story for another day," Cooper answered easily.

The door opened behind them and all three turned to look.

"Hello, ladies!" Caro said loudly, waving widely. "And gent, of course."

"Hey, Caro," Rose said with a welcome smile. She looked to Genni and Cooper. "Why don't we head to the back and we can introduce Cooper to everyone."

"Oh, I've already met him," Caro said airily. She grinned as if she held a secret, and Genni stiffened.

Caro was spunky and gorgeous and that had always been a little intimidating to Genni, though she'd never worried about it...before now.

"Who do you think got him a job with Old Frank?" Caro said with a laugh.

Cooper smiled back, but his hand never left Genni's, for which she was grateful. "She caught me stumbling through the grocery store and gave me the directions I needed in order to find Frank's."

Caro laughed. "He was like a blind squirrel trying to find an acorn." She clapped her hands together. "Are we ready to get this going? Now that we don't have to hate Cooper, I'm eager to figure out what exactly is going on."

Rose nodded and turned to lead the way. Cooper squeezed Genni's hand, catching her attention, then winked at her, easing her tension.

"Who all's here?" Caro asked.

"I think we're the last ones," Rose said, pushing open the back door. "Come on in."

Once more, Genni felt a flash of dread and worry, but she was getting better at pushing those feelings aside. They'd ruled her life for too long. Now that she'd felt the sun, she had no intention of going back to live in the shadows.

Shouts and greetings met the group as they walked into the work space. It wasn't a large room, but the dozen people there fit comfortably.

"What's up, man?" Bennett called from a seat in the back. He was leaning on the back two legs of his chair, a wide grin on his boyish face. His nut brown hair was nearly covering one eye, only adding to his charm.

Cooper raised a hand. "Hey, Benny. Long time no see."

Bennett shrugged. "Eh, you know how it is. Everybody wants their mail and they want it now."

Cooper chuckled and Genni found she enjoyed watching the exchange. She'd known Bennett a long time. He had always been the happy-go-lucky boy next door. His sister, Melody sat next to him, nearly bouncing in her seat.

"Hi, Genni!" she said with a bright smile, waving her hand quickly.

Genni smiled and gave a little wave in return.

"Who's next to Ben?" Cooper whispered as they took their seats.

"That's Melody, Bennett's sister."

"Ah. That would explain why they look like the same person."

Genni snorted quietly. "Yeah, and if you ever meet their mother, you'll see they look exactly like their father."

Cooper gave her a weird smile. "That is not what I expected you to say."

Gennie laughed quietly. "I know, and it's kind of a long-running joke around here. Truth is, their father left when they were little, and they were raised by their mom. Their hair color and stuff definitely comes from Marcia, but their personalities, thankfully, do not."

"Why's that?" Cooper nodded to another guest at the meeting.

"Because Marcia is certifiably insane," Genni whispered, making sure her voice didn't carry. "She moved down to California years ago so she could live a free life on the beaches. She thinks if you own a home, the government uses it to track your every move."

Cooper's eyebrows shot up. "Uh, wow. So, like a hippie or a conspiracy theorist?"

Genni nodded. "Yep."

His eyes trailed to the siblings. "I never would have guessed. Benny seems cool."

"Oh, he is. They both are. Which is why we all joke about them being nothing like her."

"Got it..I think." He grinned. "Small town humor is still something I'm learning."

Before Genni could tease him any more, Rose brought the room to attention. "I want to thank everyone for coming tonight," she said, her confident voice carrying well in the space. "I believe everyone knows why we're here, but just in case our ever-present gossip line failed you" —she paused while the group laughed— "we're trying to help Genni and Cooper save the Boardwalk Manor. Apparently there were some back taxes on it that no one knew about and now they only have..." She looked to Genni, an expectant look on her face.

Genni swallowed hard. "Twenty-one days," she croaked out.

Rose nodded. "Twenty-one days to do something about it." She clapped her hands. "Now. Let's start brainstorming."

COOPER FOUND HIMSELF impressed with how quickly everyone in the group threw themselves into the fray. Ideas, questions, concerns...all were talked out immediately.

"I'm still concerned about the legality of what's going on here," Ken said, rubbing his chin. "I know several of us have said that this thing smells fishy, and I agree. I think we should dig a little deeper into the background of this company."

"Each day that we do that means one less day to get the money we need," Charli pointed out.

"True..." Ken scowled. "Maybe we should split duties, then." He turned to look at Cooper. "Can you two give me the names of the lawyer guy and the company again? Maybe the police database will turn up something." He went back to the rest of the room. "The rest of you can use your resources to help with the other side of things. That way we cover both bases."

Rose nodded regally. "I think that would work."

Cooper noticed Ken's eyes flash as he looked at the beautiful redhead. There was a maturity about her that the other women lacked, yet she only looked a little older. If Cooper had to guess, he would put her in her early thirties, where the rest of the group appeared to range from just out of college to late twenties. He tilted his head, considering. *Does Ken have a thing for the flower lady? Why doesn't he do something about it?*

"So what should we do to raise some money?"

Genni sniffed beside him and Cooper looked over to see her bottom lip trembling. "Hey...what's wrong?"

She shook her head and rubbed her cheeks. "Gah. I'm sorry. I'm just...overwhelmed with all this."

Cooper noticed a hush had gone over the room and he glanced around to see most of the room watching them. "You're upset about the house?"

"No," she said thickly. "I mean...yes, of course I'm upset about the house. But that's not what's turned me into a blubbering idiot tonight."

"You're not an idiot," Melody shot out.

Her smile was compassionate, and Cooper felt another tick go on the "stay in Seaside" list. He'd have been left high and dry if something like this had happened back East. He *was* left high and dry. Even after his name had been cleared, none of his former friends or family had come back to apologize or reclaim him. But this small town was proving to be just the opposite. The people actually cared about each other. It was a novel and welcome experience for him.

"This isn't your fault," Melody continued. "And what are friends for if it's not to lift when someone is down? What affects you, affects all of us." She grinned, a slightly menacing feel to it. "And we're not about to go down without a fight."

Genni sniffled again and Cooper put his arm around her. "Thank you," she said, addressing the entire group. "I never thought...I mean, I didn't expect...Gah!" Genni threw up her hands. "You guys are awesome, okay? That's all I've got."

A few chuckles broke the tension of the room before Caro jumped to her feet. "I've got it!" she shouted. Everyone quieted and turned to her. Caro put her hands on her hips and preened. "It's tourist season, right? So we've got tons of people in town who are willing to spend some money. Why don't we do something like a weekend festival and donate all the proceeds to helping save Boardwalk Manor? I'm totally willing to put on a baked goods table." She tapped her chin. "We can even advertise it as saving an historic landmark. People will love it!"

"I'll donate the drinks!" Melody piped up.

"I can certainly have a flower booth," Rose added.

"I can donate profit from fishing tours that weekend," Felix threw in.

"I can do a booth for my shop," Brooklyn said. "But I might need some help."

"Since I can't offer a booth for construction, I'll be your assistant," Charli answered, her face slightly pale.

"Sweet!" Brooklyn said with an evil grin. "Maybe I'll get you in something other than leggings and sneakers!"

"Don't count on it," Charli grumbled, folding her arms over her chest.

Cooper turned to Genni for clarification.

Genni laughed softly, wiping the corner of her eye. "Brook runs a little boutique in town. It's as girly as it comes. Charli is our resident tomboy. She doesn't do dresses or accessories, even if it means life or death." Genni grinned. "Brook is always trying to change that."

"So what does Charli do?" Cooper asked.

"She's a jack-of-all-trades." Genni ticked her head back and forth. "I suppose jill-of-all-trades would be a better description. She does remodeling work, like, *all of it*. Plumbing, the woodworking, painting, construction, you name it." Genni nodded. "And she's good too.

There are a lot of old homes here and she's the main reason they're all as nice as they are."

Cooper whistled low. "That's impressive. Usually people have one specialty."

Genni shrugged. "Charli always said she gets too bored sticking with one thing." She patted Cooper's leg. "And if that's not enough, the woman does iron man's. She has more energy than any person I know."

"Uh, I'm tired just listening to you," Cooper said, making a face.

Genni laughed. "Yeah. But she's so nice, we can't hate her."

He tugged her a little closer into his side, kissing her temple. "Your friends are all pretty awesome."

"Yeah..." Genni agreed. "They are."

"And I'll help wherever I'm needed," Bennett hollered. "I've got absolutely no skills, but I'm sure someone can put me to work."

"Oh, don't worry," Melody quipped. "I know just what to do with you."

The group laughed while Bennett growled. "How is it you're so much younger than me, but so bossy?"

Melody folded her hands in her lap and schooled her features. "It's a gift."

Genni shook against his side as she laughed at their antics.

"This all sounds wonderful," Rose said, her voice slightly louder than normal. Once the room calmed back down, she spoke again. "Does everyone have a job, then? Or anything else to add?"

Jensen raised his hand. "I don't have anything to do yet," he said. "But I'm happy to go where I'm needed. I don't think the school is going to be much help to us for something like this."

"Hey, man!" Bennett called out. "You can help Ms. Bossy Pants over here, and I'll work at Caro's booth!"

"You just want to eat everything at my booth," Caro quipped.

Cooper watched Melody slink back into her chair, her face growing bright red as the others teased and laughed. *Oh, ho. Another one? This group is growing more interesting by the minute.*

"I promise to save some for the customers," Bennett said solemnly, his hand in the air as if making a vow in court.

Caro sniffed. "Fine. But the first time I find frosting smeared on your face, I'm kicking you out."

Bennett grinned. "Deal!" He put a hand to his mouth and leaned toward Melody, speaking in a loud faux-whisper. "Hey, sis, can I borrow a stack of napkins that day?"

Cooper couldn't help but smile as the group once again broke into laughter and teasing. He settled back in his seat, knowing they had more planning to do, but he was finally feeling like they might actually have a chance to beat this thing. Things were once again looking up.

CHAPTER 20

"You think they'll be able to pull this off by next weekend?" Genni asked, brushing another cobweb from her face. She and Cooper were back in the attic today, once again attempting to find paperwork of any kind that might give them information about Grandma's taxes.

Since she and Cooper didn't have skills they could sell at a booth, they had been assigned to continue their search while the rest of the group put together the fundraiser. Genni had been more than happy to comply. Searching her house was much more comfortable for her than speaking to businesses about donations.

"Yeah..." Cooper drawled. "At least, they sounded confident they could." He paused in his work and brought his head up.

Genni grinned at the ponytail and hat he wore. He wasn't taking any more chances at spiders landing on his head.

"Why?" Cooper pressed. "You're not?"

She shrugged. "I certainly hope so, and honestly, with Caro and Rose front-running it, I have no doubt it'll be exactly what they want it to be. But...there's no way we'll make the kind of money we need, and I'm worried it'll all be for naught."

Cooper nodded thoughtfully. "That's definitely a concern. But maybe the collectors would be willing to take payments? Maybe if we can offer them a sizable down payment, they'll let us work slower on the rest."

"I hadn't thought of that," Genni mused, her eyes becoming unfocused as she grew lost in her thoughts. "Maybe we should call them now and offer that?"

"We don't know what the down payment will be though," he pointed out.

"True." Genni shuffled through a few more papers, then leaned back with a sigh. "I don't think we're going to find it in here."

"Why's that?" Cooper's voice was slightly muffled.

"All I'm seeing is junk. Wouldn't she at least have all the tax records together?"

"I'm not putting anything past your grandmother at this point," Cooper grumbled.

"Nope." Genni slammed the cardboard lid back on the banker's box she was going through. "I'm going to look somewhere else. I don't think half the stuff I'm looking at was even hers."

Cooper muttered under his breath. "Fine. But where?"

"I don't know..." Genni thought frantically. "I'm going to the carriage house."

Cooper straightened, looking curious. "Yeah...I've been meaning to check that place out anyway. Let's give it a try."

Genni headed toward the stairs and hurried down them. Something had to give soon. Even with her friends' plan, Genni was worried it wouldn't work out. What if the tax collectors wouldn't accept a partial payment? What if they couldn't find the papers? What if she lost the house? *What if that means I also lose Cooper?*

She could feel her usual darkness creeping in, and Genni felt an added measure of panic at going back down that cold road. Just as a cold sweat broke out on her forehead, a warm hand slipped around hers. She turned her head to fall straight into warm, green eyes.

"If we're going to walk across the property, I might as well get a few moments holding my girl's hand," he said with a grin. He kept their stare, bringing her fingers up to his mouth and leaving a soft kiss on the skin.

That wonderful warmth pressed the shadows back down and Genni took in a long, deep breath. "Your girl, huh? Is that what I am?"

Cooper's eyebrows went up. "Did you have a different term in mind? Like girlfriend or something?"

Genni smiled and turned away, feeling a little shy. She'd never gotten this far in a relationship before. "I, um...I'm not really sure," she admitted softly. "I like the idea, but don't really have any experience." She looked at him through the corner of her eye. "In some ways, I feel like I know everything about you, but if I really think about it, I can't answer certain basic questions."

Cooper was quiet for a minute and Genni worried she'd crossed a line. "What would you like to know?" he asked.

She let out a soft sigh of relief. "How about your favorite color?"

Cooper stopped and let go of her hand in order to pull open the large, sliding barn door on the carriage house. Before he moved, he grinned at her. "That's easy. Brown."

Genni's skin flushed all over at the emphasis in his voice. "You're ridiculous," she scolded, though she loved his comment.

"I thought we went over that," Cooper said with a grunt. "Geez, when was the last time you opened this place?"

"Too long," Genni admitted. The air inside the detached building was stuffy and full of dust. She coughed slightly and waved a hand in front of her face.

"Well," Cooper put his hands on his hips, "where do we start?"

She pointed up the stairs. "Let's try the apartment. I think there were filing cabinets in there."

She let Cooper lead her up the stairs. "You didn't tell me yours," he said as they neared the top.

"My what?" Genni was breathing embarrassingly heavily for a staircase. The fact that it was nearly twice the size because of the high ceiling in the carriage house didn't matter. *I have GOT to start exercising. Good grief.*

"Your favorite color."

Genni looked over, surprised. "You want to know my favorite color?"

Cooper gave her a wry look. "Genevieve Winters, haven't you figured it out yet?" He stepped a little closer and ran his knuckles along the underside of her chin. "I want to know everything about you."

If she was a swooner, Genni would have done exactly that. *I guess I kind of did when he first arrived. Would he hold me again if I let myself go?* "I think that's the sweetest thing anyone has ever said to me," she whispered.

Cooper leaned in to kiss the end of her nose. "Maybe we can start there. Tell me why you're so unused to compliments."

Genni blinked several times. "Wow. That was a big jump."

Cooper shrugged and turned to the wall to turn on the light switch. "Sometimes you gotta go for the deep end first."

Genni blew out a long breath. "Are you sure you want to hear the story?" The old Genni would have held onto her past like it was a nationally treasured secret. But Cooper had more than earned her trust. *If anyone is willing to listen and not judge...it'll be him.*

"I do," he said, taking her over to a row of old metal filing cabinets. "You start here and I'll go down there. We can work our way to the middle."

Genni nodded and tugged open the first screeching drawer. "My mother died when I was two," she started, forcing her shaking knees to stiffen. "And no one knows who my father was."

COOPER MADE SURE TO keep his face impartial as he listened to her story. It told him so much about her and he finally began to put together the pieces that were uniquely Genni.

Mostly, he found himself impressed with her. She came from a difficult background, lacking in support and love, and yet...here she was. Determined to keep her family legacy alive and build a place where people would come to celebrate the exact virtues that Genni had been kept from.

She's too good for you, his inner critic stated coldly. *She's dug herself up by her bootstraps from nothing. You had it all and still fell apart.* He paused in his scolding. Maybe saying he had it all was too much. Cooper had had money, parents and he thought he'd had friends. He had a career and an education. The world had been at his fingertips for the taking. Until one stupid decision had wrecked it all. *One decision? How about a lifetime of choices that led straight down the road to purgatory?*

"Coop?"

He turned, grateful for the lifeline to get out of his own head. "Yeah?"

"Sorry." She chewed her lip. "You just looked so upset. Did I..." She dropped his gaze. "Are you upset with me?"

"Oh, man, no!" Cooper hurried to say. He stopped thumbing through the files, walked over and took her face in his hands. "I got caught up in my own thoughts, but sweetheart, I'm so amazed by you." Her eyes were wide, and Cooper felt like he could drown in those chocolatey pools and die a happy man.

"You are? You don't think I'm stupid for wanting to open a bed and breakfast? Or for keeping everyone an arm's length away my whole life?"

He shook his head and brought their foreheads together. Ahh...she was the best tonic for his guilt-ridden thoughts. "I don't think you hold any blame, Gen. You've had a difficult life and true to your family name...you survived. The best part is that now, you're not just surviving, you're beginning to thrive." He kissed her softly. "And I'm grateful to have a front row seat to the show."

"It's because of you, you know," she whispered, her voice thick with tears. "You're the one who opened my eyes."

Cooper shook his head. "No way. The only thing I did was make you mad." He smirked. "You make your own choices."

She got on tiptoe and brought their mouths together for a longer exchange. "You make me want to be warm," she whispered against his mouth after they separated in order to breathe.

Cooper wasn't quite sure what she meant by that, but he could tell it was meant as a compliment. Instead of breaking the moment, he returned it. "And you make me want to be a better man." Pulling her in tighter, he let himself get lost in her. It wasn't difficult. Genni made his head spin, projecting thoughts of futures and homes and children...all things he would never have considered before meeting her.

I'm not sure I'm falling anymore, he thought. *I'm pretty sure I'm completely gone.*

After a few more minutes, Genni put her hands on his chest and pressed back. "I can't get enough of kissing you, but we really need to look through these papers."

"Spoilsport," Cooper grumbled, then gave her one last peck, which turned into three. "Okay, okay." He put his hands in the air and backed up. "I'm under control now...I think." He winked, prouder than he wanted to admit when she flushed at his flirting.

Forcing himself to turn away, he went back to the drawer he'd been looking through. His mind was still racing and his adrenaline pumping, but if they had any chance at making this dream work, first they needed to save the house.

"So what about you?"

He stiffened. *Crap.* "Hmm?" he tried to deflect. It didn't work.

"I told you my story. What about yours?"

"Mine, huh?" Cooper didn't look at her, hoping that if he stayed distracted enough, she wouldn't press. A minute went by and he cleared his throat at the awkwardness hanging in the air between them. "My story...is pretty boring," he said.

"Can I hear it anyway?" Genni laughed softly. "I could use boring after giving you mine."

He nodded. "I grew up in a big city. My parents were bigwigs, and I was mostly raised by nannies."

"Oh, Cooper. I'm sorry."

He looked at her and shook his head. "No, it's fine. I mean, they were nice ladies, so it wasn't all bad. Besides, my parents were gone, like yours."

"Yeah, but to have parents and still not have them around..." She shook her head. "I think that's worse than them being deceased."

Cooper swallowed, trying to clear the lump in his throat. Truth was, his parents' inattentiveness is what started his rebellious behavior. All he wanted was for them to notice him. "No, really. It was fine. I graduated high school, went to college and got a job."

"You have a mechanics degree?"

He frowned and turned to look at her. "What?"

Genni scrunched her nose. "Sorry. I don't know all the right terms. But you're a mechanic, right? Isn't that what you went to school for?"

"Uh, no, actually." He rubbed the back of his heated neck. "I just really like motorcycles, so I picked that up along the way."

"Oh." She nodded. "So what did you study, then?"

Cooper pinched his lips together. "I was an architect."

Genni's jaw dropped. "Really? Wow. You don't seem like the suit type."

He shrugged and went back to work. "Yeah. But it was nothing. I didn't really love it all that much."

"So why did you go into it?"

He didn't know what to say. He was already lying to her, or at least lying by omission. But they were getting into dangerous territory and he didn't want to tell a flat-out falsehood. "I..." He paused, a paper in his hands. "Hey, Gen? I think I found something."

"What?" She wiped her hands on her jeans and rushed to his side.

Cooper squinted. "I'm not sure, but it has my grandpa's name on it..." He trailed off when she snatched it from his hand.

"I think I know what this is," Genni said, her voice cracking slightly. She folded the paper really small and stuffed it in her back pocket. "We don't need to worry about it. It has nothing to do with the taxes." She spun on her heel and went quickly back to her cabinet.

Cooper stood stunned as he watched her. The fact that she had basically stolen the paper from him had him insanely curious, but mostly, he was grateful for a chance to break their line of conversation. *Do I push? Or let it go? If it was something I needed to see, Genni would tell me...right?*

His old fear of mixing business with pleasure reared its ugly head, but Cooper shoved it aside. Something weird was on that paper, but Genni had given him no reason to mistrust her. He was the one lying in this relationship. *If anyone has the right to be hurting, it's her. Not you.*

"You know what?" Genni asked, breaking the tense silence.

"What?"

"We need music." Genni went to the stairs. "Be right back. I'm just gonna grab a speaker."

Cooper nodded. "Why don't you grab Scottie and we'll let her play while we're in here."

"Sounds good!"

He saw a thumb go up as she agreed to his request. With a grateful sigh, Cooper turned back to the cabinet. He'd dodged a bullet, but somehow it felt like he'd still lost the battle.

CHAPTER 21

"Oh my goodness," Genni said, her trembling fingers covering her lips. "I can't believe they did all this."

She and Cooper had come to the festival an hour before it opened in order to try and help set up, but apparently her friends were way ahead of her. The vendor spaces along the boardwalk were perfectly decorated. Bright banners waved in the ocean breeze, the smell of flowers mixed with the brine and when Genni took a deep sniff, she could smell a little bit of Caro's chocolate goods as well.

Cooper whistled low. "I had no idea it would turn out so well."

Genni nodded, her vision once again blurring over. She had cried more in the last month then she had in her entire life. Most of the changes she was experiencing were wonderful, but Genni never would have guessed she was such a blubbering pot.

"Gen!"

She found Caro waving her down.

"Over here!"

Genni's wide smile was completely genuine as she tugged on Cooper's hand and took him down to Caro's little tent.

"What do you think?" Caro asked, doing a little "ta-da" with her hands. Plates of wrapped goodies filled the tables. She had used stands to create dimension and each layer was filled with finely decorated sweets.

"Oh my goodness, Caro," Genni gushed. "It's so gorgeous!" She shook her head. "I don't know how to thank you."

Caro smirked and cocked a hip. "Just admit I'm the best candy maker this side of the Mississippi and we'll call it good." She winked and leaned in. "Plus, when that bed and breakfast opens, I expect an exclusive dessert contract."

"Done." Genni didn't even hesitate. If she could still get her dream up and running after this, it would be a miracle and Caro would have more than earned the right to a little side business. Genni paused, realizing suddenly that the bed and breakfast wasn't just hers. "Uh...I mean..." She looked at Cooper. "If that's all right with you?" Her voice cracked slightly. This was the first time she'd openly admitted that Cooper was part of the Manor and therefore part of its future.

By the warmth in his gaze, he recognized the moment and Genni was glad she'd set aside her own pride. "I have no problems with that," Cooper said with an easy smile. "But I might need to test the merchandise first."

"Well, duh," Caro said, rolling her eyes. She grabbed two ribboned goody bags out of a bucket under the table. "These are for friends and family." She pumped her eyebrows. "I always make a little something extra for us." A long, pink fingernail pointed to Genni's nose. "Don't eat it all in one place."

Genni laughed. "We won't." She swallowed the lump of emotion still lodging in her throat. "And thank you."

Caro pushed out her bottom lip, then grabbed Genni around the neck, pulling her into a tight hug. "We're all in this together, sweetie," Caro whispered. "Don't worry. We've got your back."

The tears Genni had been holding back spilled over and she stood from the embrace, wiping them away. "I'm going to be a mess, and the festival hasn't even started!"

Caro's laugh was also a little watery. "Maybe you better move on before you mess up my makeup."

"Expecting someone special?" Cooper said with a chuckle as he pulled Genni to the tent entrance.

Caro fluffed her hair. "Always. You never know what tourist might walk in off the street."

Cooper's laugh grew louder as he and Genni emerged into the sunlight. "That woman is a handful," he said with a grin.

"She is," Genni agreed. "But the more I get to know her, the more I realize what a good heart she has." She sighed, feeling amazingly light, despite the pressure sitting on her shoulders. "They all do."

Cooper squeezed her hand. "Come on. Let's check out the next one."

"Rose!" Genni cried as they drew closer. She skirted around a man drawing on the sidewalk. "Whoa...he's good."

Cooper nodded. "Seriously."

Genni paused to watch as a dolphin slowly began to form. The creature looked as if it were leaping out of the concrete. "That's amazing," Genni said to the man. His hair was hanging down around his face and she didn't recognize the back of his head.

He looked up and grinned. "Thanks, Gen."

"Oh my gosh! Bennett!" She put her hands to her cheeks. "Where the heck did you learn to draw like that?"

He dusted off his fingers and shifted his weight onto his heels. "Nowhere. I've always doodled."

Genni pointed to the picture. "That's not doodling. The dolphin looks like it's 3D."

"Wassup, Coop." Bennett thrust his chin toward the quiet man behind Genni's shoulder.

"Benny," Cooper greeted back. "Pretty impressive, man."

Bennett threw his head back to get the hair out of his eyes. "Eh, it's a hobby."

"I mean it, Bennett. It's really good," Genni's voice had quieted a little. *No more crying!* she told herself.

"Better stop, Gen," Bennett teased. "You might make me blush." He tilted his head and pursed his lips. "Or go ahead and build my ego, but if my sister is to be believed, that would be a horrible thing to do."

"It's too big as it is!" Melody shouted, catching their attention. She grinned and waved as she walked toward them. "Don't say anything else, Genni. The guy is already impossible to live with."

"Like you would know," Bennett shot back. "You don't live with me."

"Thank heavens," Melody said, throwing her head back in apparent relief. "You leave your socks everywhere."

Genni felt like she was watching a tennis match, her head bouncing back and forth between the siblings. Instead of her usual pang of longing, however, she found herself amused. Their banter was funny, but there was an underlying love that was easy to spot. That type of relationship used to make Genni feel like an interloper, but now she was experiencing a love of her own, both that of friends and that of a more romantic nature. Not that she had admitted it to Cooper. They'd only known each other a couple of months, and they'd only been dating for a couple of weeks. It felt far too soon to be talking of love.

But that didn't stop Genni from thinking it, and it didn't stop her from enjoying the fact that she was no longer on the outside looking in. Maybe, just maybe, she really did belong with these people.

COOPER WAS IN COMPLETE awe. There was no other word for it. The amount of effort that had gone into this festival was almost more than he could comprehend. It didn't look like something that had been thrown together in two weeks. Rather, it looked like the type of situation where there'd been months of planning with a full committee and an entire town sponsorship behind it.

The colors were bright, the smiles were wide, the smells were enticing and the overall feeling in the air was enough to melt even the coldest heart.

"Excuse me...can I have your attention, please?"

Cooper turned away from the booth he and Genni were admiring. They'd come early to help, but hadn't lifted a single finger. All the locals they'd run into had been sympathetic and Genni had been the recipient of so many hugs that Cooper kept waiting for her to spontaneously combust.

It was either the hugs or the fact that the whole town seemed to know about the situation with the Manor that was going to eventually get to her. He glanced over from the corner of his eye. He'd been surprised at how well she'd been handling things. She was a far cry from the distant, anxious woman he had met when he'd first shown up in Seaside Bay.

"That's right, folks, come on over here."

"What's going on?" Genni asked as they began to meander toward a small stand with a microphone.

Cooper frowned when he saw Rose and Caro up on blocks. It was Rose who had been calling everyone over. The festival was set to officially open in five minutes and Cooper had no idea what was going on. "Beats me," he admitted quietly. They stopped at the back of the crowd, holding hands and waiting to see what the announcement was.

"Thank you so much for coming," Caro gushed into her microphone. A shrill blast rang through the air, causing everyone to cover their ears. "Darn it," Caro mumbled, the words getting picked up by the microphone as she turned to adjust the speaker behind her.

Cooper chuckled, then tucked Genni under his arm as they waited for things to get settled. He frowned when he saw Rose turn to the side and her hands began moving wildly. "What's Rose doing?" he murmured.

"She's talking to Lilly."

Cooper jerked back. "What?"

Two lines formed between Genni's eyebrows and Cooper had the quick thought to rub them away, but she spoke before he could react. "Lilly is her daughter... She's deaf. Rose is signing to her."

His own eyebrows shot up high. "I didn't know she had a kid." He looked back over and shifted so he could see who Rose was addressing. A darling little girl, who only looked to be about five, was smiling up at her mother. Her bright red tresses seemed to float in the breeze, while a white sundress fluttered around tiny legs. The girl's skin was creamy and looked like the type that would easily sunburn. "Huh."

"Isn't she the prettiest thing you've ever seen?" Genni said breathlessly. "I always think I remember how darling she is, but then I see her again and am amazed once more. I've never seen such a perfect-looking doll."

"And she's deaf?"

Genni's jaw tightened. "Yes."

"What's with the face?"

Those dark eyes softened. "Sorry. All of us women tend to be a little...mama bear when it comes to Lilly."

Cooper shook his head. "I was just surprised, is all. I don't have a problem with her being deaf." He craned his neck to look at the mom and daughter again. "That only makes it more impressive." Rose was shuffling the little girl toward an older woman, who held out her hand to Lilly. The child went willingly, waving her hand at her mother as she disappeared into the crowd. "Is that the grandmother?"

Genni shook her head. "No. As far as we know, Rose is alone." Genni pursed her lips. "We really don't know a lot about her past. We think she's divorced, but no one knows for sure. She came to Seaside a few years ago with a tiny baby in tow and opened up the flower shop." Genni shrugged. "She was too sweet not to love, and now we all work together."

"As evidenced by this festival," Cooper responded thoughtfully. As much as he was enjoying making new friends and spending time here, he was starting to realize that almost everyone had secrets. Most probably weren't as severe as his own, but they were still there.

Even the little things, like Genni having no idea of Bennett's artistic skills, or the secret crushes in their group, and now Rose's mysterious past... It was all just a reminder that no matter how well you think you know someone, you can't know everything.

Cooper forced down the bubble of fear that thought brought to his throat. His relationship with Genni was still difficult sometimes. When the shadows of his past crept into his present, it was like fighting a rising tide. Cooper had thought he'd been in love before. He'd trusted someone he worked with before. He'd set aside worries and enjoyed the moment before...and then he'd paid the consequences.

Genni ISN'T Cianna, he reminded himself for the millionth time. *She's naive, a little shy, and most importantly...kind. All qualities that Ciana lacked. There's no way this is going to blow up in your face like before.*

"Okay...did we get it fixed?" Caro asked into the mic, tapping it with her lacquered fingernail. She smiled when the crowd cheered. "Wonderful! Now, as I was saying before, we want to thank y'all for coming." She glanced at her partner. "Rose and I, plus many others, have worked hard to put this last-minute festival together, and we have to say how pleased we are with everyone's cooperation."

When those blue eyes landed on Cooper and Genni, Cooper felt Genni stiffen against him.

"Many of you know, but for those who don't, I'll explain. This isn't just any festival."

Uh-oh. Cooper tightened his hold, praying Genni didn't try to run.

"We have a situation on our hands that we're hoping to help alleviate." Caro handed the mic to Rose.

"Thank you," Rose said softly, then brought the mic to her lips. "The Boardwalk Manor is an institution in our town. It's been here longer than any of us have and is a vital heirloom in our community." She paused while the crowd clapped politely. "But now it's in danger of being lost to us." She nodded as she continued. "Maintaining such a beautiful landmark has taken its toll, and one of our own needs our help. So today...all the proceeds of the day go to helping keep the Boardwalk Manor where it belongs. In the hands of Genevieve Winters and Cooper James."

Genni's arms went around his waist as the crowd turned and began offering their support. Many individuals had already done so this morning, but having so many at once was difficult even for Cooper. He could feel Genni trembling slightly, but her smile was gracious, if strained a little.

She accepted all the words of encouragement that were offered, hugging when necessary and shaking hands with others. Cooper kept his hand on her lower back, knowing she was struggling with the attention. He wanted to offer a reminder he was there, but the truth was, these people were here for her. As kind as it was for Rose to include him in this situation, the people weren't here for him. They wanted to support Genni. And she needed every ounce of it.

CHAPTER 22

G enni's smile felt like it had become a permanent fixture on her face. Everyone wanted to speak to her, and as much as Genni hated the attention, she had come to realize that everything was being done in friendship and love.

An *entire* town had shown up to support her and Cooper. It didn't matter that Margaret Winters had been an aloof, quiet woman. It didn't matter that Genni had kept to the shadows, working hard never to disturb a single soul. It didn't matter that their family had no money or influence in the community. All that mattered was that she was a part of the community. And even brand-spanking-new Cooper was welcomed with open arms. She felt herself sway slightly on her feet, before stiffening her knees. The weight of her situation had been sitting on her shoulders for so long, the relief today was bringing now was making her light-headed.

She grimaced slightly. If the amount of women dancing around Cooper was to be believed, he was *more* than welcomed. Genni had spent a lot of her life wondering what it was like to be part of something bigger than herself. She often found herself longing for family and belonging, but never would she have described herself as a jealous person...until now.

If one more woman in tiny cut-offs and a too-small V-neck spoke to Cooper, Genni knew for sure she would blow a gasket. "It's the Oregon Coast," she grumbled to herself, hugging Scottie closer to her chest. "It's not even that warm for heaven's sake." *I hope they get pneumonia.* She closed her eyes and instantly berated herself. *Get a hold of yourself, Gen. Cooper isn't going to leave you for some tourist with too much skin showing. If that was his type, he would never have kissed you.*

"Pathetic, isn't it?"

Genni's eyes snapped open, taking a moment to focus her sight. "Hudson," she growled. The anger in her tone must have alerted Scottie to the situation because the puppy began to squirm hard against Genni's chest. Keeping her eye on the sleazeball, she set the dog down, keeping a tight hold on the leash. "What are you doing here?"

He grinned, that perfect smile looking more sinister than ever before. "Just admiring the efforts of these quaint people." He tilted his head to the side, smirking. "You really think you have a chance to win the suit?"

Genni stuck her chin in the air. "Are you seriously just here to poke fun at us?"

Hudson snorted and put another bite of caramel corn in his mouth. "Nope. Like I said...just admiring the efforts." He jerked his head down and scowled. "Get off."

Genni realized that Scottie was trying to chew on Hudson's shiny shoes. She had a quick thought that they were a weird choice for the beach. "No, Scottie. Leave it." Genni pulled her back, eventually picking up the squirming bundle. "Did you have anything else you wanted to mock? Or am I free to go?"

Hudson stepped forward, his pleasant demeanor gone. "You won't win, sweetheart," he said in a low, steely tone. "While bringing your town into it is a nice touch, it won't make a dent in what you owe us."

Genni backed up. The threat seemed to come out of nowhere and she wasn't sure how to respond to it. "Why do you even care?" she asked. "It's not like you'll benefit if I lose the house."

Hudson cleared his throat and stepped back, smoothing his hair. "I didn't say I would."

"But you—"

"What are you doing here?" Cooper's angry words burst into their conversation and Genni's head spun as she spun to look at him.

Hudson smirked again. "Funny...I seem to be hearing those words an awful lot lately."

"Yeah, well, maybe you need to realize they're a nice way of saying you're not welcome." Cooper stood right next to Genni, his muscles tight and a vein thrumming near his jaw.

Genni had a hard time taking her eyes off of him. He was magnificent in his anger, but slightly dangerous as well. She had a feeling Cooper knew how to fight, and considering how much bigger he was than Hudson, it wouldn't be much of a contest.

Hudson clicked his tongue. "It seems small town hospitality isn't quite what I've heard."

"Leave."

Genni stepped back a little. The testosterone-filled air was getting a little too thick for her.

Hudson's eyes went to her, then back to Cooper. He put his hands in the air. "No harm, no foul. I'm just here to enjoy." He backed up. "Good luck to you both." The smile dropped. "You'll need every bit of it."

Cooper didn't move until Hudson was long gone and Genni found herself watching him warily. This was a side she'd never seen of Cooper, and it frightened her. She didn't think he would hurt her, but the tattoo and motorcycle seemed to make a lot more sense after that little display.

Slowly, Cooper turned around, his face gradually relaxing. After a moment, he shook himself and gave her an apologetic smile. "I'm sorry. It took everything I had not to deck the guy, but I was afraid Ken would throw me in the slammer."

An inappropriate giggle slipped through Genni's lips and she covered them with her fingers. "You were..."

"Terrifying? Overbearing? A Neanderthal?" he offered, scrunching up one side of his face.

Genni relaxed, grateful he was back to himself. "A little bit," she admitted.

"Sorry." He blew out a long breath and shoved a hand through his hair. It was blowing in the breeze and was a little wild-looking at the moment, fitting the situation. His eyes came back to hers. "Did I really scare you?"

She shrugged and used the excuse of setting Scottie on the ground to buy more time. "I didn't think you would actually hurt me, but I don't think I've seen you get so worked up before." Her eyes were on the dog, but thick fingers slipped under her chin, bringing her face up. The warmth in his eyes immediately melted her reserve. She knew this man. She knew he had feelings for her, and she knew that he was only trying to stand up for her. She might have gone about it a little differently, but at least he got his point across.

"I'm sorry," Cooper whispered, his fingers caressing her skin. "Scaring you was never my intent."

She gave him a sheepish grin. "I think you scared Hudson too. He hadn't been the least bit inclined to leave until you showed up."

Cooper snorted and dropped his hand.

The loss of touch was acute.

Scottie yipped and tugged at her leash.

Genni watched for a moment. "Want to go get a smoothie?" she asked. "I don't know if you've had one of Melody's concoctions yet, but they're amazing."

Cooper's slow smile was enough to heat her more than the afternoon sun. "You sure you want me along? I might scare off anyone in our path."

"Works for me," Genni quipped. "I have to admit, as nice as everyone is being, I've kind of reached my people quota for the day."

Cooper laughed and held out his hand.

Genni slid her fingers into his, enjoying a feeling of coming home as they began to walk down to the bright pink booth with bananas hanging from the opening.

"THIS IS BETTER THAN I thought it would be," Cooper said after swallowing a cold mouthful of fruity slush. He eyed the cup. "Who'd have thought spinach could taste good?"

Genni laughed and Cooper smiled at the sound. After their tense moments with Hudson a bit ago, it was good to see her feeling better. Shame coursed through his veins as he remembered how he'd frightened her. It had never been his intent, but when he'd seen that slick lawyer standing over Genni, her face pale and tight, Cooper had lost his cool. Despite the frustrating circumstance, however, he was curious what Hudson had said that had frightened Genni so badly.

"You men," Genni scoffed, waving a wild hand in the air. "You're all alike." She dropped her voice and banged her chest. "Me man. Me eat meat."

Cooper leaned back, his eyes wide at her little speech. "Wow. All these years and I had no idea that's how I sounded." He shook his head. "Someone should have told me." He put a hand to his chest.

Genni laughed some more, the sound a little more shrill than usual. "Oh my word," she said breathlessly, putting a hand to her forehead. "I think I'm giddy or something. This really isn't that funny."

"Did they spike your smoothie or something?" He took another long sip. "Maybe Melody isn't your friend after all..."

Genni laughed again.

Cooper couldn't help but smile. "You really are giddy. Being around too many people has finally gotten to you."

She nodded. "I think you're right." Genni wiped at her forehead. "I think I should go home and go to bed. I haven't been sleeping well lately."

Cooper checked his phone. "It's late anyway. We've been wandering around for hours, so we should get Scottie home as well." He looked down to see the pup curled up in a ball, sleeping at Genni's feet. "Come on, squirt," he grunted, lifting the dog into his arms. "Time to go home."

Genni got to her feet and swayed slightly.

"Whoa...Gen!" Cooper cried, his worry skyrocketing. There really was something wrong. He dropped his cup and pulled Genni into his chest. "Are you going to be able to walk?"

She nodded. "I think so. Just give me a second to catch my breath."

He held her while she breathed deeply. Normally Cooper loved having her close, but his fear overshadowed his pleasure at the moment. She definitely wasn't acting herself.

"Hey..." Felix walked up to them, his words trailing off and a smile fading from his face. "Gen...are you okay?"

She laid her head on Cooper's shoulder. "I'm fine."

Felix raised an eyebrow and looked to Cooper, then back at her. "You don't look fine."

"I think I'm just overtired," she said, her voice soft. The words were followed by a loud yawn. "Oh my word. I'm sorry."

"How much sleep have you had in the last few nights?" Cooper asked, shifting the weight of her against him and trying to keep Scottie in his other arm.

"I don't know," Genni admitted.

Her weight was growing heavier and heavier, sending Cooper's worry through the roof.

"A couple of hours, I think, in the last week."

Felix cursed. "Are you kidding me, Gen? What the heck have you been doing?" He scowled and reached out. "Here. Let me take the dog. I think you're gonna need both hands."

Cooper handed off Scottie, grateful for his new friend, and then swung Genni into his arms. He laid his cheek against her forehead. "She feels really warm," he muttered.

"It's hot today," Genni mumbled.

Cooper scoffed. "Not hot enough for this." He turned to Felix. "We walked. Do you have a vehicle here?"

"Yeah. Come on." Felix turned and led the way to his truck. "Throw her in the middle and we'll hold her up between us."

"Right." Cooper did his best to maneuver Genni where he needed her. "Come on, sweetheart. I know you're not feeling good, but let's get in the truck. We'll cool you down and get you home."

She nodded her head and helped him get her in the seat, where she scooted to the middle. Her muscles shook with the effort. "I'm sorry," she whispered.

"For what?"

"For this." A tear rolled down Genni's cheek. "I don't know what's wrong with me."

Cooper scowled. "You're sick, Gen. You've worked yourself into the ground trying to find that stupid paperwork, and now you're getting sick." He sighed as he fastened her seatbelt for her, then kissed her temple. "Between the sun and all the excitement of the festival, I think your body is just crashing." He took Scottie from Felix, so the captain could drive.

The dog curled up in his lap, whimpering slightly.

Cooper let his fingers run through the animal's fur, his other arm around Genni. It only took a few minutes to get to the house.

"Hand me Scot," Felix said, reaching across Genni. "Then we'll get Gen taken care of."

"Sounds like a boy name," Genni said with a soft smile.

"It is a boy name," Felix said with a wink. "But that's lover boy's fault, not mine. If he'd given her something feminine, the nickname would be feminine as well."

"*Scottie* is the nickname," Cooper grumbled.

Felix laughed. "Are you saying the rest of the name is more lady-like? What should I call her? But? Ter?"

"Shut up," Cooper whined as Felix got out, still laughing.

"Scottie is a cute name," Genni said. She still leaned heavily against him, but at least she seemed to be more in control of herself than before.

"You just said it was a boy name," Cooper said, more to keep her talking than anything else. He was afraid if they were quiet, she would faint again, or something worse.

"No. I said Scot is a boy name." She reached out her arms and Cooper lifted her down from the truck. "Scottie is cute and could go either way."

"Good to know," Cooper said. He held her around the waist. "Can you walk?"

She nodded and let out a shaky breath. "Yeah. I really do think I'm just overtired. But I'm really sorry to be a burden."

Cooper sighed and pressed a kiss to her forehead. "You're not a burden, sweetheart. I'm just worried about you." He walked her inside, leaving the door open for Felix when he finished with Scottie outside. "Do you want to go to your bed?"

Genni didn't answer for a minute. "Would it be horrible if I said no?"

Cooper stopped walking. "Where do you want to go?"

She glanced up from under her eyelashes. "Umm...I'm not sleeping well in my bed, and I don't really want to be in there alone. Would you mind sitting with me on the couch?"

A smirk crossed Cooper's face. "I don't mind, but you have to promise to go to sleep."

She nodded. "Sure, sure."

"Why does that sound so suspicious?" Cooper asked as he started leading her to the sitting room.

She laughed quietly and plopped onto the couch, accepting the blanket that Cooper handed her. "Thank you."

"I'm going to get you a glass of water, just a sec." He was back quickly and stood guard until she drank the whole thing.

"Here's Scot!" Felix called, putting the dog down at the door. Straightening, he waved a hand. "All under control here?"

"I got her," Cooper hollered. "Thanks for taking care of the dog."

"Anytime," Felix said with a grin. "They're much easier than humans."

Cooper chuckled and raised a hand. "See ya." The front door closed and Cooper turned back to Gen. "What do you need?"

She patted the seat beside her. "Just you."

Those words went straight through his chest, knocking every part of Cooper for a loop. He'd suspected he was falling for her, but the last nail had just been put in his coffin. Two simple words were all it took for him to know he'd found the home he'd always wanted. Who would have ever guessed it would be in Oregon?

CHAPTER 23

Genni had never felt so loved...and so exhausted. All weekend, Cooper stayed by her side, checking on her, talking to her, making sure she ate and drank what she should. Having someone take care of her was addicting and Genni was slightly worried she'd never be able to go back to taking care of herself again.

All her days of anxiety and fear had finally caught up with her, and she'd slept a lot of the weekend. But now it was Sunday night, just two days before their deadline with the tax company, and Genni was waiting to hear the results of the festival. Rose and Caro had both promised to bring by the proceeds that night.

"Doing okay?" Cooper asked quietly, gently massaging her shoulders.

"Oh my word, that feels good," Genni groaned, letting her head hang forward.

Cooper laughed quietly. "Nervous?"

Sighing, Genni forced herself to straighten. As good as the massage felt, she was too worried to enjoy it for long. "Do you think we have a chance?" she whispered.

Cooper shifted on the couch, careful not to disturb Scottie, who was lying at his feet. "If I'm being honest? No."

Genni's heart sank. She wanted to believe they could make it. So much work and effort had been put into everything and it had been a roaring success. But she had to admit that a quarter of a million dollars seemed insurmountable.

Cooper scratched his chin. "I think it will help. But I don't think one weekend will cover what we need."

"Maybe I can get a loan for the rest..." Genni trailed off, her mind running rampant. Fatigue was once again draining her. When would she ever find peace? It seemed as if her entire life had been one hit after another. *Why, Grandma? Why leave me this way?*

A warm hand on her lower back brought her out of her depressing thought. "I don't think a loan is a good option." He paused. "But with only two days to go, who knows if we can do it in time, and I'm not prepared to take out that kind of money."

"Can you think of any other way to get around this?" Genni wrung her hands. "Maybe I should go back to looking for that paperwork. I mean, it has to be somewhere." A pulse began in her forehead and she pressed clammy fingers against it. "There just has to be something we're missing. It's so hard to believe that Grandma would leave me in this position, or that no one else would have caught it before now."

"Hey..." Cooper said softly, pulling her into his chest. "It's gonna be okay."

"But how?" Genni asked. "How is it going to be okay?" She leaned back to look into his eyes. "How do I walk away from the only home I've ever known? From the dream that I've had since I was a small girl? How do I simply drop everything and give up?" Her bottom lip trembled. "I don't think I can do it."

Cooper sighed and tucked her head under his chin.

His presence was sweet, comfortable and soothing, but not quite enough. This thing they were facing was bigger than them both and Genni was terrified they would lose. They'd been kidding themselves, trying to think positive thoughts. Maybe her grandmother had been right all along...

Genni thought of the paper Cooper had discovered in the carriage house. It wasn't the full contract between Grandma Maggie and Verl James, but it was a portion of it. As luck would have it, it included a line about a buyout.

Genni had been so caught up in the festival and trying to save the house that she hadn't bothered to go back and find the rest of the document. She wasn't completely sure she wanted to. But now, with them so close to losing everything, she couldn't help but wonder if she would have been better off on her own. If Cooper wasn't here, could Genni have gotten a loan for the whole amount? She wouldn't have to have anyone else's input or worry that they would let down their end of the bargain. If she'd just taken it on herself, it would have gotten done.

The doorbell rang, forcing Genni to put aside her ugly thoughts. *Stop it,* she scolded herself as Cooper opened the door. *He's been the best thing to happen to you during this whole ordeal. Not having him around would have made it ten times worse.*

Genni stood, unable to sit still any longer. She could hear voices and walked briskly toward them.

"Hey, Gen!" Caro called out as Genni drew nearer. The petite woman held up a thick manila envelope. "Guess what we have?"

Genni's heart nearly beat through her chest. She was sure those in her foyer could hear it. "Lottery tickets?" she teased weakly.

Caro snickered. "Nope. Hopefully it's a lot more helpful than that." She handed it to Genni. "We know it's not the full amount, but we're pretty proud of what we did and hope it'll be a big help."

Genni waited, hoping not to have to ask the question, but Caro just continued to grin and bounce on her toes.

Rose tisked her tongue. "Oh, for heaven's sake, Caro. You'll give the girl a heart attack." Rose turned her kind smile on Genni. "We managed fifty-thousand dollars."

Genni gasped. "Really?"

"Wow," Cooper said with an impressed nod. "I'll admit, I didn't think it would come in that high."

Rose shrugged. "Everyone wanted to help. We even had flat-out donations." She smiled. "No one wants to see you lose the Boardwalk Manor."

"I don't know if I can accept this," Genni said, her voice shaking. The weight of that much money sat heavily in her hand. All these people were counting on her to save the house. What if she couldn't do it? What if the tax people took the money, and then took the house? Or what if they refused the money? How was she supposed to give it back to everyone?

"Of course you can," Caro urged. "This whole thing has been for you." She stepped through the middle of the group and grasped Genni's hands. "Now, you listen, and you listen good, Genevieve Winters." Caro paused and an expectant eyebrow went up.

Genni nodded.

"We love you. We love you too much to let you get kicked out of your home. The whole town came together just for you today, so you take this money, and you tell those tax people to go to—"

"I think she gets it Caro," Rose said wryly.

Genni looked over to see Cooper smiling, but it wasn't his usual genuine one. It looked polite, slightly distant...and worried. He met her gaze and immediately smiled wider, but he wasn't fooling anyone.

"We're glad to see you on your feet," Rose said, bringing the attention back to herself. "But I'm sure you're still tired, so we'll let you have your evening."

Genni stepped forward and hugged both of the women. "Thank you," she rasped. "You've done more than I could have ever asked for." She stepped back and wiped at her eyes while Caro and Rose smiled.

"Anytime." Rose turned to Cooper. "Take care of her, Coop," she said, then bustled Caro out into the cool night air.

Genni stared at the envelope, her anxiety from earlier once again coming to a boil. It wasn't enough. As amazing as the town was, they would never have enough. Genni's heart broke into tiny shards and she fell to her knees. *What am I going to do?*

COOPER KNEW EXACTLY how Genni felt. The amount from the town was insane, but would it even make a difference in the end? He walked over and held out his hand. "Come on, Gen. Let's get dinner and we can call the company in the morning."

She shook her head. "We'll never make it." She barked out a laugh through her tears. "After all these years, I finally get my chance at the house and I lose it within a couple of months." Her voice dropped. "Are you proud now, Grandma?"

A flicker of irritation stung Cooper, but he bit back the snarky response he wanted to give. These dramatics weren't helping anyone. He might not be losing his ancestral home, but it was the first place Cooper had truly wanted to call home, and that should count for something. She wasn't the only person hurting right now. Still...he knew snapping at her wasn't going to help anything. She was still fragile physically as well as mentally. He didn't need to add to her weight. "Come on, hon. Things'll look better in the morning."

"Stop saying that," she said.

"Saying what?" Cooper frowned.

Genni jumped to her feet. "Stop saying it's going to be all right." Her face crumpled. "It's not going to be all right. It's horrible. My home is about to be taken away! I'm losing the only good thing in my life!"

"Wow." Cooper put his hands on his hips. "The *only* good thing, huh?" He pointed toward the door. "So those friends who just gave their time and money, *to the tune of fifty-thousand dollars* aren't worth more to you than this house?" Before she could respond,

Cooper continued. "All your memories, the ancient furniture in this place, the knowledge of hundreds of ancestors isn't worth more to you than this house?" His chest was heaving now, though he fought to keep his voice even. "And me? After all we've been through together? The fights, the kisses, the falling in love..."

She gasped but didn't speak.

"None of it means more to you than this house?" His voice broke at the end, but Cooper didn't care. He wanted the house too, but he wasn't going to claim his life was ruined if he lost it. He'd lost it all before and he'd survived. He could survive again. Although he was hoping that this time he'd have something or at least someone to survive for. But Genni was acting as if none of that really mattered. She was saying he didn't matter, and that hurt more then he would have ever thought possible.

Her entire body was shaking, but she proudly held her chin in the air. "Without this house, I am *nothing*. I won't have a home, a business or anything to call my own." Her face was flushed and her nostrils flared. "And if you hadn't come, maybe I could have saved it."

Cooper's head snapped back as if she'd delivered a physical blow. "Are you kidding me right now?" He pointed to his chest. "You think this is all my fault? That I somehow brought the wrath of the tax gods down on you because I showed up on your doorstep?"

"I could have taken out a loan!" she shouted, her shoulders caving. "You said not to get one. You kept saying we would fix it. WELL, WE HAVEN'T FIXED IT!" she screamed, swinging her arms wildly. "And now it's too late. Now I can't do it in time and if you won't take out your own loan, then I can still only pay half of what's owed!"

Cooper shook his head and stumbled back. All this time he'd thought she was growing...changing. He thought she'd been willing to let him into her life, and now here she was, throwing him back out. It wasn't quite the same as Ciana using him as a scapegoat, but somehow, the betrayal hurt worse. He'd thought Genni was different.

"That's just fine," Cooper said through clenched teeth. "I guess I should have just listened to you in the beginning." Storming past her, he headed to the sitting room.

"Cooper?" she asked, the words trembling. "Cooper! What are you doing?"

He picked up his sleeping dog and headed to the stairs. He wouldn't stay in this house one more minute. There was nothing for him here.

"Where are you going?" she demanded as he headed up the stairs. "Cooper! Answer me!" she screeched.

He set the sleepy puppy down on the bed and stuffed a few things in his backpack. Just enough to get him by for the night. He'd come back when she went to work next week and clean out the rest.

Letting his boots slam against the hardwood, the loud noise making him feel marginally better, he stormed to the front door, little Scottie tucked into her kennel.

"Coop," Genni said as he reached for the doorknob.

The distress in her voice called to him. He paused, every instinct in his body screaming for him to go take care of her.

"Coop, don't go."

He squeezed his eyes shut, nearly strangling the doorknob with his hold.

"You just can't understand what this means to me," she continued, her voice growing stronger as she came up behind him.

Those words brought back the explosive anger. *Can't understand? She has no idea what I understand.* "I understand just fine," he snapped, not daring to look at her. Scottie whimpered and he took a breath, trying to calm the tone of his voice. "In fact, I think I understand better than before. You never wanted me here. You've made that plain. So I'm finally understanding and getting out of your hair."

"But I—"

Cooper didn't stick around to hear anything else. He threw the door open and marched down the front steps, tying everything to his bike. "I'll be back for the rest later," he hollered over his shoulder.

No noise came from the house, and after straddling the bike, he couldn't help but look up. Her silhouette in the doorway tore his heart in half. Her hands were over her face and her shoulders shook. *You're in love with her. Go to her.* Cooper shook his head. *No. She made her choice and in her anger told me how she really feels. It's better to leave now and just let the chips fall where they will.*

Gunning his engine, he hit the gas so hard, gravel pinged off a nearby tree, but Cooper paid no attention. Ignoring the speed limit and not caring if Ken found him, Cooper hit the freeway as quickly as he could. His only concern right now was to let the cold wind hit his face and to get away from the gorgeous, hard-hearted woman who held his heart. The cold air quickly began to numb his cheeks, and he could only hope that it would spread to his heart.

CHAPTER 24

G enni clenched and unclenched her fists. She couldn't decide whether she should break down in tears, or throw something after the motorcycle. Her skin was flushed and she knew her eyes must be blood-shot. *He left. Just like everyone else...he left.*

The anger won.

"FINE!" she screamed after the bike. Taking in a shuddering breath, she stormed back inside and slammed the door behind her, locking it fiercely for good measure. "I don't need you," she snapped. "I don't need anyone. I've spent most of my life on my own, and it'll just be easier that way."

Turning, she put her back against the door and faced the home. Despite its size, it felt claustrophobic, as if the walls and ceiling were caving in on her. Her breathing grew shallow and her vision spotty, letting Genni know she was on the verge of a panic attack.

"No," she ground out through clenched teeth. "No. I can do this. I don't need him or his dog. I. Can. Do. This." Pressing her fists against her temple, she stumbled through the house to the office. She needed a distraction and she still needed to save the house.

Starting in one corner, she began to work her way through the room, searching every nook and cranny, even pressing against the walls for secret compartments she might not know about. She peeled back rugs and curtains and shifted furniture, but nothing revealed the tax papers she needed.

Screaming in frustration, she moved on to the next room. And the next. And the next. The hours passed without her notice, and soon she found herself blinded by the rising sun breaking through the east-facing window in the dining room, covering everything in an orange-colored glaze.

Shaking with exhaustion and loss of adrenaline, Genni collapsed into a chair, no closer to finding the records than she had been the day before. Hopelessness began to press in on her, stealing her breath and robbing Genni of her logical thinking.

A broken sob tore out of her throat and she slapped her hands over her mouth to keep anything else from breaking loose. *No. I can't let it go like this. I can't. My whole life...wasted. NO!*

She pushed herself to her feet, then had to catch the edge of the chair when her vision went black with a head rush. Squeezing her eyes shut, she forced herself to breathe, though each breath felt like she was being stabbed with a kitchen knife. "You don't need him," she reminded herself. "You're a Winters woman. Winters women are survivors."

Though she had tried to ignore it, the pain of Cooper's departure was growing stronger each minute. All through the night it grew, like a festering boil without a cure, poisoning each part of her body until it hurt to move at all. "The house. I've got to focus on the house." She sucked in a forceful breath. "Cooper made his choice."

Yeah...because you drove him off.

Genni shook her head. She didn't have time to argue with herself right now. The fact was, Cooper was gone and the deadline for the house was here. If she couldn't find those records, she would lose everything. *And losing Cooper is enough. I won't survive losing them both.*

She took a step, her knee almost buckling. "But maybe I need to get my blood sugar up first." Holding onto the wall, she walked to the kitchen and managed to swallow a yogurt without having it come back up. She took a minute to let the sugar hit her system, then went right back to her search.

By the time the grandfather clock struck eight, Genni was losing her focus. She was exhausted mentally and physically. The destruction of her heart on top of everything else seemed to add an extensive amount of weight to the pressure already riding her shoulders.

She plopped into a seat, fighting back tears. "This is impossible." Her head fell forward and a tear slipped down her cheek just as she remembered the envelope of money sitting in the front entry. She'd dropped it when she'd chased after Cooper the night before.

Grasping the tiny lifeline, Genni bolted to her feet and ran to grab the money, then found the envelope with the tax papers in it.

Praying harder then she ever had before, she found the office number and punched it into her phone.

"Tax Mediation Incorporated," a familiar voice said.

Genni frowned and pulled back to look at the phone.

"Hello?"

"Hudson?"

There was a thump on the other side of the line and a bunch of shuffling before Hudson came back on the line. "Genni? Is that you?"

"Yes," she said warily. "I thought I was calling the tax company."

"Y-you did." He cleared his throat. "I'm in the office today."

"But why would this go to your phone? I thought you were just their legal help."

"I am," he snapped. "What did you need?" The sneer was audible in his voice. "You do remember that your deadline is midnight tonight?" He chuckled darkly. "Did your little party manage to pull in enough to clear your title? Or will you be sleeping in a new bed tonight?"

Genni felt the depression trying to take back over, but she forced it down. It was difficult, but she kept a picture of her grandmother in her mind's eye. Grandma wouldn't have backed down. Genni wouldn't either. "I've called to make an offer," she said, proud of her strong voice.

"An offer?" he scoffed. "What did you have in mind?"

"We have fifty-thousand that we can give you now," Genni stated. "I'm willing to work on a payment plan for the rest."

"Genni, Genni, Genni," he crooned in a voice that gave her shivers. "It doesn't work that way."

"That's not true," Genni insisted. "People do payment plans all the time."

"Well, we don't," he sneered. "I'll be there at eight a.m. sharp tomorrow. Have the money in hand or the deed to the house. Your choice."

Genni opened her mouth to beg, but the line went silent. "Hello? Hudson?" The cell clattered onto the desk and Genni's forehead followed. The last twelve hours of emotions broke loose and Genni's entire body began to shiver. Great wracking sobs from her core filled the room with the sounds of anguish and she did nothing to stop it. Tears flooded the wooden desktop and her cries echoed off the walls.

It was gone. Everything of value in her life was gone. The house, her dreams of a bed and breakfast, her plans for the future...stolen from her with the snap of a finger. She felt hopeless and useless, not worthy of the name her grandmother had left her.

Because despite how much she was losing, it was the company of a certain pair of hazel eyes that made her feel, for the first time, as if she didn't want to survive at all.

COOPER PULLED HIS HELMET from his head and took a deep breath. He'd come to his senses enough last night to drop Scottie off at Frank's before getting out of town. But now he was stopped for gas somewhere in south Oregon and Cooper wasn't even sure where he was.

He got off the seat and pulled out his wallet, pushing the card into the gas dispenser. While he filled the tank, his mind wandered back to Genni and how she'd looked when he left.

Broken.

He scowled. *She's the one who started all this. She's the one who said it would have been better if I hadn't come.* "Like any of this was my fault. It was *her* grandmother who didn't pay the taxes."

He paused. The taxes still didn't sit right with him. Suspicion still niggled in the back of his mind that it was all a scam, but he just couldn't prove it.

Sighing, Cooper tapped the gas hose against the side of the tank and put it back. After getting everything put back together, he slung his leg over the seat and began to pull out. Instead of gunning it for the highway, he slowly drove through the town, admiring the old nautical feel of the area. When he reached a sign for the marina, he let curiosity win out and followed the signs.

"Geez," he murmured as he came up to the docks. Large wooden boats were lined up in their slips, tipping slowly back and forth with the light waves of the ocean. The size of the boats made Cooper feel small, and for a moment...his anger slipped away.

Without the red haze clouding his thoughts, the pain of losing Genni began to creep back in and a stabbing sensation beat against his sternum. He hunched in on himself, pressing his palm against the spot. *It didn't hurt like this with Ciana.*

Back East, Cooper had thought he'd had it all. Having grown up with little to no supervision and unlimited funds, he had become an arrogant playboy who thought he owned the world. College was nothing but a party and he barely graduated with his degree in architecture.

Although his parents didn't offer much in the way of love and attention, they were more than happy to share their connections and soon Cooper was working for the biggest architect company in the state.

When Ciana Fowers had entered his office one day with a proposition, life had only gotten better.

Cooper snorted and shook his head as he thought of his ignorance. All it had taken was a beautiful woman with mile-long legs and a perfect smile to bring about his fall. And fall he did. Hook, line and sinker.

Ciana had lured Cooper in with her attention and whispers of getting him all the best jobs from the city offices, where she worked, if he would just be willing to let her have access to his email accounts.

"I know exactly what they're looking for," Ciana had assured him. "Rather than us playing telephone with each other, just let me write all the emails from your account and I'll be able to win you every job you could ever dream of."

Young, stupid and thinking he couldn't fail, Cooper had agreed and given her every password she asked for. He hadn't even known anything was wrong until the police had shown up to arrest him for embezzling from the city.

Cooper had spent four days in jail before his lawyer had managed to prove that Ciana and her mayoral boyfriend were behind the whole thing. Four days with nothing to do but think about how stupid he'd been. All the signs had been there. Every red flag was shining brighter than Rudolph's nose now that he was looking backward.

Once he'd been sprung, Cooper had sold his house, all of his possessions, given most of the money to charity and begun again. The only things he'd kept were a few clothes and his motorcycle. His hobby of working on his bike had led to his new job as a mechanic and that had been all he'd needed...until the call that had brought him to Oregon.

Coming to the coast had been both the best and worst decision he'd ever made. It had been well worth wiping his slate clean and meeting people who didn't know about his rotten past. What he wasn't sure about was whether it had been worth meeting Genni.

Cooper sighed and pushed a hand through his hair. It teased his ears in the breeze and he wished he had a rubber band.

Genni...

That pang in his chest pulsed again. He'd tried to stay strong. He'd told himself over and over again that he shouldn't mix business with pleasure, but he'd fallen anyway. He'd fallen for her sassy comebacks, and her sweet center. He'd fallen for her independence and her need for companionship. He'd fallen for the way she'd softened and begun to not just want him, but need him.

Her luxurious hair and addicting kisses had been icing on the cake.

Yep. His heart was well and truly gone and Cooper found that he wasn't quite ready to walk away. Not now that his mind was clearing from the anger of last night. "I can't just leave her like that, letting her take the fall for the house." He huffed. "What kind of man would that make me? No matter what she thinks of me, she shouldn't have to face Hudson alone."

Cooper blinked a few times and scratched his chin. Something was sitting just on the edge of his mind as important. He was exhausted from driving all night and his brain wasn't quite grasping whatever it was that he'd overlooked—

"JAIL!" he shouted as it came flooding back to him. Cooper turned at a squeak of distress and gave an awkward smile and wave to an older couple who were walking by. "Sorry. Talking to myself," he explained lamely.

The woman looked affronted, but the man chuckled. "Not a place I'd recommend," he quipped.

Cooper snorted. "Me either."

Still laughing, the man pulled his wife along and Cooper was back to himself and the gulls. He scrambled for his phone, remembering what was important about his trip down memory lane. In all the excitement about searching for records and the town fundraiser, Cooper had forgotten he'd sent the papers to his lawyer.

The phone rang several times before a professional-sounding woman answered.

"Binger, Binger and Stern. How may I direct your call?"

"Hey, Gloria, it's Cooper James."

"Cooper!" the secretary gushed. "How are ya, honey?"

Cooper couldn't help but smile. Gloria was a sharp, older woman who watched those around her like a mother bear. If Cooper could have chosen his mother, he would have picked someone just like her. "I'm doing all right, thanks." He cleared his throat, hoping she didn't hear the lie in his tone. "But I have a question for Gene."

The secretary clucked her tongue. "I told that old coot he needed to call you back. Kept saying something about some papers, but I doubt he got around to sending the email."

Cooper heard some shuffling.

"Hold on, hon. I'll get him on the line."

"Thanks, Gloria. I owe you one."

"You just come back and visit me sometime and we'll call it even."

"Deal." Cooper waited while elevator music played in the background for a few seconds, only to be interrupted by a gruff voice.

"Gene Stern, how can I help you?"

"Gene? It's Cooper James."

"It's about time you called," Gene grumbled. "I've got news for you."

"Oh?" Cooper's heart began to race. "What did you find?"

"Make sure you're sitting down, Cooper. This is worse than we thought."

CHAPTER 25

N umb.

Genni felt completely numb, right down to her backside that was sitting on the top step of her front porch. Part of her recognized that it was better than the pain she'd experienced all through the previous day and night at the loss of Cooper and the imminent loss of the house, but the more rational part of her knew this was not in her best interest. It was just another step in the grieving process, which meant Genni had given up. For the first time in her life, she'd lost her determination and grit. Her well was as empty as her tear supply. Every ounce of it had been used and Genni had nothing left.

She'd spent most of the day yesterday searching every place she could think of for those records and hadn't found anything. Finally, around dinnertime, she'd crashed on the couch for a few hours of sleep. But her rest hadn't lasted. Waking up from a nightmare, Genni had gotten herself a mug of hot herbal tea and came outside to wait out the sunrise.

She squinted as light began to flood her porch. Everything was covered in a reddish orange haze that seemed oddly macabre, fitting Genni's mood perfectly. Another shiver wracked her body, shaking her so hard that the board underneath her squeaked. With a sigh, Genni forced herself to her feet, grasping the rail when her knees shook and pins began to prick her thighs in earnest.

She gritted her teeth as her legs came back to life and shook them a little until she felt strong enough to walk toward the house. Nothing had changed. She didn't have a way to hold off the repossession of the house, and she was feeling more alone than she'd ever been. But she'd be hanged if she was going to present herself as a greasy, grungy mess when Hudson came knocking on her door.

After her shower, Genni almost felt human again. At least as much as she could with her heart no longer beating in her chest. She ran on auto pilot, fixing her hair and makeup, then heading downstairs for a breakfast her stomach threatened to get rid of.

She was just pouring her oatmeal into the garbage when a car door sounded outside. Genni's stomach lurched and she dropped her bowl into the trash can. Not bothering to retrieve it, she stumbled to the entrance of the kitchen, then stopped and held onto the wall, waiting.

Loud pounding came only moments later and she had to fight down a sob. Forcing her lungs to accept more air than they wanted, Genni fluffed her hair, straightened her shoulders and used every ounce of energy she possessed to walk to the door.

This was it. This was the moment of truth where she had to face the consequences of her family's actions. And because of her own actions, she would be doing it alone.

Just as she reached for the doorknob, her phone buzzed in her back pocket. Genni paused, then jumped when the pounding started up again.

"I know you're in there, Genni. Let's not make this any more difficult than it has to be, huh?" Hudson's voice wheedled.

How in the world did I ever find him attractive? she thought, shaking her head.

"Just sign the paperwork and we can both go about our own business. Don't make me get the authorities involved. It won't go well."

Genni backed up, a shaking hand going to her throat. Losing the house was going to be horrible enough, but having Ken do the eviction would be ten times worse. She started forward again when her phone buzzed a second time. Sighing, Genni took it out of her pocket to turn it to silent, but froze instead.

There on the screen were two texts...from Cooper.

Hold him off.

I'm coming.

Five words. Five simple words from the right person was all it took for Genni to feel a spark come to life inside of her. Her grip on the device tightened until her knuckles were white. "Hold him off," she whispered.

The pounding started up again. "Genni! Open the door! I know you're there!" Hudon's voice was growing in pitch and volume, making his frustration clear.

Genni looked up from her phone and made a decision. She didn't know what Cooper was planning, but she trusted him. In her hurt the other night, she'd driven him off, said things she didn't mean, but none of it was true. She loved him with everything in her being, and knowing he was coming back despite their fight was all she needed to fight for herself as well.

Walking forward, she grabbed the knob and wrenched the door open.

Hudson jumped back, his hand in the air, shock clear on his face.

"Good morning, Hudson," Genni said coldly. "What brings you by this morning?"

Hudson's shock turned to disdain. "Come on, Genni—"

"It's Ms. Winters," she interjected.

Hudson rolled his eyes. "Fine, if that's how you want to play it. *Ms. Winters...* Don't play dumb. Your time is up." He grinned. "I'm assuming you don't have the money? I can't imagine how you would have gotten it between our little chat yesterday and this morning."

Genni folded her arms over her chest and cocked a hip. "Whether or not I have the money doesn't matter. You can't have the house."

His eyebrows rose high on his forehead. "I beg your pardon Ge—Ms. Winters, but the government says otherwise."

She tapped her bottom lip thoughtfully. "Yeah...see, I don't really understand all that legal jargon. All I know is that you showed up and my life immediately turned to crap. I think you're cursed or something." She waved a hand in the air. "So I refuse to deal with you. If your company is so set on taking my house, they'll have to bring in someone else."

Hudson's face began to turn bright red underneath his carefully trimmed three-days' growth. "It doesn't work like that, *Genevieve.*" His voice had darkened and Genni felt her first pulse of fear. "My employers don't bother with little details like this. That's why they hire me." He began to walk, crowding her back into the house. "Shall we do this in the dining room?"

Genni stumbled back. "You can't come in here."

"I can. I represent the people who now own this house." Hudson's lip curled on one side.

"Not until I sign over the deed and I haven't done that," Genni shouted back. *Please hurry, Cooper. I don't know how much longer I can do this.*

"Which is exactly why I'm here," Hudson said, straightening his tie and sleeves as if calming himself down. "Let's get this done and you can begin to move out." He gave her a sardonic grin. "I believe my employers left you a week in order to vacate the premises, which is more than generous."

"You think I can move a lifetime of memories and history in seven days!" Genni screeched.

"I don't really care," Hudson said over his shoulder as he walked to the dining room entrance. "All I care about is doing my job." He pushed open the swinging door and paused. "Ugh. What threw up in here?"

It was Genni's turn to smirk, although in the back of her mind she grudgingly gave the point to Cooper. Waltzing past Hudson, she walked around the room. "What's the matter? Losing your nerve?"

His eyes hardened and Hudson came in, slapping the leather briefcase on the table. "Let's get this over with."

"COME ON, COME ON," Cooper grumbled as he passed yet another sightseeing car. "You'd think people have never seen the ocean before." The city boundaries for Seaside Bay were only a few minutes ahead and Cooper prayed that Gen had not only gotten his message but had been able to keep Hudson busy.

It was possible that Hudson hadn't arrived yet that morning, but Cooper doubted it. The shark was chomping at the bit to sing his teeth into Boardwalk Manor and Cooper figured that meant Hudson would be there first thing now that the deadline was past. *Hopefully he didn't show up at midnight last night.* He cursed at the thought, again regretting his decision to leave.

"Finally." He sped across the town line and began to watch for the old road that led to the house. Another curse slipped Cooper's mouth when lights and a siren went off. Looking in his mirror, Cooper saw the car behind him and automatically began to slow down. *Wait...* Grinning, he waved his arm at the police officer and picked up speed. Being caught speeding just might be the best thing that could have happened right now.

The siren let out a loud welp, followed by a familiar voice. "Pull over, Coop."

Cooper sighed in relief that it was Ken. He'd have a much easier time talking his way out of the situation with a friend than a stranger. He waved his arm again, pointed forcefully toward the house and kept going.

"This better be good," Ken called over the loudspeaker.

Cooper grinned, doubling down on the bike and whizzing to this destination. He forced himself to slow down as he approached the house. No need to spray gravel everywhere, especially on the already angry cop car behind him.

He gritted his teeth when a black BMW came into view. His instincts had been correct. Hudson was already here. *And Genni's all alone with him.* His anger surged and he almost leapt off the bike before it was at a complete standstill.

Jumping up the front steps, Cooper tore his helmet from his head and burst through the front door. "GENNI!"

"Cooper?"

"Mind telling me what's going on?" Ken asked, coming up behind Cooper.

Cooper ignored the police captain and raced for the dining room. The relief in Genni's voice was enough to drive everything else from his mind. "Genni," he breathed as the dining room door swung open under his touch. He rushed forward and swept her into his arms, beyond grateful that she went willingly.

"You came back," she cried, hugging him tightly around his neck.

Cooper could feel her tears on his skin and it made him tighten his hold. "I shouldn't have ever left," he murmured in her ear. Her hair smelled so good and her frame against his was like water for a dying man. He'd been trying to keep from getting too personal, knowing they had an audience, but when a soft sob came against his shoulder, Cooper broke. *Hang this.* He cupped her face with his hands and brought their mouths together.

The world faded away. Somewhere, shouting and other noise existed, but not right here. Cooper hadn't realized how hungry he was for Genni, and he knew he was probably being a little more aggressive than he should have been, but there was no stopping him now.

By her reaction, Genni didn't mind. Her hands tightened around his neck and he felt her go up on tiptoe in order to get closer. He wasn't sure how long he enjoyed her, but far too soon, a strong hand landed on his shoulder.

"I hate to break this up," Ken said, laughter in his tone, "but I need to know why I'm here."

Cooper pulled back, his chest heaving and his heart soaring as he looked down into Genni's warm, chocolatey gaze. "Sorry," he rasped, then cleared his throat. He looked over his shoulder with a sheepish grin. "I got carried away."

"I can tell," Ken said wryly.

"As touching as this little reunion is," Hudson said sarcastically, "I really do need to get going." He pushed a paper across the table. "If the two of you will just sign here, I'll get out of your hair."

Ken tilted his head. "What's all this about?"

"He's trying to get me to sign the house away," Genni answered, her arms wrapped around Cooper's chest. He held her in place, not willing to let her go just yet.

Ken raised an eyebrow. "Are you telling me that the amount we raised this last weekend wasn't enough for a down payment? Or at least an extension?"

Cooper watched closely as Hudson swallowed, then straightened his shoulders. "No, it's not. My employers don't deal with payment plans."

"You're telling me they simply expected this nice young woman to come up with a quarter of a million dollars at the drop of a hat?" Ken pursed his lips and pushed back his hat from his forehead. "I've never heard of it working that way. Mediation companies are meant to help solve the problem, not create a bigger one."

Cooper glanced at his watch. As much as he was ready to be done with this slimeball, they had to wait just a little bit longer.

"Every company runs themselves a little differently," Hudson defended, shifting his weight from side to side. "Mine takes on the impossible cases and isn't afraid to put their foot down." He turned to look at Genni. "Most of the time, delinquent accounts are simply because people don't want to pony up. They're too lazy to follow the law." He straightened his tie. "My company isn't afraid to fight for what's right."

Cooper growled low in his throat and started to move. Hudson was a jerk, but Cooper wasn't going to stand around and let the man speak that way about Genni, or her grandmother.

"Don't," Genni whispered, her eyes watery. "He's not worth it."

"I don't know," Ken drawled, studying his fingernails. "I'm finding myself mighty thirsty." He jabbed a thumb over his shoulder. "If I go get a drink for a minute, who knows what might happen in here."

"Are you kidding me, Sheriff?" Hudson screeched, finally losing his composure. He pointed to Cooper and Genni. "These two owe the government a lot of money, and you're just willing to overlook that?"

Ken shrugged and folded his bulky arms over his equally bulky chest. Even Cooper had to admit the guy was ripped, and it made him grateful they were on the same side.

Hudson's nostrils flared and his face reddened. "Well, I'm not. And I'm authorized to handle this however I need to." He turned back to the couple and shoved the papers even further. "Sign this or I have the paperwork in my briefcase to have you arrested."

Genni gasped, but Cooper chuckled. "Prove it."

"W-what?" Hudson asked, his sneer falling from his face.

Cooper shifted his body to look more directly at the lawyer. "I said...prove it. Show us the paperwork."

"Cooper, what are you doing?" Genni asked.

Cooper looked at her and winked. He had this under control and help would be here very soon.

CHAPTER 26

C ooper was up to something and Genni wished she knew what it was. *And why is Ken here? In his uniform, no less.*

"I don't have to show you anything," Hudson said, straightening his suit coat. "I'm here to collect your signatures. Nothing else." His expression softened. "I feel like we all got off on the wrong foot here." His smile was sheepish. "I suppose I should never have taken you out on those dates, Genni. I'm sorry. It muddied the waters for both of us."

Anger, hot and fierce, exploded in Genni. "Considering I was never attracted to you, I don't think the waters were muddied at all." She held a straight face as the other two men bit back laughter. That statement wasn't completely true, but she'd never felt more than a normal, shallow attraction, and for now, that was enough.

Hudson shook off her insult and kept going. "It doesn't matter now. I've learned my lesson and will make sure I know better for next time." He folded his hands in front of him in a penitent stance. "Since all of that is water under the bridge, we don't need to fight now. Just sign the papers and everything will go smoothly. Getting the authorities involved only creates an ugly mess, and since you've lived here your whole life, I'm sure you wouldn't want to ruin your reputation."

Her anger died down a little and she had to admit he was right. An arrest would be devastating, but Genni just couldn't bring herself to do it. "I'm with Cooper on this one. Prove you can arrest me."

By the flash of fire in his eyes, Hudson wasn't happy with her response. "Officer, am I to assume you aren't willing to listen to my authority on this matter?"

Ken widened his stance and looked at ease, other than the bulging muscles in his arms. "I have yet to see any sign of authority, Mr..."

"Baumgartner," Hudson responded. "Hudson Baumgartner."

"When you can show me your papers, I'll be happy to help you then, Mr. Baumgartner," Ken responded agreeably.

Genni held her breath, waiting for the other shoe to drop, but Hudson only sighed and put the contract back in the briefcase. "I can see this is a biased situation. You've given me no sign that you'll follow through with my company's authority, so I'll be taking my orders elsewhere." He snapped the locks closed and looked up at Genni. "This isn't over." Straightening, he moved to leave, but Cooper left Genni's side and meandered to the doorway, blocking the exit.

"Just wait a second," he said, holding up his hands. "I don't think we're done just yet."

"Are you willing to sign, then?" Hudson asked. "Not quite ready to have this spot on your clean..." A smile tugged on Hudson's lips. "Oh wait, you don't have a clean record, do you, Mr. James?"

Genni frowned. *What?*

Cooper's eyes darted to hers, then back to Hudson. "Don't try to turn this on me, you skunk. Right now we're talking about you and your audacity to come here and try to fleece Ms. Winters out of her home or her life savings."

Genni gasped. "Fleece? Are you saying this is all a scam?" She turned wide eyes to Ken, who straightened.

"What proof do you have, Coop?" he asked, his hand resting on his gun.

Cooper grinned, looking slightly blood-thirsty. "It's on its way."

Hudson scoffed. "On its way? Really? That's all you've got?" He shook his head and turned back to the table, setting the briefcase down again. "I don't have all day, Mr. James." He folded his arms over his chest and leaned his hip against the table. "Why don't you just tell us what you think it is I'm scamming?" A fine line of sweat began to bead on his brow, catching Genni's attention.

"Fine," Cooper spat. "We'll start with Tax Mediation Incorporated." He cocked his head. "The company doesn't exist."

"Au contraire," Hudson responded. "It does. You can look it up online." His words were amicable, but the tightness of his jaw was in direct contrast to his actions.

"Yeah, you put together a pretty good website," Cooper admitted. "But you know where you can't be found?"

Genni watched with rapt attention. They had wondered if this was a scam from the beginning, but had found no evidence. Just what had Cooper discovered to tip him off?

"You can't be found in the business database," Cooper finished.

"We're not stationed in Oregon," Hudson said easily. "We're a national company, making contracts directly with the government. Your reach wouldn't let you look someone like us up."

Cooper shook his head. "Any company can be found under the Better Business Bureau. Except you."

Hudson's jaw clenched. "Apparently you just need better searching skills. Or maybe there was a glitch in the system when you were looking."

Cooper snorted. "Except I wasn't the one looking."

"Oh?" Hudson raised his eyebrows. "Pray tell who this internet professional was who somehow missed my employer?"

"You wouldn't know him," Cooper explained. "He's a lawyer back East."

The look of immediate glee in Hudson's eyes startled Genni and she took a step back.

"Lawyer back East?" Hudson's lip curled. "That wouldn't be Gene Stern, would it?"

Cooper stiffened. "How do you know that name?"

Hudson chuckled darkly. "Unlike your Mr. Stern, I do my research well, Mr. James. Gene Stern is the man who helped get you out of prison."

Black spots burst through Genni's vision. "What?" she gasped, grabbing for the back of the dining chair to her right. "Prison?"

"Gen..." Cooper started, holding out a hand and walking her way. "Give me a minute and I'll explain everything."

"Somebody better," Ken bellowed.

"Tsk, tsk, Ms. Winters," Hudson said smoothly. "You didn't think you actually knew this man, did you?" He shook his head. "Your little boy toy here spent time in prison...for embezzlement."

"I was released!" Cooper shouted.

"On a technicality," Hudson said, splaying his hands.

"On account of the fact that I was innocent," Cooper retorted. "The technicality was the proof they needed to catch the real criminal."

Hudson continued to shake his head, while Genni felt her world once again falling apart. She hadn't known him at all, not really. After all they'd shared, after all she'd told him about her own life, Cooper had still kept this a secret.

"And before you think you're the only one with secrets, Mr. James," Hudson crooned. "You might want to know that little Miss Innocent over here has paperwork that gives her the right to buy you out of the house."

Cooper's jaw dropped and Genni thought she might throw up. "Is that true?" he asked her.

Genni shook her head. "No...I mean, yes, but no...not really...I—"

"Let me explain," Hudson inserted. "Since Ms. Winters seems to have lost her tongue, I'll give it to you straight."

Genni's knees shook as hard as her head. "Don't—"

"All that time you've spent looking through the house?" Hudson plowed on. "She used it to find the contract between your grandparents, all with the intent of using a loophole to get you gone."

The hurt on Cooper's face was the last thing Genni saw before she collapsed just as she had the first time he arrived.

COOPER LUNGED FOR GENNI as soon as her eyes rolled back in her head, but Ken was closer.

"Easy, Gen, I've got ya," he said softly, helping her down to the floor.

"Genni?" Cooper asked, stepping to her side. He let out a long breath when he realized she hadn't truly fainted. Her eyes were open, though slightly glazed over, and she looked confused rather than hurt.

Ken looked up and nodded to Cooper before rising and stepping back, leaving room for Cooper to help.

He got down on his knees. "Hey. You can't make such a habit of this."

She gave a watery smile. "Sorry. I didn't realize I was a fainter until you showed up."

He forced a chuckle. "Yeah, well, that's not really a recommendation."

Her smile fell and her bottom lip began to tremble. "It's not how it sounds," she tried to explain. Shakily, she rose from the floor, taking Cooper with her. "It was when we were fighting, before I got to know you. I—"

Cooper put up his hand to stop her rapid explanation. "You and I will have plenty to talk about when this is over." He turned his head to glare at Hudson's smug face. "But right now we have a rat to deal with."

Ken scratched his head. "I'm still lost as to how Hudson plays into all this."

"He's the one who sought Genni out in the first place," Cooper said, walking slowly toward the con artist.

"If you call asking out a pretty woman as seeking her out, then yeah, I suppose I did." Hudson shrugged. "But it's not like I knew who she was when I did. We were in a home improvement store, for heaven's sake."

The radio on Ken's shoulder crackled. "Sir?"

Ken leaned into the mic. "Go ahead, Officer Windsor." He looked around the room. "Excuse me." Ken walked out as the voice on the speaker began to talk.

When the chatter died down, Cooper smiled. Behind Hudson, he could see several black SUV's slowly coming up the driveway. The end was near.

"You didn't just ask out a pretty woman," Cooper continued, hoping to keep Hudson's attention on him and not the arriving help outside. "You followed her and approached her when her guard was down."

Hudson rolled his eyes. "And why would I do that?"

"So you could get information out of her." Cooper leaned forward. "You wanted the house, but you needed to find the right angle to take it."

"That's an awful lot of work," Hudson said. "It doesn't sound like something I'd be interested in." He grabbed his briefcase. "It's clear we're not going to see eye to eye today. If you'll excuse me, I'll have my employer contact you himself. Maybe when the big guns come in, you'll be willing to listen to reason."

Genni grabbed the back of Cooper's shirt as Hudson stormed out. "You can't let him leave!" she hissed. "If he's a scam artist, we have to stop him!"

Cooper nodded toward the window. "Come on."

"Cooper!" Genni argued.

He held out a hand. "Come on. I think you'll want to see this."

Sighing, Genni took his support and they went to the window. She gasped as the scene in front of them unfolded. "What in the world?"

"He really is a scam artist," Cooper said, pulling her in front of him and bringing her back to his chest so he could wrap his arms all the way around her. After the bombs that Hudson threw at them, Cooper knew a long talk was ahead, but it didn't matter. He had faith they'd be able to work it out. *Hopefully she feels the same way.*

"Tony Wesel, you're under arrest," one of the officers was saying outside. Hudson was screaming his head off as men dressed all in black, plus a couple of high-powered suits, surrounded the home. His hands were cuffed and soon the noise died down as Hudson was shoved into the back of one of the SUV's.

"Tony?" Genni asked. "Hudson wasn't his real name?"

"Nothing about him was real," Cooper grumbled. He reluctantly let go of her. "Come on. There's some people we need to meet." He took her hand and led her outside where all the action was.

"Cooper James?" one of the suited men asked, walking up to the porch.

Cooper nodded. "That's me." He reached out and shook the man's hand.

"Nice to finally meet you," the man said with a wide smile. "Gene nearly chewed my ear off telling me about you."

Cooper groaned.

The man laughed. "Don't worry. He's on your side."

"I didn't catch your name," Genni said, stepping into the conversation.

"Agent Starling, ma'am," the man said. "FBI."

Genni's eyes widened and Cooper prepared himself for her to collapse again, but she managed to keep standing. "FBI?" she breathed.

Agent Starling nodded. He looked over to the SUV. "I'm sorry you all got caught up in this, but I'm not unhappy that piece of crap has finally been caught."

"Who was he?" Cooper asked. "I mean, Gene told me some of it, but mostly we were trying to get things rolling before Genni lost the house."

Agent Starling nodded. "Understandable. His name is Tony Wesel. He's a known con artist and has a few stings he likes to pull. Back taxes being one of them. He was stupid enough to pull one over on one of my agent's grandmothers a couple years back, and we've been chasing him down ever since." The agent scratched his cheek. "He's good at changing his name and his story. Which has made it hard to stay ahead of him. Usually by the time we arrive, the goods have been handed over and subsequently sold." He blew out a breath. "We've been unable to follow his trail." He grinned. "Until now. You're lucky Gene had worked on a case like this before and recognized the signs."

Cooper nodded. "Yeah. We almost didn't make it in time. He was in the middle of a big case when I sent him the paperwork, so he only looked over it a couple of days ago."

Agent Starling nodded. "That's what he said." He stuffed his hands in his pockets. "Well, I think that about wraps things up around here. Someone will be in touch to take your statements, and there'll be way more paperwork than any of us want, but soon it'll be over and you two can get back to your normal lives." With a nod, the man turned, called out to the rest of the agents and soon the driveway was cleared of all the large black vehicles.

Genni stepped over and took Cooper's hand as Ken walked up from where he'd been chatting with some of the other officers.

Her initiating the contact gave Cooper hope that she would be willing to hear him out from hiding his past from her.

"I guess that's my cue to go as well," Ken said. He shook his head. "That was the craziest thing I've ever seen." Pushing back his hat, Ken scratched his head. "Nothing like that ever happens in our small town."

"It'll make a good story for the precinct, huh?" Cooper teased. "You can tell everyone about how you took down one of America's Most Wanted."

Ken laughed, then squinted at Cooper. "You know what else I get to tell them?" He pulled a notepad out of his pocket. "How I won the bet about you speeding again within a month."

Cooper's face fell, but Genni snickered at his side. "Just you wait," he whispered to her.

"I am," she whispered back, looking up from under her eyelashes.

Cooper relaxed and accepted the ticket with a grumbled complaint. He winced when he saw the amount, fighting the urge to call Ken every name in the book. Looking down at Genni, however, his frustration melted away. "Oh well," he said softly, tugging Genni close enough to kiss the top of her head. "At least you're worth it."

CHAPTER 27

"So..." Genni began. She held a warm cup of tea between her hands, still fighting off residual tremors from the earlier rush of adrenaline.

"So," Cooper echoed, lounging back in his seat on the couch.

She pinched her lips together, not quite sure where to start. "I suppose we should discuss things..."

"I suppose we should."

Genni huffed and met his amused gaze. "This isn't getting us anywhere."

Cooper's right eyebrow slowly rose up his forehead. "Nope." When she made another face, he laughed and leaned forward. "Would you like me to go first?"

Genni started to say yes, but then she paused. While she was immensely interested in Cooper's past and why he'd been in jail, she knew in her heart it wouldn't make a difference. The man he'd shown her since coming to Boardwalk Manor told her everything she needed to know. No...the most important thing to be cleared up at the moment was the ownership of the home, and she wanted it taken care of right now.

She shook her head, then tucked a free strand of her hair behind her ear. "Let me go first, please."

Cooper leaned back again and waved a hand at her in invitation.

Genni's gaze went to the dark liquid inside her mug, as if it held the answers she sought, but nothing came to her. "I'm not quite sure what all to say."

"Why don't you tell me about the papers?" Cooper pushed softly.

She nodded, taking a fortifying sip of the hot drink. "When you showed up on my doorstep, I panicked. I was terrified of losing my dream of opening the bed and breakfast." She shook her head. "It just seemed like everything was against me. I never had a father, my mother died when I was little, my grandmother never even told me she loved me. I'd always been on the outside. Unwanted, unloved, but now...now I was going to have something better. Something that was mine. Something I could be proud of." She forced herself to look up.

"I was going to turn this dark, dank house into a place filled with light and laughter. Couples and families would come from all over to bring a little joy to Boardwalk Manor." Her eyes dropped again, unable to be brave in more than one way at the same time. "So when you got here, and refused to be bought out, I figured the best thing I could do is find a legal way to get you booted." She glanced up quickly. "You were the only thing standing between me and my dream, and I had worked and sacrificed for too many years to let you ruin it now."

Cooper's mouth drooped in the corners and he started to speak, but Genni put up her hand.

"Let me finish, please."

He paused, then closed his mouth and nodded.

She sighed. "We both know what happened during your first month here. I mean, we fought like cats and dogs." She paused, straightening with a sudden panic. "Speaking of which, where's Scottie?"

"I left her with Frank yesterday. I'll go grab her in a bit."

"Oh, okay. Whew." Genni relaxed. "I was worried something had happened." She waved a hand in the air. "I mean it did, but not..." She shook her head. "Whatever. Back to the story. While we were still fighting, I began searching the house, looking for the contract between our grandparents." She took a drink. "I was hoping it would give me some insight into how I could buy you out."

There was silence for a bit until Cooper asked, "And did you find it?"

Genni shrugged. "Part of it. First, I found part of Grandma's diary. It alluded to the fact that there was a buy-out clause."

He sucked in a quick breath. "What?"

Genni looked up just in time to see his eyes widen.

"That's why you took that paper from the carriage house," he said hoarsely. "You knew it would have the information on it. Your way to get rid of me." He jumped to his feet. "I've been such an idiot!"

Genni's heart began to race as he spoke. This wasn't what she wanted to convey to him at all.

"All this time I was falling for you and you were looking for the key to eviction." He barked out a sarcastic laugh. "How could I fall for it again?"

Slamming her mug on the coffee table, she stood quickly. "I LOVE YOU!" she shouted.

Cooper stopped his pacing and slowly turned to see her. "What?" The question was barely audible.

Her knees were shaking harder than they'd been with Hudson, and Genni realized with a start it was because more was riding on this conversation. Losing the house would have been catastrophic, but losing Cooper for good...would have been the end.

"I love you," she said, her voice just as shaky as her body. "I was already falling for you by the time you found that page of the contract and I was confused, unsure what to do with it." She swallowed audibly. "That's why I took it from you and tried to hide it. I was afraid if it mentioned the clause, you would feel obligated to leave or something." She dropped her voice. "And I couldn't stand the thought of that."

He took a step in her direction. "You want me to stay?"

Genni nodded jerkily. "Yes. I do."

"Because you love me?" He took another step.

"Yes."

They stared at each other for an infinite moment. "But will you still feel the same when you find out what I've done?" he asked. This time, it was his voice trembling.

Genni had to use every bit of the little strength left in her body to keep from leaping at him. "I will," she said firmly.

He huffed a laugh and gave her a crooked grin. "Let's hope so." His fists clenched and unclenched and he began to pace once more.

His agitation was so tangible that Genni began to question her answer. *Maybe it's worse than I thought? Did he...did he kill someone?* She shook her head. *No. There's no way that's what happened. Hudson...Tony said it was embezzlement.*

She slowly dropped back down to her seat and folded her hands in her lap. She loved him. She'd never been more certain of anything in her life, and that meant that she also trusted him. So, she would be patient. When he was ready to speak, he would...and Genni would be willing to listen.

COOPER'S HEART WAS going to break through his ribcage at any moment. Genni had just admitted in no uncertain terms that she loved him, giving him everything he wanted, and he couldn't even celebrate with her because he had to spill his guts about a sordid past he'd rather keep hidden.

"You have to understand," he began, his voice slightly gravelly. "I was a different man then."

Genni nodded calmly. "Just tell me, Cooper. It's all right."

He pushed a hand through his hair. "It doesn't feel all right." He blew out a breath. "I've told you I was raised with money..."

She nodded again, tilting her head as she watched him.

"Well, I might have had every luxury man can buy, but like you, I was lacking the one thing I truly wanted." He took in a fortifying breath. "Attention." He shrugged. "And love, I suppose." His hands flexed. "My parents were too busy enjoying the good life and their influential friends to pay much attention to their kid."

"Oh, Cooper," she whispered, her eyes growing glassy.

"No. Don't feel sorry for me," he said, harsher then he'd intended. He paused. "Sorry. I didn't mean to snap. My parents weren't horrible people, just...easily distracted. I was a time suck and they preferred to enjoy life." He went back to pacing. "So, as I got into my teenage years, I did what any good teenage boy does." He smiled without humor. "I got even more obnoxious, barreling into adulthood with both guns of rebellion blazing. I did it all. Partied, stayed out all night, underage drinking...you name it, I tried it."

She wasn't even trying to stop the tears coursing down her cheeks, and Cooper ached to beg her forgiveness and hold her close, but he wasn't done yet. In fact, the worst was yet to come.

"I gained a reputation as a party boy and took it straight into college, barely graduating with my degree in architecture because I was too busy living life to the fullest." His voice was bitter and angry. Cooper stared at his feet, struggling to go on with the story and scared stiff that Genni would change her mind about having him stick around.

"What happened?" she asked quietly.

Cooper snorted. "My parents got me a job in the best firm in the city."

"And?" she prompted when he didn't continue.

"And I met a woman." The statement was just the bomb that Cooper knew it would be. All the happiness in Boardwalk Manor was sucked into the black hole that was his past, and Cooper wasn't sure if it would ever be seen again. "Her name was Ciana Fowers," he continued, his voice hoarse.

"Was she beautiful?"

Cooper dared a glance at Genni's stricken face. "Yes," he admitted. "But her beauty wasn't the same as yours."

She frowned, two lines forming between her brows, and Cooper's fingers twitched with the need to smooth them.

"She had a...manufactured beauty. Perfectly done nails, hair and tailored clothes. Nothing was ever out of place."

"I see," she murmured, her sad eyes dropping to her lap.

"No, you don't." Cooper took a couple of large steps in order to drop to his knees in front of her. He hoped she didn't notice his shaking hands as he brought her chin up. "You aren't manufactured, Genni," he assured her. "You're beautiful naturally." He ran his fingers along her brow to the back of her ear, tucking the stray hairs out of her face. "Your eyes are like deep pools of chocolate and your skin warm and soft. Your hair always smells like lemons and I find myself wanting to touch it just to see if it's as luxurious as it looks."

He used his thumb to wipe a dripping tear. "But the best part is, you're beautiful on the inside too. You came into this world with nothing, and your dream is to create something wonderful, giving others the chance to have what you didn't. You want others to smile and laugh, even though your life had almost none of that." He smiled softly. "And you're not a manipulative liar."

Her bottom lip trembled and the tears began in earnest. "But I was. I lied about the papers, I hid the fact that I was trying to get rid of you."

Cooper shook his head. "No. You were trying to survive and save yourself." Gently, he kissed her forehead. "But the fact that you changed your mind says it all. Everyone's first reaction is to take care of themselves, but you shifted. You started to take care of me instead."

He cleared his throat and shifted back into a crouch so he wasn't quite so close. "But I need to tell you the rest."

She nodded. "Okay."

"Ciana and I began a relationship..." He looked away, too ashamed to see Genni's reaction. "It started when she showed up in my office with a business proposition that included giving her access to all of my email accounts." He stood and walked away from the woman he loved. "Ciana worked for the city and she was convinced she knew a way to get us all the best jobs, but it would have to come from an outside bidder, like myself." His hair fell into his eyes and he shook it back. "Still in the 'the world is at my fingertips' stage of my life, I agreed, and soon our relationship went from the workplace to home." Cooper rubbed the back of his neck. "I thought it was just another step on the ladder to success. I was making money, had a beautiful woman on my arm and the esteem of my colleagues for my ability to land contracts right and left." He chuckled darkly. "Little did I know, I was just an idiot waiting to be hung out to dry."

"What happened?"

Cooper turned back to look at Genni's anxious face. "Ciana's little scheme included embezzling funds from these projects, and she used my name and accounts to do it."

Genni's eyes widened and she gasped. "No."

He nodded. "Yep. And I'm the stupid guy who gave her the key."

"Cooper..."

"Don't feel sorry for me. I learned my lesson." His grin was bittersweet. "What I learned first was don't mix business with pleasure. Which is exactly why you were such a horrible roommate." He gave her a significant look. "Far too much temptation."

Her blush was enticing, but he needed to finish his story. "Anyway, long story short, I was arrested and spent four days in jail."

She let out a distressed squeak.

"But in that vast black book of good business contacts my parents had, there was also a good lawyer."

"The one you mentioned earlier, Mr. Stern?" Genni guessed.

Cooper nodded. "The very same." He blew out a breath. "He sprung me free, then went to work proving that I'd been taken like a lamb to the slaughter and got me cleared of all charges."

"And Ciana?"

"She and her accomplice—the mayor, of all people—are still behind bars."

"That's quite a story," Genni said softly.

Cooper shrugged. "Almost as crazy as what happened today."

"Close," she agreed.

He waited a beat for her eyes to meet his. "But through both of them, I've come to learn an invaluable lesson."

CHAPTER 28

Genni felt sure that her heart was showing all over her face at the moment, but she wasn't sure how to pull it back. Between his little speech about her beauty and the anxiety of listening to how he was played for the fool, she felt as if she'd been on an extreme roller coaster. Right now she wasn't sure if she should squeal in glee or throw up.

"First I learned to be smarter. I learned not everything that glitters is gold." He took a step in her direction. "I learned that leaping before looking could have dire consequences." He knelt in front of her. "And I learned that only the right kind of attention mattered."

Her tears began anew and she sniffled as his hand came up to cup her face.

"During my time here, I learned even more." That delicious slow smile of his grew. "I learned that determination and hard work are good qualities, but can also create loneliness."

Genni jerked back a little. His confession was coming a little too close to home now.

"I learned that the line between love and hate is very thin." He chuckled and wiped his thumb over her cheek bone. "I learned that slowing down and starting over aren't as scary as they appear to be."

She laughed through her tears. "It sounds to me like all you've done is learn a bunch of cliches," she teased.

Cooper brought their foreheads together, laughing softly. "That might be true. But if that's the case, there's one more I'd like to clear up."

"And that is?" Genni held her breath.

"I'm hoping that when they say love conquers all, they mean it."

She leaned back to look him in the face. "And what exactly does it need to conquer?"

He shrugged, looking unsure. "My past. My mistakes. Our roommate situation..."

Genni brought her hands up to frame his face, enjoying the feel of his stubble against her fingers. "I don't think it has to overcome those," she whispered. "They overcame themselves. And that left love free to move forward, if you're willing."

His eyes widened. "You don't mind about my history?"

Genni shook her head. "I don't. We've all done things we're not proud of. I'm just grateful that nasty woman was such an idiot."

Cooper frowned and leaned back a little. "*She* was an idiot?"

Genni nodded, slowly closing the distance between them. "She was. Because she let you go." Their lips were so close, Genni could feel the heat of his skin against her own. "But I have to be grateful because it was her idiocy that led you to becoming my roommate." She gave him a soft kiss. "And it's the best thing that's ever happened to me."

Speaking was absent in the house for a long time after Genni's words. Cooper quickly pulled her to her feet and wrapped his arms around her back, and she stepped willingly into his chest.

The normal explosions of color and sensation that accompanied Cooper's touch and kiss were more prevalent than ever. Something about openly admitting her feelings had changed Genni's perspective and suddenly, everything felt...more.

His skin was warmer, his smell stronger, his hold more comforting, and his hold over her more powerful than ever.

"In case you missed it from the other day, I love you too," Cooper whispered in a husky tone against her neck. His breath washed over her skin, leaving behind a trail of goosebumps. Cooper chuckled and kissed just under her ear when she wiggled. "A little ticklish?"

Genni laughed softly and swatted his shoulder. "Maybe."

"I'll remember that." He pulled back to look her in the eye.

Genni fought back a girlish sigh. She loved the fact that his eyes were green today. He was wearing a forest green T-shirt and the brown was almost completely absent from his gaze.

"I guess the question is, where do we go from here?" she asked, running her fingers through his hair. She never would have guessed that the man she'd fall for would have hair past his ears, or that he would have barbed wire tattooed over his bicep, but right now, both of them were very high on her list of attractive things.

"Where do you want to go from here?"

She chewed on her bottom lip, then laughed when he kissed her and stopped the action.

"You can't do things like that," he teased. "It just makes me want to kiss you."

"I don't really mind that," Genni said with a smile.

"Maybe so, but we'll never finish getting things figured out if I kiss you all day long."

"Mmm..." She hummed, leaning into him more heavily. "That sounds nice."

"Focus, Gen," Cooper said, then gave her another quick kiss.

She laughed and pushed off his chest. "If I must." Turning around, she began to walk toward the kitchen. "I'm starved. Let's get something to eat."

"Perfect. I haven't had breakfast yet."

"I tried, but most of it went in the garbage," Genni admitted.

Cooper sighed and headed toward the pantry. "Sounds like something more substantial is in order."

Soon the smell of pancakes floated through the air as the two sat down to a hearty meal.

"What are we going to do with the money?" Genni asked between bites.

Cooper pursed his lips. "That's a good question. Giving it back isn't going to be easy. Unless someone kept a record of how much came from each vendor?"

Genni shook her head. "I have no idea. I can text Rose and see if we can have a get-together to figure it out?"

Cooper nodded. "That might be best. Since the danger of losing the home is over, we really should try to give it back."

"I agree," Genni said, stuffing another bite in her mouth. "I'll text as soon as I'm done here."

"Sounds good."

"SO TELL US WHAT THIS is all about," Caro said as soon as Cooper and Genni walked into the flower shop.

"Back here, Caro," Rose drawled. "We don't need them to explain it twice."

Caro rolled her eyes. "Yes, Mother."

Cooper looked down when Genni laughed. "It's good to hear you laugh again," he whispered.

She smiled up at him shyly. "It's good to laugh. I hadn't realized how nice it was until you brought it into my life."

"And then Hudson tried to take it back out again," Cooper growled.

"No thinking of the slimeball," Genni ordered, tugging on his hand. "Let's go get rid of fifty-thousand dollars." She paused and ticked her head. "I can't say I ever thought I would say those words."

Cooper grinned and kept walking, forcing Genni to follow. "Me neither, but I've been through a lot of firsts with you." He gave her a sly glance. "And all of them good."

She rolled her eyes. "That's not quite true, but I'll take it nonetheless."

"Okey dokey, folks," Caro called out. "Now that everyone's here, let's find out what's going on."

Ken laughed and laced his hands behind his head. "This might take the whole evening," he said. "You sure you got time for that, Caro?"

Caro glared at the officer, then at Genni. "What does the popo know that I don't?" she snapped.

"Oh my word, Caro," Melody said with a laugh. "How old are you? Five?"

Caro sniffed. "Just sayin'."

"How about we let Cooper and Genni talk, hm?" Rose suggested, going to sit on the far side of the space.

Cooper immediately looked to Ken, whose eyes were stuck on the beautiful florist. It would be interesting to see how or *if* things developed there. "We've got kind of a long story to tell you," Cooper began. He turned to Genni, letting her have the stage.

She took a deep breath, squeezed his hand and then began.

Twenty minutes later, everyone but Ken, Cooper and Genni were sitting with their jaws on the ground.

"It's times like this that I wish I was a writer," Bennett said with a shake of his head. "You can't make this stuff up."

"Truth is stranger than fiction," Jensen agreed. He scratched the back of his head. "I can't believe that happened in Seaside."

Genni leaned into Cooper's shoulder, resting her head against him. He turned just enough to kiss her hair.

"So, our question now is, what to do with the money?" Cooper asked. "Is it possible to give it back? Did anyone keep a record of who gave what?"

Rose frowned and turned to Caro. "Not detailed enough to split it up precisely," she said, rising up at the end like a question.

Caro shook her head. "Nope. I don't think giving it back to the individuals is going to be feasible." She tapped her lip. "Buuut..."

"Here it comes," Bennett teased.

Caro's blue eyes snapped in his direction. "What would you suggest, Oh, Wise One?"

Bennett put up his hands. "Pardon me. We bow to your genius."

Caro put her nose in the air. "That's better."

"Caro," Charli warned.

"All right, all right." Caro stood, looking at Cooper and Genni. "That money was raised so you wouldn't lose the house, right?"

"Right." Genni nodded and the rest of the room responded in kind.

"What are your plans for the house now?" Caro continued.

Genni squinted up at Cooper. "I don't know if we've—"

Cooper turned to the group. "We're opening a bed and breakfast."

"You're going to do it?" Charli asked, her smile wide. "For reals?"

Felix whistled low. "Gonna be a lot of work, man."

Melody bounced in her seat. "I'm so happy for you!"

Despite all the excitement, Cooper only had eyes for Genni, who was currently staring at him with wide, glassy eyes.

"I thought you didn't want to share your home," she whispered.

Cooper smiled and rubbed a thumb along her jawline. "My home is with you," he whispered back. "The rest doesn't matter. If a bed and breakfast would make you happy, then that's what I want too."

With a loud squeal, Genni leapt at him, wrapping her arms around his neck. Cooper laughed as he caught her, only stumbling a step or two at her sudden jump.

"Hold on!" Caro shouted, putting her hands in the air.

It took several seconds for the room to calm down after the announcement, but eventually they were all focused on Caro again.

Cooper could feel Genni vibrating with excitement and it sent him soaring. There was nothing better than seeing the woman he loved so happy. Their time together had been rocky, but he knew as long as they stuck together, everything would turn out just the way it was supposed to. Even if it meant he had to share a house with a bunch of guests.

"I was hoping you would say that," Caro hedged with a grin.

"Spit it out," Bennett whined.

"Well, the house still needs a lot of fixing up, so what if the money was used for the renovations instead?" Caro splayed her hands. "It might not be saving the house from taxes anymore, but it's still saving the house, right? We're preserving a landmark that'll make the town proud and help bring in more tourism. I don't know if there's anything better than that."

Genni's hands went to cover her mouth. "Do you really think that would be okay? People won't be mad?"

"I won't be mad," Felix said with an easy shrug. "The money is yours. Use it how it helps best."

"I feel the same way," Rose said with a smile.

"Me too," Melody threw out. There was a pause, then Melody elbowed her brother in the ribs.

"Ow..." he rubbed his chest, glaring at his sister, who gave him a meaningful look. "I mean...me too!" His grin was wide and goofy and most of the room laughed.

Caro clapped her hands. "It's unanimous! Boardwalk Bed and Breakfast, here we come!"

The room erupted in clapping and Cooper pulled Genni into his chest. She buried her head in his chest. "I can't believe it," she mumbled against his shirt. "I can't believe it." She looked up. "We're going to have a home, a real home," she said, her eyes shining.

Cooper kissed the tip of her nose. "It's going to be wonderful, but I think I should look at moving out."

"What?" she gasped.

"Just to the carriage house," Cooper quickly responded. He gave her a seductive look. "Under the circumstances, I don't think you and I should share a roof at the moment."

"That place is a pigsty!" she argued.

Cooper shrugged. "Dust is cleanable." He sighed. "But really, I do think it's best. A man only has so much self-discipline."

Her cheeks turned pink and she buried her face again. "As long as you don't go too far, I'm sure we can make it work."

"It'll work all right," Cooper said, kissing her head again. "We won't let it turn out any other way."

EPILOGUE

Genni put her hands on her hip. "I can't believe it." She admired the new paint job, which was the crowning glory to the completed renovations.

Cooper wrapped his arms around her from behind. "Believe it, sweetheart. The grand opening is tomorrow and we're going to have a houseful."

She spun, immediately wrapping her arms around his neck. "You are the most amazing boyfriend ever! I had no idea you would be so handy!"

Cooper gave her that slow grin she loved so much and pulled her in a little tighter. "Just how amazing are we talking here?" He nuzzled her neck, right under her ear where he'd discovered she was slightly ticklish, and Genni squirmed. "Amazing enough for a kiss?"

Genni pretended to consider the idea. "I don't know...that would have to be pretty amazing..." She laughed when he went into full tickle mode, causing her to jump away from him.

His strong arms didn't let her go far before he caught her again. "Care to try that answer again?" he asked.

Genni sighed. "So needy!" She patted his chest. "You were definitely amazing enough for a kiss." She got up on her tiptoes, but Cooper leaned back.

"Hold on," he said and she thumped back down to her heels. "Was I amazing enough for two kisses?"

Genni raised her eyebrows. "Okay..." she agreed, curious where he was going with this. "Two kisses."

"What about three?"

Genni gave him a wry look. "Now you're just getting greedy." A deep bark had her turning to see Scottie come barrelling around the side of the house. Genni tried to step away to greet the dog, but Cooper held her tight.

"I'm not done," he said.

Genni rolled her eyes, but waited.

"What about a lifetime's worth of kisses?" he asked, his voice low and slightly uncertain.

Genni froze. "Cooper, what are you asking?" Her heart went into high gear and those darn knees began to shake. When Cooper dropped to one knee, keeping a hold of her hands, her vision went blurry with tears.

"Genevieve Winters, these last six months putting together your dream have been the happiest time of my life. I love you...all of you. I love your grit and determination, but I also love your kindness and sass. I love how you fight for what you want, especially since what you want most is to make other people happy." He gave her a crooked grin. "Would you do me the honor of letting me join you in that journey? Of letting me tag along as you build a home full of happiness to share with others? Will you let me be your go-to guy who fixes sinks during the day, but gets to hold you all night?" His face grew serious. "Genni, my love, will you let me be your roommate for good?"

"Cooper James, you were so unexpected in my life, but it turned out to be the best surprise ever. I love you so much that I don't know how to breathe when you're gone. I always thought that opening the bed and breakfast was my dream, but it turned out that having *you* open the bed and breakfast with me was the real dream." Her voice broke. "And now it has come true."

Cooper kissed her fingers, then stood and reached into his back pocket and pulled out a ring. "Then I think we should make this official, huh?"

Genni gasped at the beautiful solitaire that was slipped onto her finger. "I don't know how life could get any better," she whispered, throwing herself against him.

Genni shook against his chest as he laughed.

"I've got another surprise for you," he said against her hair. "Come on, and then I'll definitely show you how things can get better." Cooper backed up and pumped his eyebrows at her.

Genni laughed, having to acknowledge that his kisses definitely made things better. She tripped happily after him as he led her to the carriage house. Genni frowned. "Are you sure we need to go in there before I get to kiss you?"

Cooper grinned over his shoulder. "Yep."

She huffed but followed. Once inside, he led her up the stairs to the apartment area and Genni came to a standstill. "How?" She was at a loss for words. She had helped Cooper do the initial cleaning for the room he was going to stay in, but he had kicked her out eventually, saying he wanted to do most of it himself. Now she knew why.

The old, dusty studio apartment had been turned into a bright, airy space, complete with a small kitchenette, queen bed and sitting area.

"What do you think?" he asked, his fingers playing with hers.

"It's beautiful," she breathed. "Every bit as nice as the house ended up being."

Cooper nodded. "Good...would you be willing to live here with me?"

Her head snapped to look at him. "What?"

Cooper scratched at his chin. "As much as I wanted you to have your dream, I'm still struggling with the idea of sharing my house with strangers." His gaze dropped to the floor as he shrugged. "So I thought maybe we could live out here, for the time being, and rent the main house." His eyes were unsure as he peeked a glance at her. "Between Charli and I, I think we could turn the carriage house into our own full cottage. It's not huge, but it should be big enough for a couple of kids."

"Cooper..." Genni shook her head. Would she ever cease to be surprised by this man? "It's perfect," she gushed.

"Really?" His shoulders collapsed and he let out a rush of air. "I was so freaked out—Oof!"

Genni cut off the rest of his words as she basically assaulted him with her kisses. Cooper, however, didn't take long to jump in with both feet. Soon he had her backed up against the wall, showing just a glimpse of what their future would hold.

"I found it, you know," Cooper panted against her cheek.

"What?" Genni asked, her mind on anything but speaking.

"The rest of the contract with the clause in it."

Genni stilled. "What?"

Cooper pulled back just far enough to look her in the eye. "I found where it says you can buy me out. The papers were in the filing cabinets." He raised his eyebrows. "Would you like them?"

Genni smiled and shook her head. "Burn it."

His eyes widened. "Burn them?"

She nodded. "Yep. Burn them. They don't mean anything now." She made a point of examining her ring. "Besides, I think you more than bought your way in, don't you?"

"I'd pay a hundred times more if I needed to," he said before giving her a searing kiss.

"The only thing I need is your heart," Genni said breathlessly between kisses.

"You have it."

"Then we don't ever need to bring it up again," she said, framing his face with her hands. She smiled and rubbed her thumbs against the short beard, still enjoying it after all this time. "All that matters is our future." She gave him a soft, lingering kiss. "Our future *together.*"

After that, their future consisted of very little talking for a long...long...time.

Thank you so much for joining me on
Genni and Cooper's journey!
I hope you enjoyed reading it as
much as I enjoyed writing it!

Not ready for the romance to be done?
Keep scrolling for a peak at book #2 in the series!
<u>"Her Unexpected Second Chance"</u>

CHAPTER 1

A little bell rang as Mel pushed open the door to the flower shop, "The Hidden Daffodil". She grinned at the familiar sound and hurried to the back room where she knew her friends would be waiting.

"Mel!" Caro called out, bringing everyone else's attention to Mel's entrance.

"Hey, Caro!" Mel called back.

"Hi, Mel!"

Wassup Chiquita Bonita!"

Mel grinned and greeted all her friends. She waved and hugged those she was closest to, smiling at the others that were more like acquaintances. Upon reaching her designated table, she sighed, then took in a deep breath of floral scented air. Mel loved arrangement night.

Rose, the shop's owner was a genius when it came to plants and had started a class where she taught arranging and the language of flowers. Surprisingly, it had blossomed into something more, giving Mel and the others her age, a common interest that had built a group of friends stronger than anything Mel had ever had before.

"So...what are we making tonight?" Mel asked Genevieve, her table partner.

Genni shrugged. "I'm not sure." She fingered the petals of the flowers. "But the colors sure are pretty tonight."

Mel studied the array of shades. "You're right." She grinned at Genni. "It would clash horribly with that pink dining room of yours."

Genni dropped her head back and groaned. "Oh man...don't remind me." She brought her head back, a wicked grin on her lips. "I almost left it that way, just to show Cooper's who's boss, but I just couldn't bring myself to stick with the plan."

Mel laughed as she toyed with a leaf. Her heart ached as she thought of the wonderful couple Genni and Cooper made. Their story had started out difficult, but now they were happy as clams, almost sickeningly so. Jealousy thrummed inside Mel's chest, and it took a little more force then normal for her to push it aside. "I'm sure Cooper's grateful for your change of heart."

"It was true to the era," Genni grumbled, her bottom lip pushed out in a pout. The argument over room colors had occurred while Genni was renovating the old seaside mansion she'd inherited from her grandmother.

Mel patted her friend's shoulder. "I'm sure it was. But sometimes it's okay to go against tradition."

"Are we ready, ladies?"

Both women looked to the front, seeing Rose standing with a welcoming smile on her face.

"Let's do this!" Charli, another good friend, shouted.

The room rumbled with laughter and chatter before Rose got it back under control.

"Thank you everyone for coming tonight," Rose started. Her stunning red hair was pulled back into a high ponytail and her bright blue eyes seemed to glow in the fluorescent lighting. "I'm always so thrilled to have you here." Her smile grew. "Tonight, with fall on the horizon, I thought we would focus on an arrangement about saying thank you. Each flower...sweet peas, hydrangeas..." Rose fingered the blooms as she spoke. "White, pink and yellow roses...they all say thank you in unique ways. So, hopefully when you look at this arrangement, you'll remember all the wonderful things in your life. Or!" She put a finger in the air. "You can give it as a thank you to someone else." Her smile was beautiful, nearly perfect. "In any case, let's get going."

Mel paid close attention as Rose directed them on how to mix the colors and arrange the heights just so. When she was done, Mel stepped backed and eyed her vase carefully. "Not bad," she muttered.

"It's beautiful," Genni offered with a sincere smile.

Mel smiled back, an automatic reaction, but also an excited one. Before meeting Cooper, Genni had always been nice, but just a little aloof. Now, however, the gorgeous brunette had warmed considerably and Mel enjoyed her even more. "Thanks, so is yours."

Genni laughed. "Maybe that's because they're almost exactly the same."

Mel pursed her lips. "Nah. I mean, I have two pink roses, you only have one. They're absolutely, completely different."

Genni shook her head, her smile still wide. "Of course. How ridiculous of me to think otherwise."

Mel grabbed her vase and sniffed. "I think I'll take my completely unique arrangement home, thank you very much."

"It's about that time, isn't it?" Genni responded, grabbing her own vase.

"You ladies heading out?" Rose asked, walking in their direction.

"Yep." Mel paused and looked around. "You want me to stick around and help clean up?" Most of the women had already filtered through the door, but a few were in clusters, chatting and gossiping just the way small towns were known for.

Rose waved her off. "Lilly and I will take care of it. She loves counting all the stem pieces as she dumps in the garbage."

Mel's smile softened. She adored Rose's daughter, Lilly. Lilly was a stunning beauty at only five years old, her only flaw being that she was deaf, though Mel and all the other women in their friend group, didn't find that to be a flaw at all. Lilly's ability to sign and communicate was beautiful to watch and her expressive face could have even the hardest person captivated for hours. "Well, I definitely don't want to take away from Lilly's fun, so I'll leave them."

Rose chuckled softly. "She'll thank you in the morning."

Giving her goodbyes, Mel headed out the door, shivering slightly at the drop in temperature. Fall was definitely on its way. Hunching in on herself, she got in her car and put the vase between her legs in order to keep it steady, then headed for home. It took less than ten minutes for her to pull into her parking spot at the small row of condos.

But before getting out, Mel stared at the attached homes. Most of them had lights on and silhouettes of people or families moving about within. All except hers. The darkness of her home fell foreboding, unwelcoming and cold. *But where else are you going to go?*

The truth in that statement made Mel reluctantly step out of the vehicle and trudge up her front steps. Once inside, she flipped on the lights and took the vase to her tiny kitchen. She set it in the usual corner and smiled softly at the burst of color it provided against the white space. "Grateful," Mel murmured. "I'm supposed to be grateful."

She grabbed a twinkie from the cupboard and headed back to her couch. Despite the enjoyable evening with friends, Mel wasn't feeling very thankful. More than ever, she was feeling lonely and left behind. Everyone had somewhere they were going in their life, whether in love or business and Mel felt...stuck. "Knock it off," she scolded herself, wiping a stray tear from her cheek. "You have a wonderful business, good friends, live close to the ocean, a semi-nice brother close by, and now a vase full of flowers. What more could you want?"

To share it with someone.

Mel groaned and shoved the sweet treat in her mouth, hoping it would quell the longing inside of her.

To share it with Jensen.

"Well, you can't have him," she sneered, knowing she must sound crazy talking to herself. "You're just a little girl to him, and that's all you'll ever be." She licked her fingers in dismissal. "You might as well aim to land on the moon."

Grabbing her kindle, Mel forced her mind onto other things. Her life might not be perfect, but right now she could focus on someone else's who might be. *Besides... landing on the moon is probably easier than capturing Jensen's attention anyway.*

"MR. TANNER?"

Jensen turned around from the white board he'd been writing on. "Yes, Hunter?'

The sophomore boy lounged back in his seat. "I'm confused. You said free verse poetry is basically just writing whatever you want. How is that any different than writing a story? If you're making stuff up, you just write whatever you want, right? What makes it poetry if it doesn't rhyme?"

Jensen snapped the marker lid back into place and turned around to the class. "Does anyone know the answer to Hunter's question?" He looked around the room. "Andrea?"

The young lady tucked her hair behind her ear and shrugged. "I don't know. Poetry is...shorter. I guess. I mean, a free verse poem wouldn't have all the descriptions of a story right?"

Jensen nodded, grateful at least one person was on the right track. "Correct, but there's a little more to it."

"It's about the imagery."

Jensen's heart dropped as he turned to look at Micah Derringer. The young man was slouched so far down in his seat, he was almost a puddle on the floor. Dark, long hair covered most of his face and the hoody of his jacket covered the rest. "Very good, Micah." Jensen tapped his desk. "Hood off please."

Micah groaned, but complied, pulling his hair farther over his forehead as if the feathery strands could hide him from the classroom.

"Thank you. Now...would you care to explain any more?" Jensen waited, hoping the boy would continue. He leaned back against his deck, folding his arms across his chest. He tried hard to hide the fact that he was studying the boy's face, looking for clues. Micah was a good student when he decided to be, and actually had a pretty good gift with the english language. However, some of the poems coming across Jensen's desk had him worried. Talk of monsters, demons and other dark comparisons had Jensen on edge.

He knew some teenage boys just went through stages where they were obsessed with dark things, but this felt like more than that. Micah was being raised by a single dad, who didn't have a good reputation. If Ken, the local police captain and Jensen's friend, was to be believed, Mitchell Derringer often had to be kicked out of the bars when they closed in the early hours of the morning. He was also known for picking fights, and it was that threat of violence that had Jensen keeping an eye on his student.

Micah shrugged at the question. "I don't know."

Jensen wasn't falling for it. "I think you do, Micah. You display it in your work often enough." He smiled encouragingly. "Should we share some of your writing with the class as an example?"

Micah shook his head rigorously. "No!" He sat up a little, then caught himself and slouched again. "I mean, nah. It's just about creating a picture in the reader's head. Poetry tries to use as few words as possible, each word becoming a symbol, whether the lines rhyme or not. But stories create a moving picture, like a movie in your head. The words work together, but aren't necessarily symbolic."

"Excellent." Jensen turned to the student who had originally asked the question. "Did that make sense, Hunter?"

Hunter shrugged. "I guess."

Jensen held in the desire to sigh. Just as he went to turn back to the white board, the bell rang and the kids started scrambling to get their things together. "Don't forget your poetry portfolios are due tomorrow! If you've forgotten what all should be included, please check the school portal!" Jensen waited a beat, then called out, "Micah?"

The teenager shifted his backpack and looked up from under his hair.

"Can I see you a minute?"

Micah looked around, appearing ill at ease before shuffling up front. "Did I do something wrong?"

Jensen shook his head. "Nope." He tilted his head, trying to see through the hair. "Actually, I just wanted to tell you how impressed I've been with your work. You really have a way with words."

The young man kept his gaze on the floor, but nodded. "Thanks." Long, slim fingers tightened on his backpack straps, one of which was attached with duct tape and Jensen felt his worry ratchet up a notch.

"Have you ever thought of doing anything more with your work?" Jensen tried to prolong the conversation, his eyes searching for any signs of anything suspicious. It was so hard to tell, since it wasn't uncommon for a boy to be reserved or shrunken into himself. Right now, Jensen was running on a gut feeling, but that wasn't enough to give his principal.

Micah shook his head again. "It's just a bunch of words, Mr. Tanner. They don't mean anything." Without saying anything else, the young man bolted, making Jensen jump at the swiftness of his departure.

Following the fleeing boy, Jensen's eyes widened when Micah grabbed the doorframe and a distinctly blue color emerged from under his sweatshirt. Before Jensen could do much more than notice the bruise, however, Micah was gone.

"Shoot," Jensen muttered, walking back around his desk. He sat down and tapped his foot impatiently. "But what can I do about it?" Again, a bruise wasn't real evidence. He could have done any number of things to receive that kind of wound. It's not like teenagers were known for staying out of trouble. Jensen sighed and rubbed his temples. He wanted so badly to help if one of his students was in trouble, but right now his hands were tied. There simply wasn't any evidence...yet.

He glanced at his watch. There was still plenty of time in the day before evening fell, so Jensen settled in to grade some papers, but his mind kept wandering. It was torn between a melody he'd been picking out last night and the problem with Micah. "I can't do anything about Micah right now," Jensen scolded himself. It was better to just push that to the back of his mind. Unfortunately, only time would tell if Jensen needed to intervene. The song, however...

Looking at his watch once again, Jensen stuffed all his stuff together in his briefcase and decided to head out early. If he hurried, he could get a track laid before dinner tonight. Something about this melody just kept speaking to him and in his heart, Jensen knew it was good.

It might even be good enough to send to an agent.

The thought percolated in his brain not for the first time. When he was lonely or feeling depressed more than usual, the idea of trying his hand at a professional music career would rear its head. So far Jensen had never indulged the thought too much. Musician's lives were too unpredictable and flighty, or at least that's what he'd been taught. *Yeah...nothing like the wonderful monotony you have right now.*

He picked up his pace, struggling to ignore the fact that the idea of playing under the stage lights were intoxicatingly enticing. Jensen didn't share his music often. It wasn't like there was much opportunity in his small town, and he wasn't one to play just to show off. So his talents had been reserved for bonfires and other small social gatherings with his closest friends. Even those, however, had only been him strumming whatever was popular at the time. Nobody knew that he actually wrote his own stuff. Well...no one but his furniture anyway.

Jensen burst inside his home, his eagerness stronger than usual as he grabbed his beloved instrument and headed to the small spare bedroom he used as a recording studio. It wasn't fancy, but it got the job done.

Sitting in his chair, he let his fingers begin to move, that persistent melody line vibrating through the air as he built upon the tune. After a few minutes he grinned, pressed the record button and let himself go, every other worry forgotten in the excitement of knowing he was creating something worthwhile.

CHAPTER 2

"**M**r. Muscles! Your green, almond-milk, strawberry smoothie with a shot of wheatgrass is ready!" Melody sang out with a wide smile on her face. She waited while an elderly gentleman, Mr. Roy Smithers, shuffled to the front.

He grinned at her. "They get better every time," he rasped, taking his drink.

Mel laughed. "Glad you enjoy it!" She wagged her finger at him. "But I've seen those pics of when you were in the navy." Mel fanned her face and pretended to swoon. "I don't know how the ladies kept their hands off of you."

Mr. Smithers chuckled. "You do this old heart good, girl. Keep at it."

Mel winked. "See ya next Thursday," she said. If Mr. Smithers was anything, he was predictable. They went through this routine every week, like clockwork, and Mel loved it. She also loved her job. Starting "Smooth Moves" had been a leap of faith for her, but as a people person, it was perfect for Mel.

She's come out of college with a degree in hospitality and a homesickness that brought her right back to her beloved Seaside Bay on the Oregon Coast. Her brother, Bennett, was here, and though her hippie mother had moved south to California, Seaside Bay had a wonderful small-town dynamic that Mel just hadn't been able to find anywhere else.

Plus, Jensen is here.

"Whoops," she whispered, grabbing the next ready styrofoam cup. "Ms. Legs for Miles, I've got a Razmatazz with a dose of antioxidants with your name on it!"

Caroline, or Caro, rolled her eyes. "You're hilarious," she drawled in her southern accent. Her tiny five-foot frame wasn't quite how Mel described her.

Mel grinned and handed over the drink. "Hey. We've got to have dreams. My job is to help encourage you toward yours!"

Caro gave her a look. "What if I don't want to be taller?" Her small hand went to her perfectly curvy hip.

A flash of jealousy hit Mel in the gut, but she quickly pushed it aside. She'd gotten good at that over the years, plus she loved Caro way too much to let jealousy get between them. "Then I'll work on talking about all your wonderful perfect characteristics rather than teasing you about your height."

Caro smiled and shook her head, her blonde hair swaying just right. "God couldn't give me *all* the good characteristics. He had to leave a few for other people, ya know."

Mel laughed as intended. "Thanks for stopping by, Caro."

Caro waved over her shoulder. "See ya later!"

"Absolutely!" Still smiling, she grabbed the next cup and stuttered.

Jensen.

Speak of the handsome devil...

"Teacher extraordinaire, I've got a blueberry, mint, and kiwi special just for you!" Her smile was too wide, as it always was when he was around, but Mel kept her feelings in check for the most part...another thing she'd gotten good at over the years.

Jensen Tanner walked up, that slight swagger in his step that had been a part of him for as long as Mel could remember. He chuckled, reaching out for the cup. "What's up, Mellie?"

Her smile drooped a little. She hated that nickname. It was much too 'little sister' for the woman she was now. Unfortunately, as her brother's good buddy, Jensen would probably always see her as that little girl who used to follow him around. "Not much. Just doing my best to help people have a good morning." She tilted her head, fluttering her eyelashes playfully. "You ready for another day of teaching?"

Jensen shrugged and stuffed a straw into the top of the drink, completely ignoring her flirtations. "Just another day," he said with his usual smile. He tipped the cup at her. "See ya later!"

Mel waved at him, deflating as his strong shoulders disappeared through the doorway.

"You got it bad, girl," Emily, one of her shift managers whispered.

Mel snapped to attention. "I don't know what you're talking about," she said through a stiff smile. "Hot Stuff Junior? Here's your Smoothie Kabloozie!" Mel shared chin tilts with the sixteen-year-old boy who was the son of a local football hero. The young man was on his way to following in his dad's footsteps and the whole town was thrilled for him. "I added a shot of protein," Mel said in a loud whisper. "Wanted to help out that throwing arm."

Parker blushed. "Thanks, Mel."

She waved as he left. "He's a nice kid," she said to no one in particular.

"Yep. But not as nice as Mr. Teachy."

Mel sighed and turned to give her employee a look. "Mr. Teachy?"

Emily grinned. "Would you rather call him Hot Teacher? The love of your life? Your heart's desire?"

"Okay, okay, I get it," Mel hurriedly tried to shut her employee up. "But I'll say again. You don't know what you're talking about."

Emily rolled her eyes. "I'm not blind, Mel."

Mel could feel a heat rushing up her neck and she set her hands down on the cold stainless steel counter, hoping the temperature would help quell her body temperature. "I never said you were."

Emily blew out a breath and went back to the blenders. "If you decide you want to talk about it, let me know."

Mel didn't bother responding. There was nothing to talk about. Mel had been watching Jensen for too many years to think she had any chance with him. She'd been in love with her brother's friend since she was a teenager. She'd watched him graduate, go on to college, find another woman, get married, become a widower, then come home to teach. Nowhere in that life line, was there any indication that he viewed her as anything but Bennett's kid sister. The five years between them might as well have been a million for the distance between them.

Through the years, Mel had lost all hope that she could ever change his mind. She'd tried once, back in high school. The night had ended in disaster and embarrassment. Now as a full fledged adult, she knew better than to think she'd ever get a second chance.

So, she'd resigned herself to being a friend, mooning from afar, and living her life trying to help others be happy instead of worrying about herself. Her smoothie shop helped her do just that, and it made Mel happy...for the most part.

The one hole in her life would never be filled though, so there was no point in complaining to her friends, or gossiping with employees. Choices had been made, lines had been drawn and Mel's life was laid out for her.

And she was content. Or at least, that's what she told herself when the nights were lonely or she'd had a difficult day. She had friends, family, and a successful business. Who needed anything more?

Not me.

"Eyes So Green They Look Like Jade!" Mel shouted. "Your kale and blueberries are waiting for you!" She laughed lightly with her customer as they picked up their drink.

Yep. I've got everything I need.

JENSEN SIPPED THE SWEET yet tart confection as he walked down the street to the high school. Stopping by Mellie's had become a daily routine for him. She was his best friend's little sister so he'd first come to Smooth Moves in order to support her, but now he came because he honestly enjoyed the breakfast. He'd convinced himself that drinking Mellie's smoothies was a better hit than coffee, and he'd been indulging in them ever since.

His new melody began floating through his mind as he walked and soon Jensen found himself humming the tune. His fingers twitched against his styrofoam cup as if they could pluck the notes out of thin air. He had the basics for something great, but he just couldn't seem to finish the piece. There was something he was missing, but he wasn't sure what.

He scoffed and shook his head. *Music is just a pipe dream.* Ever since he was a young kind, Jensen had been fascinated with the guitar and had taught himself to play in his teens. Once he had even entertained the idea of creating a band, but like many young dreams, the plan had never come to fruition.

Instead, Jensen had headed to college, gotten married and eventually become a teacher. All things that were safe and predictable. Everything his parents had taught him were the best parts of life. As the only child of two school teachers, his path had been laid out long before Jensen had ever taken his first step, and he'd gone along with it, not willing to rock the boat.

He sighed. "It's not like you mind any of it," he grumbled under his breath. "There's nothing wrong with teaching."

And there wasn't. For the most part, Jensen enjoyed the job. Only one part of Jensen's life hadn't gone according to plan and that was the unexpected death of his wife. Jensen missed her, but if he was being truthful with himself, he wasn't as heart broken as he thought he should have been.

Those words brought on a burden of guilt he'd dealt with for a long time. The weight of that emotion felt second nature at this point, which just added to the monotony that was his life.

"Hey, Mr. Tanner!"

Jensen set aside his maudlin thoughts to wave at a student. "What's up Ian?"

The young man grinned and wrapped his arm tighter around the girl at his side. "Not much. We were just discussing those poem thingies you were telling us about in class." His grin was pure mischief. "You know, the ones by that beard guy."

Jensen nearly choked on his smoothie. "Beard guy?" His eyes widened. "Oh, you mean *bard!* Shakespeare's sonnets?" His eyes darted to the girl and back. "I take it you mean the love sonnets?"

"Yeah...that's it." Ian gave a little thrust of his chin. "I was just sharing some of them with Nina here."

Jensen held back his laughter. "I'm sure she enjoyed that," he stated even as Nina rolled her eyes. "Good luck." Jensen grinned and shook his head as he heard the two teenagers begin to bicker behind him.

Jensen's humor faded, replaced by a ridiculous trickle of jealousy as he passed more couples on his way to his classroom. *That's a new low. Being jealous of a bunch of teenage kids.*

He unlocked his classroom and headed straight to his desk, dumping his backpack to the side and plopping into his seat with a sigh. Glancing up at the clock, he noted that the bell would ring in less than five minutes, giving him little time to prepare for the morning's classes.

"Should just do a pop quiz and call it good," he muttered, setting his drink down. His phone buzzed and Jensen glanced at the text.

Dinner tonight? Mel's cooking.

Jensen grinned. Bennett was always inviting him over. "Yeah...but does Mellie know she's cooking?" It seemed the Frasier family was constantly worried about whether or not he was eating. Even when Mrs. Frasier still lived in Seaside Bay, he'd spent a lot of dinners at their house.

Sounds good. Thanks.

He sent the reply, not being one to turn down a good home cooked meal and then got back to work. Jensen could hear the kids starting to roam the hallways and knew he'd be inundated soon.

Hours later, when school was over, Jensen sat back down, exhausted from being on his feet all day. He leaned back, letting his head rest against the back of his chair. It was usually at this time of day that he felt way older than his almost thirty years.

His back ached, his feet hurt and his temples pulsed with a headache. To top it all off, the idea of going home to his empty cabin was about as appealing as eating raw geoduck. His phone buzzed, catching his attention again.

False alarm. Had something come up. How about tomorrow?

Jensen didn't take long to answer.

No prob. See ya then.

Jensen set his phone back down and let his shoulders slump. Truth was, it didn't matter what night Bennett invited him over, he'd be free. Other than teaching and the occasional night with his buddies, Jensen had nothing going in his life.

No excitement, no goals, no anticipation...every day was exactly the same as the day before. *If only Melissa was still here...*

Jensen growled and shook his head, making his headache pulse harder against his skull. "That wouldn't have helped," he reminded himself. During their one year of marriage, life had changed little. Melissa had been a nice, quiet girl he'd found in the library one day during a study session.

She was exactly the type of person his parents had wanted for their studious son. Focused on her academics, intelligent, easy to get along with and planning to become a teacher.

She'd been very lovely in a natural way, her medium brown hair was long and straight and there was nothing unwelcoming about her features, but like everything else in Jensen's life, he hadn't found himself *excited* about her. She was just another step in the life that had been presented to him.

Maybe things would have been better if she was still alive, but Jensen didn't think so. If there had been no true spark as newlyweds, how in the world would one have happened after they become working professionals? Jensen had been sad and hurt when she'd died, but more from the loss of a young life than the fact that she was his wife. It had felt like losing a good friend instead of his soulmate.

Mostly he felt guilty for how little time he'd spent with her during their short marriage. He would never stop being sorry that her time on Earth was cut short, but he struggled to continue to be sorry he wasn't married. None of it was her fault, he knew. She'd done nothing wrong. But there was a deep, mostly buried, part of Jensen that wanted...more. He wanted sparks, he wanted adventure, he wanted a woman in his life who inspired music and poetry and made him stupid-smile whenever he thought about her. He wanted something, *anything,* that was out of the ordinary, but he hadn't been raised to believe in fairy tales. He loved his town and his friends, but they definitely didn't inspire the kind of excitement that he secretly craved.

Another heavy sigh escaped him as he gathered his papers for the evening and left the building. The day was still bright as they were in the early stages of fall, so the sun still set late into the evening.

The walk home was more painful then it should have been. It seemed like everywhere he looked there were couples. Couples walking their dog, couples holding hands, couples swinging a child between their arms. Every smiling face reminding him of the cold, dark house he was headed toward.

Jensen scowled and picked up his pace. *I must be the most boring thirty old in existence. Go to work, go home, go to work, go home...nothing ever changes.*

He paused slightly upon reaching his little house, but a cool breeze rushed over his neck, forcing him to forgo the lonely trepidation he felt and step inside. He immediately dropped his backpack on the coffee table and proceeded to turn on all the lights. The sunlight through the windows was still enough to let him see in the home, but having the overhead bulbs glowing always seemed to help a little with the emptiness of the place.

A beautiful acoustic guitar stood in the corner, resting peacefully in its stand and Jensen found himself walking toward it. "You've been waiting for me to come home, haven't ya?" he cooed, refusing to feel guilty for speaking to an inanimate object.

Lovingly, Jensen picked up the instrument and nestled it against his body, loving the perfect fit of the guitar's curves. He thumbed the strings, and closed his eyes at the soothing chords.

This...this was the one thing that never felt boring or useless or lonely. He never seemed too tired to create music and the sounds filled every corner of the cottage, dispelling the starkness that seemed to permeate every part of his life.

Deciding he wasn't hungry, Jensen walked over to the leather sofa and sat down, losing himself in the melody he'd been working. With just a little bit of work, he might turn it into something worth listening to. *Then at least there'd be one part of my life that was making progress.*

Find the rest of the story at

amazon.com

Find All my Books at
Lauraannbooks.com